From "Unforgettable, That's What You Are"

My vision went flat. All I saw was her fingertips as she slowly reached for me, fingertips that glowed golden. They brushed my jaw as she leaned into me and lifted her mouth for my kiss. For a moment I couldn't breathe, then I realized I had been holding my breath as those fingertips mesmerized me. I fell dizzily into her, tasting all that she offered. It was a kiss that gave up everything and yet painted mysteries and fantastic promises. I was suffused with a dazzling array of sensation throughout my hungering body. She was strong under all that soft skin, thank God, because I held her tight and hard and close as I kissed her.

FROSTING ON THE CAKE

BY
KARIN KALLMAKER

THE NAIAD PRESS, INC.
2001

Printed in the United States of America on acid-free paper
First Edition

Editor: Christine Cassidy
Cover designer: Bonnie Liss (Phoenix Graphics)

Library of Congress Cataloging-in-Publication Data

Kallmaker, Karin, 1960–
Frosting on the cake / by Karin Kallmaker.
    p.   cm.
  ISBN 1-56280-266-6 (alk. paper)
  1. Lesbians—Fiction. I. Title.
PS3561.A41665 F7 2001
813′.54—dc21

2001018301

First and Foremost
For my Readers
And As So Many Readers Have Noticed,
For Maria, Again

Eleven is Heaven

Also by Karin Kallmaker

Unforgettable

Watermark

Making Up for Lost Time

Embrace in Motion

Wild Things

Painted Moon

Car Pool

Paperback Romance

Touchwood

In Every Port

Substitute for Love (forthcoming)

Writing as Laura Adams

Christabel

Night Vision (Daughters of Pallas 1)

The Dawning (Daughters of Pallas 2)

Sleight of Hand
(Tunnel of Light Book 1; published by Bella Books)

About the Author

Karin Kallmaker was born in 1960 and raised by her loving, middle-class parents in California's Central Valley. The physician's Statement of Live Birth plainly declares, "Sex: Female" and "Cry: Lusty." Both are still true. Her genealogically minded father recently informed her that she is descended from Lady Godiva.

From a normal childhood and equally unremarkable public-school adolescence, she went on to obtain an ordinary Bachelor's degree from the California State University at Sacramento. At the age of 16, eyes wide open, she fell into the arms of her first and only sweetheart. Ten years later, after seeing the film *Desert Hearts*, her sweetheart descended on the Berkeley Public Library determined to find some of "those" books. "Rule, Jane" led to "Lesbian-ism — Fiction" and then on to book after self-affirming book by and about lesbians. These books were the encouragement Karin needed to forget the so-called "mainstream" and spin her first romance for lesbians. That manuscript became her first Naiad Press novel, *In Every Port*.

Karin now lives in the San Francisco Bay Area with that very same sweetheart; she is a one-woman woman. The happily-ever-after couple became Mom and Moogie to Kelson James in 1995 and Eleanor Delenn in 1997. They celebrate their twenty-fourth anniversary in 2001.

Fans of romantic supernatural and science fiction should investigate Karin's alter ego, Laura Adams.

Table of Contents

To the Reader —

The information below each story's title tells roughly how much time has elapsed since the end of the novel. These stories are presented in the order that the original books were published. Some of you will undoubtedly want to read them in that order. You could, however, choose your favorite book and read that story first. It's your cake. Eat it any way you want.

— Karin

In Every Port

Published: 1989
Characters: Jessica Brian, management consultant
             Cat Merrill, hotel management executive
Setting: San Francisco, California, 1978

The First is for Filling Up

Conversations

(23 years)

"I can't find the remote." Jessica raised her arms helplessly.

Cat looked at her over black half-moon glasses. "Have you looked everywhere?"

"Yes."

"Why do you think I know where it is?"

Jessica gestured at the confines of the living room. Beyond the windows was the sleepy expanse of San Francisco, mellow in the late summer glow of a Sunday

3

morning. The remote control was not out there. "Well I don't know where it is, so I'm hoping that between us we have one brain."

Cat started to set aside her Sunday *Chronicle*.

"Don't get up! I'll keep looking." Jessica paced the living room and the kitchen, reciting her progress. "It's not on the TV, it's not on the coffee table. It's not on the counter. It's not in the refrigerator. It's not on the breakfast table. It's not —"

"Oh, all right!"

"Don't get up!"

It was too late. Cat stood up. She gave Jessica a long-suffering stare before she glanced around the room.

Jessica studied the ceiling. Why watch? It was a genetic gift.

Cat walked over to the library table and extracted the remote from where a large philodendron leaf had sheltered it.

"Thank you," Jessica muttered, holding out her hand.

"I'm the one who found it. What makes you think I'm going to give it to you? We're watching the 'Niner game."

"We're watching the Giants game," Jessica said firmly. Septembers were always full of conflict and compromise with baseball and football vying for their attention.

"That's what you think." Cat skipped back to the sofa and pointed the remote at the TV.

Jessica tackled her and they wrestled, sinking into the receptive couch. Wrestling led to tickling, and Jessica lost her tenuous grip on the remote. "Oh, all right. Kiss me."

Cat came up for air a few minutes later. "You're just trying to make me drop the remote — oh . . ."

The phone chirped, interrupting a very pleasing kiss.

"He did it!" Herine was so excited she didn't stop for air. "I mean we did it — it was amazing, and — get Momma Cat on the other phone, I want to tell you both!"

Jessica's heart was suddenly pounding. She gestured at the phone in the kitchen. "Get on the other phone."

Cat pulled at her sleeve in alarm. "What's wrong? It's Herine — is she okay?"

Jessica could only nod. She was certain Herine was fine.

Cat hurried into the kitchen with a frightened backward glance. Jessica felt a little faint.

"Mom? Good you're there — oh my God — he did it!"

Jessica held the phone at arm's length as twin shrieks of pure exhilaration blasted from the ear piece. She could hear thumps as Cat jumped up and down in the kitchen.

"Details, details," Cat chanted after she'd caught her breath.

"It was so romantic, oh Mom, it was just amazing." Herine was breathless and Jessica could hear tears threatening. "Last night we went out to dinner and had a really great talk, about the kinds of things we're hoping to do before we get too old to do them, and then we went for a walk and I realized we were in front of the store where I bumped into him that first day. He reaches into his pocket and brings out the ring box —"

"Oh my God!" Cat began jumping up and down again.

"— And he said that the future is easier to get to if we have someone to help us along the way, and that we made a great team and we had wonderful dreams and he couldn't envision a life without me and then he started to cry and I was bawling and he gave me the ring..."

Jessica was only dimly aware of the rest. She felt cold and lightheaded. Herine was getting married. Twenty-one was too young. Thirty-one was too young. Forty-one was too young. She didn't want to lose Herine.

She had lost already, she knew that. The moment she'd met Rob she'd wanted to dislike him because she'd known how Herine felt about him. She could hear Cat's frenetic questioning and Herine's answers, but the words didn't make sense. Three months in the future ... Herine was getting married ... a simple ceremony ... first day of Christmas break ... Herine was getting married ...

5

"Of course I'm excited. I'm just overwhelmed," she managed to say, when Cat and Herine demanded to know how she felt about it.

It was a long while before they all hung up, and Cat hurried back to the living room, her face glowing with happiness and tears. She took one look at Jessica and paused. "Oh, honey, it'll be okay."

After a hard swallow, Jessica managed, "I know. It's just too soon."

"I know." Cat burst into the tears Jessica was bottling up and Jessica let her cry for both of them. They cuddled and said nothing for a long while. Jessica could feel Cat's heartbeat against her ribs. She had always liked the sensation.

"It's probably the third inning."

"She'll look wonderful in white velvet."

"Holly and roses will be striking."

"I'm sure it's the second quarter by now."

"I miss Joe Montana."

"He really loves her."

"He's the lucky one," Jessica said firmly. She stroked Cat's hair. "She's her mother's daughter and I know how lucky it is to be loved by you."

"Oh," Cat said, sounding surprised. "That's so sweet."

"It's truth."

"Kiss me."

"Oh yeah," Jessica murmured. "We were interrupted, weren't we?"

"I never said I'd pick you up in front of Starbucks. That was the plan last Wednesday and the construction made me late, remember?"

"You said Starbucks."

"I said in front of the hotel."

"Was I in the room when you said this?"

"I don't talk to you when you're in another room. You just forgot."

"There's nothing wrong with my memory. You said Starbucks. That's where I was."

"There's no Starbucks in front of the hotel and so you weren't where I said I'd pick you up. I circled the block for twenty minutes."

Patiently, "Because I was in front of Starbucks, where you said you'd be."

"That was last Wednesday. The construction made it impossible to circle the block, so I would have never said Starbucks today because I knew it wouldn't work."

"You weren't late on Wednesday, I was."

"Don't you remember how hysterical I was because of the traffic?"

"I don't think you told me about it."

"I was chewing the steering wheel."

"If you'd told me about it I would have suggested someplace other than Starbucks when you told me to meet you in front of Starbucks today."

"But I didn't tell you Starbucks. I said in front of the hotel."

"Did you tell me that when I was in the shower?"

"Yes, of course. I always wait to tell you important information when you're in the shower."

"I'm glad we cleared this up." Cat laced her fingers through Jessica's. "How many times have we had this conversation?"

Jessica grinned helplessly and pulled away from the curb. "Multiply the number of years we've been married times fifty-two weeks in a year. Add six leap days and the number of times we both got our period on the same day."

Cat chewed on her upper lip for a moment. "That's like twelve hundred and twenty-five times."

"That's scary." Jessica negotiated the turn to the Geary tunnel that would whisk them from Japantown to the Cliff House at Ocean Beach. A quick glance at Cat caught a

7

worried frown. "We'll be fine, honey, everything will be fine."

"I know. It's just — I like Rob a lot. His dad sounds kind of conservative though. I don't want us to be an issue for Herine."

Jessica was worried about that too, but it wasn't worth adding to Cat's stress level. "They can't help but love Herine. As for us parents? We don't have to like each other. Just respect our kids' choices."

Cat took her hand and squeezed for the next few minutes. They were both nervous but there was no need to say so again. Long ago Jessica had thought that worrying about whether life was kind to Herine would ease, when Herine was older. She was now beginning to suspect that it never ended. Marriage wouldn't change anything.

"I don't care if she does get married," Cat said fiercely. "I'll never stop being her mom."

Me, neither, Jessica mentally echoed. She squeezed Cat's fingertips. "I never said Starbucks."

"You have never looked so beautiful." Jessica kissed the tip of Cat's nose. The heavy powder did not really hide how red the adorable nose was.

"Oh right. My mascara's still running." Cat turned back to the murky bathroom mirror. "Look at the bags under my eyes. And I've gotten so gray."

"What bags?" Jessica knew when to be blind. She backed up the lie with a full measure of truth. "And I love the color of your hair." Every year the blond was lighter and the strands of silver at the temples grew more pronounced.

"Rob's mother looks half my age."

"If you ask me, Rob's mother has had surgical assistance."

Cat made a face at herself in the mirror. "Maybe I should do that."

"Don't you dare. I love everything about you, just the way you are."

Cat grinned suddenly. "Thanks. I needed that. It's not fair that you're not crying, you know."

"You cry at *Star Trek* episodes, my dear, and I love you for it."

"I was not crying when Kirk lets Edith die, not the last time we watched it. I had a lash in my eye."

"I understand."

Cat looked suspicious of Jessica's sympathy. "You never cry at the movies, either. It's not fair."

Jessica heard the organist change pieces. The old Carpenters' tune was their cue. "It's time for us to go in, you know." She picked up the bundle of red roses and bright green holly and gently repinned it to Cat's ivory and green gown. Her own corsage was being more cooperative.

"I know," Cat said tersely. She stuffed a paper towel from the dispenser into her tiny pocketbook. "I'm out of tissues already."

The walk down the aisle, hand in hand, was easy, even when Cat burst into tears and had to dab with the coarse, brown paper towel. They found a new box of tissues waiting when they reached the front pew — no doubt Herine's forethought. Jessica tenderly dabbed at Cat's eyes, mopping at the mascara Cat should probably have just skipped.

Rob's parents came behind them. They seemed to adore Herine, which was all Jessica required of them. They'd also not in any way indicated they were uncomfortable with their son acquiring two mothers-in-law, and Jessica was content with that.

The music changed to *Con Te Partirò*, swelling with the promise of shared future. Herine had watched her mothers dance to it on their twentieth anniversary and

9

had said then that she'd use it in her wedding someday, as a reminder that relationships can last forever. *I will go with you*, Jessica hummed. To all the unseen worlds of the future, she added to herself. Cat briefly rested her head on Jessica's shoulder as if she had heard Jessica's thoughts.

Jessica abruptly realized that Rob had stepped in from the side room. He stood looking fixedly toward the back of the church, like an explorer sure that the Promised Land lay in that direction. Jessica turned in the pew to look to the rear doors.

Jessica knew most of the girls who stepped in rhythm down the aisle; she'd known some of them for most of their young lives. Camille, the wicked one who was Jessica's favorite, glanced at Cat, then pointedly rolled her eyes at Jessica. Jessica wrinkled her nose back. She and Camille shared the burden of loving emotional women. She'd seen less of Camille and the rest of Herine's friends since Herine had moved to her own apartment. She supposed that now she would see them even less. She was losing more than Herine today. She felt old.

The music changed to the traditional wedding march and all the guests rose to face the bride.

Jessica kept her hand at Cat's elbow, but she no longer noticed Cat's tears.

God, dear God, when had Herine become so heart-rendingly beautiful? She looked so much like her mother. It hurt to look at her. The memories were all there in a rush. The affable Tom who had donated the sperm to help make Herine, and his death six years later from the mysterious "gay disease" that swept through the gay male community of San Francisco. Jessica remembered Herine's screeching entry into the world and the horrible nine and a half minutes when it had appeared that Cat might hemorrhage to death. With the clarity of a movie she could see Herine's first step, and hear her first word, "More." Every broken bone from gymnastics, each broken-heart episode from junior high — it was all there.

She recalled, too, how hard both Herine and Cat had cried after that one big fight of high school, when "I hate you both!" had been instantly followed with "I didn't mean it!" They were so much alike, and here was Herine like a mirror to Cat. There were so many hugs, so much laughter over the years that the memory of it enveloped Jessica in a glow of peace. She squeezed Cat's elbow, trying to convey that they had done a good job. A spectacularly good job.

Herine gazed at Rob with ardent devotion, none of her usual humor about her. She was serious, as serious as Cat had been at their own wedding. For a moment Jessica wanted to stop everything, because there was no way that Rob was worthy of her beloved daughter. The moment passed as she realized again Rob was no longer the thief of her most treasured possession but a member of the family. He was worthy, and that fact was deeply calming. Still, her heart ached when Herine touched Rob's hand, then stood tall and proud by his side. Jessica predicted that Herine's marriage would be as happy as her own. Herine and Rob spent a lot of time gazing into each other's eyes, but they also looked outward in the same direction with steadfast passion.

Camille, the darling and most wicked of Herine's friends, was smirking at her. Jessica didn't realize why until she felt the tears on her cheeks. Then Camille's pert smile crumpled and she joined the other bridesmaids in tears.

Tissues were passed all around. Noses were dabbed in unison as the minister began, "Dearly beloved . . ."

Cat surreptitiously helped herself to a fresh tissue. She muttered, "I knew you'd cry."

"Are you going to sleep?"
"I think so."
"Good." Cat was laughing.

"We don't do that often enough."

"I know, but what we lack in quantity we make up for in quality." Her hand on Jessica's hip was lazily tracing a circle.

"It's an interesting proposition. When you like something is it better to have a little all the time or save it up for having a whole bunch all at once?"

"Doesn't matter what we prefer, it's what's practical that matters. We may have a truly empty nest now, but you travel at least one week a month and the hotel has busy seasons."

Jessica rolled over to look up into Cat's face. "You'd think our schedules would coordinate better than that after all these years."

"*Retirement*, darling. Just keep saying the word . . . I retire in three years."

"*Retirement* — who would have thought that I'd find that word a turn-on?"

Cat's fingertip moved slowly from hip to thigh. "Then we'll both be working one week a month doing conferences, and the rest of time —"

"I work more than just the week I'm on the road."

"I know, but when you finish that book we'll both have more time for this."

"Retirement," Jessica purred sleepily. "Retirement."

"We could be grandmothers by then."

Jessica's eyes flew open. "Do you know something I don't know?"

"No, but it's just a possibility."

"Stop laughing. You'll be one too."

Cat's hand went back to stroking the inside of Jessica's thigh. "Do you really want to go to sleep?"

"I can sleep later . . ."

* * * * *

"Are you going to eat all that?"

"I was planning to." Cat looked forlornly into the bottom of the carton of Dolce de Leche. "There's a couple of bites left, I guess." She surrendered the carton and spoon.

Jessica pushed them back. "You finish it."

Cat's eyes said *I adore you*, then they returned their gaze to the book balanced precariously on one knee. "A meteor really did kill off the dinosaurs."

Jessica muted the infomercial for a moment. "See, she just dumps in all the ingredients — it's oh so simple — and yet when she opens the Wonder Pot back up, the ingredients have conveniently arranged themselves for best filming."

"The cloud cover after impact lasted perhaps as long as fifty years."

"A complete three-course meal in seven minutes."

Cat padded down the stairs with her empty carton and spoon. She returned a few minutes later with a bowl. "We only had Chocolate Galaxy."

"I'll live. Thanks." Jessica savored a mouthful of the gooey ice cream, then pointed at the screen. "Right there — did you see how hard the spokesmodel had to work to move that thing? She tries hard not to let it show, but that cooker weighs a ton."

Cat turned the page of her book.

"Now how did that ground beef get stirred so perfectly into the rest of the ingredients when it was all on the bottom when she started?"

"Did you know that there has been an extinction-causing event every thirty million years?"

"I don't care how tender it is, personally, I wouldn't eat a pot roast sliced by a library card."

"It coincides with every time the earth passes through the plane of the Milky Way. Last time was the dinosaurs and the meteor."

"How can you cook a cup of rice with a quarter-cup of liquid?"

"When the meteor hit the Yucatan Peninsula in Mexico it spewed iridium as far as Alaska."

"And get this — three hundred dollars for three pots and a bunch of cookware utensils. We should have gotten the kids a set for a wedding gift."

Cat gave in to an enormous yawn. "Since she likes to cook about as much as I do, Herine would have beaten you to death with that cooker. I'm going to sleep."

Jessica set her empty bowl on the bedside table and turned off the TV. She snuggled under the covers, stifling her own yawn.

Out of the darkness, Cat asked, "Why doesn't the rice burn?"

"Must be magic rice."

Jessica drifted for a while. "You still awake?" Cat made a quiet noise that meant she was marginally alert. "When do we next pass through the plane of the Milky Way?"

"Another ten million years."

"Oh. That's a relief."

Cat hooked her ankle over Jessica's. "I'm asleep."

"We'll *really* be an old married couple by then."

Touchwood

Published: 1990
Characters: Rayann Germaine, wood sculptor and
                    advertising artist
              Louisa Thatcher, bookstore owner
              Michelle, Rayann's ex-lover and ex-friend
              Judy, Rayann's best friend
              Dedric, Judy's lover
Setting: Oakland, California

The Second is for Spilling Over

Satisfaction

(5 months)

"Hello, Rayann."

"Michelle!"

Rayann stood there with one hand on the silky lingerie undies she had been considering and stared blankly at her ex-lover. She knew she should have thought ahead to the day when she would finally run into Michelle casually. Bumping into her last New Year's Eve at the dance had provided little opportunity to chat, thank goodness.

"How have you been?" Michelle's question was accompanied by a pointed look at the undies.

Rayann smoothed the scarlet silk, then nonchalantly took her hand away. It had been almost a year since she'd walked in on Michelle and another woman. "Fine. Great, in fact." It was the truth. She wouldn't try to explain Louisa. Michelle would never get it.

"That's great." Michelle looked uncharacteristically nervous for a moment. "Are you seeing anybody new?"

She had last seen Michelle at the New Year's Eve party. Zoraida, who had understood the need for Michelle to see Rayann having a wonderful, carefree time, had escorted Rayann. Zoraida had since moved to Lake Tahoe with a new love, *sans* rancor. Louisa occupied Rayann's heart and mind now, and always would. "Yes, as a matter of fact. You don't know her. We went to Greece a few months ago for my mother's wedding. Had our picture taken on Lesbos." Chew on that, Rayann thought. Funny, she couldn't find enough resentment to add "you lying, cheating bitch" to her thoughts.

"Sounds fun."

Michelle reached over to touch the undies Rayann had been considering. She was now standing very close. There had been a time when that crooked smile, the half-closed lids and the exotic scent Michelle dabbed behind her ears had made Rayann weak in the knees and judgment.

It didn't today. It made her remember last night, when Louisa had locked the stairwell door that led to the bookstore and said huskily, "Dinner can wait, can't it?"

Rayann's breath caught in her throat at what the memory did to her, just the thought of Louisa's fingertips on her shoulders and the kiss that had started against the wall in the kitchen and led slowly, deliciously, to bed.

Michelle looked up from her study of the panties and Rayann felt herself flush. For a moment, thinking about the silk of Louisa's mouth on her thighs, she had forgotten Michelle was even there. Remembering the brush of

Louisa's black and silver hair over her stomach had even made her forget where she was.

"I've been hoping I would run into you." Michelle spoke quietly, again with uncharacteristic nervousness. "Do you have time for a cup of coffee? We could sit at the fountain and enjoy the sun for a while."

"I —"

"Give me a chance to say I'm sorry about how we broke up."

Rayann had just been killing time in the department store. She was rarely in San Francisco since moving in with Louisa, but she was meeting her mother for dinner and a movie in an hour. Louisa had urged her to take the late afternoon off, saying she never rested. As if Louisa ever rested, Rayann thought. "I have a little time, I guess." She glanced at the scarlet bikini briefs again and was momentarily awash with the fantasy of Louisa peeling them off of her.

"Great," Michelle said. "I could certainly use some caffeine."

They took the elevator down to the plaza level and chitchatted, while they waited for their coffees about the weather and the rigors of Michelle's continuing medical residency. Rayann sipped her frozen cappuccino and smiled, remembering the mess she and Louisa had made when one morning they'd become so distracted with each other they'd forgotten to put the coffeepot under the dripping filter.

The afternoon was the usual mid-October glory of blue sky and cool breezes. Workers from nearby offices basked on the fountain steps as sunlight glinted off the distinctive obelisk that sat atop the Museum of Modern Art. Rayann instinctively walked her favorite path through the gardens to perch on the edge of the long holding pond that fed the curtain of water over the Martin Luther King, Jr., tribute.

A band playing plastic drums punctuated the ripple of running water. Louisa would love it, Rayann thought.

"So . . ."

Rayann tried to hide her start of confusion. She'd forgotten Michelle was there again. "So?"

"I just wanted to say I'm sorry. I should never have said I was going to be faithful to you."

"That did start me out with the wrong expectation," Rayann said lightly. She had not thought Michelle could admit to any kind of error, so it was gratifying to hear.

Michelle fiddled with the collar of her shirt. "You wouldn't have moved in with me if I hadn't lied."

"Mm-hmm," Rayann confirmed. "It would have spared us both something if you'd just been honest."

"We still had some real happiness."

"You had your version of happiness," Rayann said without heat. There had been a time when she had thought she'd never forget the sight of Michelle wrapped between another woman's legs, but the image was now hard to recall. She could not even remember the pattern of what had been her favorite sheets. "Me whenever you wanted. Someone else whenever you wanted. My happiness was based on ignorance."

"I was selfish."

Rayann blinked. Had she heard right? In the Breakup According to Michelle, Rayann's need for the illusion of fidelity was the only reason Michelle had lied. Rayann looked at Michelle more carefully. "Thank you for admitting that. It was the lies, in the end, that hurt the most. I've kicked myself for believing you when your history should have told me that just wasn't who you were. But I never lied to you, and I hope I never invited you to lie to me."

"I thought so at first. I thought you didn't care about the other women, you just didn't want to know. I was wrong and it didn't take me too long to realize it. But I still wanted you with me. I'm sorry that it hurt you."

It was like a dream, after all the heartbreak and depression leaving Michelle had caused her. She had been broke, with no place to go except back to her mother's. At that time, it had been an untenable solution. Rayann didn't quite know what to say. She remembered one of her mother's rules for proper social behavior: Be gracious in victory. "Apology accepted," she said slowly. "We wanted different things."

"Not always," Michelle said quickly. "Sometimes we wanted exactly the same thing."

Rayann fought back a blush. "That was why we were together for three years. Because sometimes it was perfect. I can't say you did me a favor, but I'm in a better place now because of it. So in a way I owe you thanks. You made me open a new door."

A new door — never in her life had Rayann imagined she would find such consuming passion and fulfilling friendship as she had with Louisa. She had been close to rock bottom, wandering the streets of Oakland wondering what she would do. The only money she'd had was Michelle's and she'd hated needing anything of hers. She'd walked miles with a suitcase, not knowing where she would sleep. Alienated from her mother by yet another fight, she'd been lost and frightened when Louisa had offered the spare bedroom and meals in return for work in the bookstore. It had taken time, lots of it, but once they had both accepted the mystery of their attraction despite the 27 years that separated them, their lives had snapped into place. She got up every day singing inside and ended every day where she most wanted to be, next to Louisa.

Their most serious argument of the last two months had been over Louisa's flat refusal to let Rayann repaint the house and bookstore. Instead, Louisa had hired a company to do it, insisting Rayann no longer needed to earn her keep with manual labor. Rayann had argued that she should do it because they were a family now and she was capable of it.

21

Louisa had laughed with all her Garboesque tones, melting Rayann's resolve on the spot. "You want the real reason? I can't stand the idea of you being exhausted and worn out for weeks on end when I can afford to pay someone to do it."

Rayann had started to protest more vigorously, but the look in Louisa's eye, the twitch of her fingers as she gazed at Rayann's body, made Rayann stop. She crossed the room to kiss Louisa instead, whispering, "You're right. There are better ways to use my energy."

Louisa's hands had been firm under the waistband of Rayann's jeans, smoothing, cupping, stroking. Rayann had yielded instantly, inviting Louisa to slide one hand lower, to tease her, to make her ache.

"You look good, you really do."

Rayann was abruptly aware that she had uncrossed her legs as she had thought about Louisa's touch. Michelle knew her sex drive was frequently in the on position, but she couldn't know that Louisa moved her to heights and depths Michelle hadn't even glimpsed. "Happiness will do that," she said lamely.

"Well, I think I've finally finished sowing my wild oats," Michelle said. "I'm tired of musical beds. Tired of not being able to make plans. Like I want to go on a cruise, but you have to book so far ahead. I realized I wouldn't want to go alone but had no idea which girlfriend I'd choose to go with me. It made me think of you."

The memory of Louisa's fingers teasing her sent a quiver down Rayann's arms. It made it hard to follow what Michelle was saying. "Why me?"

"Because — because I want to have that again. Knowing who'll be in my life tomorrow."

"Wanting it doesn't make it happen."

Michelle seemed to be breathing hard. Her eyes were intent, her cheeks flushed. "Why not? We used to have enough want to start a forest fire. I was an idiot for letting you leave me. Nothing's been right ever since."

"Oh —" Rayann was so startled by Michelle's kiss that at first she responded. She was dry brush all the time with Louisa providing endless flame. For just a moment, Michelle's lips added to the prickles of fire already running down Rayann's arms.

They weren't Louisa's lips. Even as Michelle wound her fingers in Rayann's hair, a gesture that had never failed in the past to open Rayann's mouth for deeper kissing, Rayann was trying to pull away. Louisa was the cause of any passion she felt. Michelle just happened to be attached to the lips. She wanted Louisa's lips and all the rest of her.

She didn't struggle, and Michelle eventually came up for air. Rayann found herself grinning into Michelle's bemused face.

"I wasn't trying to make you laugh," Michelle said a trifle testily.

"I know. I'm sorry. It's just not going to work."

"Are you sure?" Michele touched Rayann's lower lip with her fingertip, but when it failed to end Rayann's smile, her hand dropped away. "I see."

"I really have found someone else."

"I wasn't sure. You seemed . . . like you always were."

Rayann knew the signs were all over her. Her breasts were straining against her bra. Her thighs clenched and unclenched. Her color was high and her hands moved nervously over her hips and stomach. Michelle knew what all those signals meant. "It's not you. I'm sorry," she said again, not wanting to seem mean.

Michelle looked resigned and unhappy, but there was nothing Rayann could do about it. Grateful for the cold chill of the frozen cappuccino, Rayann thought perhaps a dignified retreat was her best strategy. "I really need to get going. I'm having dinner with my mother, and then we're going to the movies."

Michelle arched her eyebrows. "You're on speaking terms?"

"I'm seeing a lot of things in a different way." She stood up and only wobbled a little. She really wanted Louisa to drag her into bed. "She's not the witch I thought." Neither are you, she could have added.

"You've changed." Michelle said it as she was trying to convince herself Rayann was not as desirable as she had once been.

"There's plenty more dykes in the sea," Rayann said philosophically. "I'm glad we had a chance to talk."

"Me too. I think." Michelle's face flickered with an array of emotions ranging from chagrin to confusion.

Beyond feeling good about Michelle's apology, Rayann didn't give her another thought as she hurried to meet her mother.

Muni was slow and BART had trains sitting idle on the tracks because of a delay at Oakland-12th Street. It was nearly midnight and Rayann knew by the time she reached home Louisa would surely be asleep. She'd been up herself since just after six, but she wasn't in the least bit drowsy.

She had finished her book fifteen minutes ago, and having nothing else to do, she recalled what Michelle had said. She had to admit it felt pretty good. When she told her mother about meeting up with Michelle, they agreed it had been an ego-satisfying turn of events. There were a lot of women who would love to have an ex admitting his or her wrongs and wanting them back, just for the pleasure of stomping on their ex's heart, good and hard. But whatever it was that Michelle wanted held no interest for Rayann. She didn't even care enough to stomp.

She really hadn't given Michelle more than a passing thought since falling in love with Louisa. At first Louisa had seemed simple and direct, but as Rayann continued to work with her she discovered complexities and contradictions that unsettled and ultimately attracted her.

Her own stereotypes had initially kept her from realizing that Louisa was a lesbian. She hadn't thought grandmothers with old-fashioned wooden combs in their hair could be lesbians. With the certainty of youth, she had then believed that Louisa was obliged to come out to her son, Teddy, even after all those years. Being a grandmother was exactly why Louisa had not — she had not wanted to risk losing contact with either her grandson or her son. Louisa had already sacrificed an open love with her first partner, Chris, to foster and keep the love of her son. At the beginning of their relationship, Rayann hadn't been able to understand why Louisa had felt compelled to choose between two loves.

Of course, Rayann hadn't grown up in a world where lacking three articles of women's clothing could get a woman arrested for cross-dressing. Or in a world where being a mother could be grounds for dismissal if your boss felt you were neglecting your maternal duties. Louisa had lived through those times. They had made her who she was: strong, adaptable, principled and practical. When Rayann had finally sensed the depth of Louisa's personality she had been hopelessly in love.

The train finally lurched into motion. The startled butterflies in Rayann's stomach made her think of being in Louisa's arms, feeling butterflies of wonder when grandmother transformed to lover. Her stereotypes had misled her again; Louisa was not the lover she had initially expected. Her fevered imaginings had hardly gotten past what a kiss might feel like. On Christmas Eve she had finally felt that kiss and it was everything she had anticipated: gentle, considerate, soft.

Kisses were only the beginning. Louisa had made love to her thoroughly, intensely, powerfully. Her decisive touch left Rayann wanting only more. Louisa didn't need to be told anything; she read Rayann's body with perceptive intent, and then she satisfied all the unspoken wanting, again and again.

Weeks had passed before Rayann found the courage to ask Louisa why she evaded Rayann's attempts to return the lovemaking. By then, at least, she had a clearer understanding of what it must be like to be fifty-six. Louisa had not been ready to believe Rayann really wanted her. But there was a sexual dynamic at play in addition to the age difference, one Rayann had never been exposed to and still didn't quite know how to handle. It was the Nineties now, and the lesbian nation was supposed to be past butch and femme labels, at least Michelle and her circle of friends had seemed to think so.

A grandmother with wooden combs in her hair was not anyone's image of a butch woman. Certainly never hers. As she walked briskly from the BART station to their home above the bookstore she realized how much she had grown from the narrow world she had experienced before Louisa. She now accepted that for some women the self-adopted labels had meaning, comfort and power. She had no desire for a label and was unwilling to analyze just where she might fall on the continuum, but she was in love with Louisa. Louisa was decidedly butch. Granted, she'd adopted outward trappings over the years to hide her sexuality from her son and most of the world. Some of the trappings had been peer pressure from other lesbians in her past, who had not allowed that a butch woman might also be a mother.

She turned the last corner to home and asked herself why she was mulling all of this over. Was it Michelle? Had Michelle unsettled her? She stopped walking for a moment. Michelle had been a good lover. Sex had been a mutual give-and-take. Was she missing the simplicity?

She set off again and didn't pause until she was in front of the bookstore. No. It had nothing to do with Michelle. The road not taken held no allure. She was

where she wanted to be. But sex with Louisa was complicated by Rayann's uncertainties. Bumping into Michelle
had just heightened her awareness that she was still
coping with her lack of control over what happened in bed.
True, Louisa did anything Rayann asked, if ever Rayann
needed to ask. Plus, Louisa was as ready and able as
Rayann when it came to how often. So what was she
complaining about?

She looked up the steps at the darkened bookstore,
remembering the day she had first gone inside. The
Common Reader had seduced her from the start, smelling
of old pages and poetry. She blew it a kiss, then went
around the side of the house to the back stairs. She had
no complaints about her life, just trepidation at this
moment. Rayann might send a smoldering glance, reveal in
a dozen ways that she wanted to have sex, but it was
always Louisa who made the first move. Bottom line, she
told herself, you have no idea how to ask her for sex
because you've never had to. You look at her mouth, at
her hands, and you want her. She looks at you, you go to
pieces, and she takes you to bed.

She tip-toed around the house, not wanting to selfishly
wake Louisa just because she wanted to have sex. There
was always tomorrow. It was almost guaranteed that when
they woke up in the morning Louisa would recognize
Rayann's desire and immediately, ecstatically do something
about it. Six or seven hours, Rayann thought. You can
wait. She needs her sleep. She noiselessly removed her
clothes, trying not to shudder as the crisp sheets of their
bed seemed to caress her knees and shoulders.

She sent her usual mental greeting to the pattern of
moons and stars in the tapestry over the bed, but the
familiarity of the weaving did not relax her at all. Her wet
thighs would not unclench and she locked her ankles
around each other, wondering how long it would take to
fall asleep when every nerve in her body was telling her
she was wonderfully alive.

Louisa stirred. "Did you have a nice time with your mom?"

"Yeah — did I wake you?"

"Not really. I was just dozing." Louisa rolled over, a blur of black and silver hair and alluring mouth. "You must be tired."

"BART had a holdup and I just missed the streetcar and it took forever for another to come." Rayann stopped babbling. None of that mattered.

"Okay," was all Louisa said.

Rayann tried to let Louisa fall asleep. Louisa wasn't going to get her seven hours as it was and Rayann had not failed to notice that Louisa needed seven hours to feel energetic the following day. Although Louisa often seemed stronger, she'd had a birthday a month ago. Fifty-seven was fifty-seven. Hell, Rayann thought. Thirty is thirty, too. You're a grump if you don't get at least six hours these days.

She tried to go to sleep. She reached the point of dozing and a waking dream intruded, remembering their second night together, when they'd finally admitted that the first night hadn't just been "one of those things." That night she had felt the way she did now. Hardly able to move or breathe, achingly wet and wanting to open herself to Louisa's fingers and take and take and take.

She moved slightly closer to Louisa, inhaling the scent of her hair. Louisa's breathing seemed steady and deep. She kissed the black and silver waves that spilled toward her, holding them against her mouth and face.

Let her sleep. You don't know how to ask. She takes pleasure in seducing you, so wait for her.

Gently, holding her breath, she kissed Louisa's shoulder. One taste — she hoped it would suffice. Instead her panting grew louder and Louisa was stirring.

"Ray, are you all right?"

She said nothing because the answer was both yes and no. Yes, she was fine, she was where she wanted to be, next to Louisa. No, she wasn't okay, and wouldn't be until Louisa took her, and until Louisa's mouth enjoyed all of her.

Louisa rolled over. "What's wrong?"

"Nothing." It would only be another moment until Louisa touched her. One touch and Louisa would know, like she always seemed to know. It's important, she thought. Before Louisa could touch her, she blurted out, "I want to have sex."

Louisa murmured, "Why didn't you say so sooner?" Her hand smoothed Rayann's hip.

"I didn't want to wake you." She moaned, trying not to be loud, when Louisa traced her hip with one lazy finger.

"Wake me next time," Louisa whispered. "Your skin is on fire."

"I didn't want to ... didn't want to ..." It was hard to think with Louisa kissing the side of her mouth.

"Didn't want to what?"

"I wasn't sure you ..."

"You weren't sure I would want to?" Louisa's fingertips slipped through Rayann's wetness, and Louisa gasped. "How could you think I wouldn't want this?"

Rayann shook her head. That wasn't it. She couldn't think anymore. Words required thinking. Only instinct was left. "Please. Don't tease me."

Louisa was already inside her. She knows, Rayann thought, she understands that tonight I just want to hold on. She held on, ignited by the friction of Louisa's fingers moving so quickly and surely. She let Louisa take her to a place beyond words, where her body sang need and satisfaction. She traveled between the extremes as satisfaction led to want led to fulfillment led to craving more. Every step she was guided by Louisa's hands and mouth, taking her surely from desire to completion and back again.

* * * * *

29

"How could you think I wouldn't want that?" Louisa kissed Rayann's mouth and chin as she cradled Rayann's damp, limp body in her arms.

"It wasn't that." Rayann shivered with exhaustion. "I knew that you wouldn't hesitate. It doesn't matter."

"Tell me. It does matter." Louisa kissed her eyelids. "I don't ever want you to hesitate again."

"I thought . . . I thought it might offend the butch in you. For me to start things."

Louisa pressed her lips to Rayann's temple and ear. Finally, she said, "Don't you know that you always start things?"

"No, I — you —"

"You're the flame, Ray. I don't know why you want me. All I know is that you do and I can't wait to get my hands on you. I'm just following your lead, like tonight."

"You make me want you. I don't know how you do it." Rayann smiled sleepily into Louisa's eyes, knowing she would have plenty to think about later. "I think we're having a chicken-and-egg argument."

"Do we love because we are loved? Do we want because we're wanted? I don't know the answer."

"Maybe the answer doesn't matter." Rayann sighed with deep contentment. "The only answer that matters to me is that you love me. That sounds selfish, doesn't it? After the last —" She peeked at the illuminated alarm clock. "Good God, the last hour, I'm still thinking about you loving me."

"Good." Rayann could tell Louisa was smiling.

"I'm not going to sleep yet," Rayann whispered. "Not until you're selfish for a while." She coiled one hand in Louisa's hair. "Please be selfish."

"I think I can manage it, if that's what you want." Louisa was definitely smiling.

Rayann didn't give in to her exasperation. She pushed her thigh hard between Louisa's legs and was rewarded by an earthy gasp. "It's what I want," she admitted. "How perfect that it's what you want, too."

"Perfect," Louisa answered as she drew Rayann's hand to her body. "Right now and tomorrow, and after that. Perfect."

Come Here

(Any given night)

This night is like any other. If I screen out the steady drone of traffic and the monotonous tick of the mantel clock, I hear the quiet drip of the fog that has blanketed our district of San Francisco for the last few days. I also hear the whisper of a page turning behind me. I don't turn to look. I know exactly how Dedric has sprawled in the armchair, her long legs hanging over one side. I know without looking that one slipper has fallen off; the other dangles from her toes. I shake this image of her from my mind and go back to my patient files.

My psychotherapy practice is thriving and the files are always in need of updating. I am breaking the rules by working on the night we choose every week as "date night." Dedric is immersed in the last pages of a spy thriller and so far hasn't said she minded my working. I set one file aside, my notes complete, and stretch lazily before taking another. I feel guilty for taking our special time and though the work needs to be done, I half wish she would remember it was date night and make me stop. There are many other ways I would like to spend the night: dancing in her arms, wrapped in a blanket with her in front of the fire, entwined in the softness of our bed.

The clock chimes after I finish two more files. The fog gathers closer and I no longer hear traffic on the street. I stretch again, running my hands over the small of my back, arching my shoulders. As I open another file I hear the soft thud of a book falling to the floor and the rustle of fabric as Dedric shifts position.

"Come here." Dedric's silken voice whispers.

The files become a blur. I have been under Dedric's unrelenting spell for nine years and those two words, in that voice of hers, never fail to find response in my body.

"Judy." Her voice is a low contralto. I have heard it raised in a forceful, commanding yell of "Stop. Police." But tonight her voice is soft, edged with the need that is her one weakness — her need for me.

I put down my pen, aware that her gaze is on me. I put off meeting her stare for I know when I do I will lose myself in oceans of emerald green. My hands will lose themselves in her long, thick, auburn hair. My lips will be lost to her demanding passion. So I don't look at her, not yet. I close the file on top and tidy the stacks, aware that I won't return to them until tomorrow. As a psychologist I understand why it is so important to me that I close the door on my professional life before opening the door to Dedric's love. My patients would not recognize their quiet, pillar-of-rock therapist as the woman who is trembling as she rises from the table, gaze unfocused, lips parted, breath quickened.

Dedric's features are cast in a soft Irish mold of creamy skin that sprouts freckles in the sun. When she's in uniform she pulls her masses of hair into a no-nonsense ponytail. The severity would make most women appear more angular, but it only emphasizes how her brows arch and the smooth rise of her throat. I know that she could have chosen anyone to be her mate, but she chose me. I am the only one who makes her more beautiful still. I am the only one who sees her goddess-like beauty amplified by passion and desire. I am the one she loves, the one she needs.

I stand in front of her as she looks up at me from the depths of the armchair. Just as my patients would not recognize my passion and surrender, her fellow officers would not recognize the flush on her cheeks, the hair down around her shoulders, the eyes that are pleading. Her colleagues often accuse her of coldness. Among our friends she's regarded as an outrageously bawdy flirt. No one else knows these expressions on her face, this open posture of her body, the lips that have grown fuller and redder over the past minute as my gaze devoured their sweetness.

I slide onto her knee. I know my power over her. She has been decorated for her courage and strength, but at this moment I know she is in my complete control. Arms that can bench press one-eighty sweep around me, hold me helpless against the lushness of her body. And yet I feel her trembling. I kiss her softly, quickly.

"Come to bed with me," she says, simultaneously asking and ordering. She needs to be specific. She wants me to know that we aren't tickling or teasing, snuggling or cuddling — maybe later, but not now and not for a while. I've known that since she said, "Come here."

"Yes." I kiss her again. She draws her breath in sharply and rocks me back in her arms. Her lips find my throat and the sound of her mouth leaving warm and moist kisses is no louder than the tick of the clock, but it is a symphony to me. The sound of her lips on my body moves me more than the sight of it. She presses her mouth to my breasts, which are hard and arching in their confinement, and I raise my hand to unbutton and expose myself but she stops me with a slight shake of the head.

"Not yet." Her mouth returns to them, torturing me with muffled nips and slow warmth. She tells me how soft I am to her mouth, how lovely I am to her, and then, raggedly, she says, "I want you so much."

I capture her hand, then draw it to me, inviting her to cup and stroke my answering ache through the soft fabric of my slacks. She slowly moves her palm between my legs, as slowly as her lips find mine again, as slowly as she opens my mouth and tastes me more deeply. Her breathing is faster now, her palm speeds up, rubbing me there as I thrust against it. Then her fingers press in.

I hold nothing back. She knows what she is doing to me and that I can't hold anything back. That is my power over her, that I can't resist her, that I can't get enough of her, that I want and need to take exactly what she wants and needs to give.

She is groaning as her fingers agitate me even more. "Inside," I plead. "Stop teasing." She hasn't been teasing — her touch has been direct. But she knows what I mean and her hand is under my clothing, cupping ... oh so cruel, now she teases me, making me pay for having falsely accused her. "I'm going to ... Dee, please, I want your fingers in me when I ..."

Supple, warm strokes fill me. She holds me tightly against her as I thrust myself to her, then cling. Not long. . . not long. She knows how close I am. Her touch changes, shifts, finds those places that are fluttering and quivering. The stroke of her fingers tightens me. I'm stiffening ... I want to be fluid for her but I can't help myself. My legs are rigid now, my spine straightening. But she holds me close and cradles me when all the tautness and strain explodes and I crumple against her, cooing pet names and murmuring in her ear.

Her heartbeat and breathing are the only sounds I hear. I revel in the peace that rolls over me. My work is forgotten, everything is gone. I could fall asleep in the cradle of her love, but her fingers shift slightly, then slide out of me. The peace dissolves. My cooing becomes demanding. I seek the full swells under her shirt with my mouth. She doesn't stop me when I awkwardly, hurriedly unbutton her shirt. I'm fast and direct — not teasing — as I worship her breasts, savoring these heavy treasures that arch to meet my mouth.

The world shifts and after my vertigo subsides I realize she has stood up, still cradling me in her arms. She carries me down the hallway and kicks open the bedroom door. Then she sets me gently on the bed and stands before me. Her strength would intimidate me if her hands weren't trembling on my shoulders as she clutches me to her, both for balance and from desire, drawing my head to her breast, offering herself to me.

The sight of her half-naked body excites me more than when she is completely nude. She is so lovely she becomes a statue, an artwork, something I can't touch. Nine years ago we had nowhere to go to make love so we found places for quick fumblings — maybe that is what has stayed with me, the image of her, her shirt open, her pale skin gleaming in the dim light. The pain of my desire makes me delirious. I know I'll remove all her clothing eventually, and I'll revel in her nakedness and glorious softness. Suddenly she is pushing me back. My mouth doesn't want to leave her taut and aroused breasts, but she pushes and I yield.

I yield my clothing, piece by piece, until nothing separates my body from her hungry, emerald eyes. She gathers her hair, arching her neck in aristocratic beauty as she does so, and with the thick hair she sweeps my body.

Her hair is pure, heavy silk, whispering silk, like her voice. It raises goosepimples on my thighs and stomach, over my shoulders and arms.

Her hands are on me again. Now her teeth capture and tease my bare breasts, alternating loving bites with strokes of her tongue. I wind my hands in hair, tangling them in the masses of silk and she looks up at me. I look into her eyes, oceans of emerald green.

She kneels between my trembling legs. My knees capture her hips. My hands, still wound in her hair, pull her down. Elegantly and slowly, like a swan coming to rest on a still lake, she dips into my wetness, but I am not still, I am moving, moaning, gasping. When I let go of her hair it flows over my hips. I fall back, yield myself up, to show her how much I need her. I am her weakness.

In the morning, as is my habit, I will probably analyze why I put her actions and mine in those terms — weakness and need — but all the analysis in the world can't capture what her tongue, slipping through my welcoming flesh, seeking my most private and hungry places, does to me. It's like riding a roller coaster made of cotton. I am beyond words, but she has small, crying words, pleading words gasped between kisses and strokes of her tongue until I give in, can't hold back. She crushes her mouth to me as I arch and cry out. Her strong arms slip under my body, holding me safe as I hurtle to the place where she takes me.

When I return she is preening her satisfaction at my satisfaction. She takes such pleasure in our lovemaking that I could forget that she needs more than that. She protests as I move to her side, returning lazily to my abject worship of her breasts. Her protests become a sigh, her sigh a moan, then her moan fades to silence. I know her jaw is clenched. Her body becomes rigid. This is the barrier only I have climbed. She freezes with the fear that I will somehow be repulsed by the fragrance of her body, the sounds of her passion, the texture of her wetness. She flaunts her sexual prowess but is scared of her sexual attraction. I start to talk. I tell her what I want to do. I tell her what I'm going to do. I tell her how much I want to do it. By the end of my speech I am so aroused I am rubbing myself against the sharp point of her hip bone. I pull her hand to me and show her what wanting her has done to me again.

Her body melts. I fly past her barriers, wrapping her long, muscular legs around my shoulders. Breathing her in, tasting her, I shudder in pleasure, in awe of her beautiful essence. I coat my lips with it, fill my mouth with it, ever conscious of her legs gripping me, her answering gasps breaking out of her lungs faster and faster. I take such pleasure in it that it seems the most selfish act possible.

We untangle our bodies. I close my eyes and drift. I love our tradition of date night.

"Come here." Her voice caresses me in the darkness, stirring me again. I did. I do. I will.

Paperback Romance

Published: 1991
Characters: Carolyn Vincense, romance novelist
             Alison McNamara, Carolyn's agent
             Nicola "Nick" Frost, symphony conductor
Setting: Hot spots of Europe and Sacramento,
                California

The Third is for Turning On

Key of Sea

(9 years)

The unfamiliar territory of a swimsuit, sun block and a beach towel almost kept Nick in her cabin. The undulation of the cruise ship wasn't unpleasant, and was not the reason for the fluttering in her stomach.

Nerves, she thought. *I don't have nerves.*

She glared at herself in the mirror, trying to find the steely calm that braved audiences and critics, cowed violinists and stopped venom-spewing sopranos in mid-syllable.

It was hard to do in a swimsuit.

"Take a vacation, you'll feel like a million quid," she muttered. Patricia, her ex and still a close friend, had thought an all-lesbian cruise would do her good. Even now, Nick could not believe she had agreed.

A Caribbean cruise was just the sort of thing that Carolyn would have done. Nick watched her mouth soften as she thought of Carolyn. It always did, always would. The one who got away, *bella* Carolyn.

Carolyn would not recognize her in a swimsuit. The only clothes Nick had worn when she'd known Carolyn had been men's. It had been nearly a decade since the charade as "Nick" had ended, but she still preferred more masculine attire. It had authority, for one thing. Of course she hid behind it — *shut up, Patricia, thank you, I know that* — and probably always would. It had been the clothes and the privilege that came with being perceived male that had given her the confidence to take up the baton. Tall, slender, ascetic "Nick" had provided too-tall, too-humorless, gawky Nicola an entrance into what was still an almost exclusively male club. For years, long past habit and probably need, she worked tirelessly to always be thought of as Maestro Frost, a conductor, musician and arranger. Woman, lesbian, just plain Nick . . . they were down the list, near English, Scorpio and allergic to bee stings.

A swimsuit. God, a swimsuit. At least it was a utilitarian Speedo one-piece. She was pale and drawn, having spent the last four years indoors. Patricia was right about one thing, sun would do her good. She angrily slung the towel around her neck, picked up her swim bag with book and suntan lotion and went out on deck.

She settled into a deck chair and hurriedly put on dark glasses. She did not want to overhear any barely whispered conversations that began, "Hey, isn't that Nicola Frost . . . you know, the conductor who pretended she was a man to get a job . . ." She really only wanted to be left alone.

For the next hour the only person who spoke to her was the deck waiter. Upon seeing her cabin key, he danced

44

attendance on her to an extent that was annoying. Drenched with perspiration and dizzy from the piña colada, she gave up the sun for the day and gathered her things.

When she reached the cool hatchway, she glanced back at the deck she was leaving. There were a few women in brilliantly hued caftans, but the majority had skin on display: thongs, Band-Aid-sized bikini tops or no tops at all. Now that's what I call a landscape, she thought. Hot flamenco tapped in her ears and wild Bartok skirled in her nerves.

"Relax, have some fun," Patricia had told her. Right. How did a mostly celibate, often disagreeable and thoroughly self-absorbed symphony conductor have fun?

She was not even granted the anonymity of a table for eight where she could introduce herself as just "Nick" and hope she wasn't recognized. Instead, her first dinner was Captain's Table and formal dress. The formal attire didn't bother her — she'd tied her own cravat enough times. She did miss Oscar, though, whose scathing wit had buoyed her through many ponderous occasions. There had been no warning sign of the stroke that had taken him from her. One moment her lifelong mentor had been deriding a critic and the next he had been gone. His memorial service, attended by hundreds, had been her first taste of life without his sheltering arm.

Life had not gotten any easier. Since Oscar's death four years ago she'd avoided the public occasions he would have insisted on. It had been four years of life indoors and in bad humor for the most part. Patricia had thrown in the towel on their relationship a year ago. She was a well-known novelist in her own right and had no need to put up with Nick's moods just for a little companionship.

She cinched her cummerbund and took heart from the fact that she would not be the only woman in a tuxedo this evening. Sure enough, tuxedos outnumbered dresses by at least three to one. There were women everywhere in purple, silver and black tuxedos, most in couples. Rainbow ties and cummerbunds abounded and the line for formal photographs was lengthy. She overheard one happy but tearful woman tell the ship's photographer that they couldn't risk a professional picture together taken at home. Carolyn would love this, Nick thought. *That's who should be on this trip, Carolyn and Alison, not me.*

She was deliberately late to the cocktail party. Between the captain's English and her Italian they conversed enough for him to assure her of his pleasure in her music. She scolded herself for being stuck up and made an effort to participate in the conversation with the senior crew instead of quenching their enthusiasm with a chilly "How interesting" from behind her maestro's mask.

It occurred to her that she hadn't liked herself very much for a while. Was it any wonder Patricia had decided she'd rather be alone than put up with emotional silence? What was Patricia doing right now?

She turned her mind from that line of thought, having already accepted that she should not have let Patricia go so easily. "I feel as if I'm just a handy escort," Patricia had said the night she moved out. "I like going out with you, Nick. It's never dull. Call whenever you want me. I just don't need to pretend it's more than that anymore."

Dinner was sumptuous and the table service impeccable. It had been a long time since she'd cared about what she ate. From bad moods and artistic fever that left her exhausted, she'd descended into a general depression after Patricia left. Not even word of an American Grammy award for *Variations on an Adagio: A Tribute to Samuel Barber* had cheered her much. She'd loved doing the recording. The vocal arrangements of the well-known adagio had been some of her finest work. Oscar would have loved it. Patricia had called to congratulate her on the award, but there had been nothing else, certainly not the Champagne and sex they'd shared to commemorate each other's successes in the past.

She abruptly realized she was listening to the Barber adagio now, very faint in the background of the chatter-filled dining room. It was indeed her recording, and she thanked the captain for the compliment. She listened to it for the rest of the meal, the pleasure of her work loosening her tongue as she found she had a little small talk in her after all.

The next morning she elected to stay aboard ship instead of hauling about in hot caravans to look at the sights of Nassau. She had no desire to see marching flamingos. On her way down from the sundeck she purchased some postal cards in the gift shop and picked up some lunch at the ever-present buffet. Her stateroom was comfortable and cool, with a small veranda.

Patricia —

She had to stop there, not wanting to write "wish you were here." It sounded so insincere, and the ironic part was that she meant it. She became so irritated with herself that she set the card aside and started a new one.

Carolyn —

You and Alison would love an all-lesbian cruise. Women everywhere, lots of them celebrating anniversaries with all the romantic trappings that you so adore. I am enjoying myself, except for the sunburn. Picture me in a swimsuit. Now stop laughing. Love to both of you.

She stared at the card for Patricia. This cruise had been Patricia's idea. How could Patricia, for even a moment, have thought Nick would fit in? Being single was handicap enough, but having celebrity made it impossible to buddy around with strangers.

A demon of ill humor wrote the rest of Patricia's card.

Patricia —

You were right, darling! Just what the doctor ordered. I haven't slept a wink but can attest that the beds in several of the cabins are quite comfortable. Wish you were here?

It was what Oscar would have described as a singular lapse in judgment to carry the two cards directly to the purser's desk to be mailed while they were in port. She waited a moment for the assistant to be free, then handed the cards over.

"We'll charge the airmail stamps to your cabin, Ms. Frost," the woman said. She had a charming voice, edged with a Nordic lilt — Swedish, perhaps. Certainly the short, nearly white hair indicated Scandinavian roots of some kind. She efficiently dabbed two postal stamps on a damp sponge and applied them so as not to cover Nick's bold, block lettering. The words seemed to leap off the cards and Nick flushed, wondering if the woman had read the message to Patricia. She was suddenly aware of her swimsuit-clad body and then abruptly even more aware of the other woman's white uniform that molded a body far more statuesque than Nick's own. Having completed her task, the woman straightened up for the first time, and Nick realized they were eye-to-eye. She did not often meet women her own height. When she did, they were usually not in attractive uniforms while she stood awkwardly in nothing but a swimsuit.

Thoroughly flustered, Nick sought out the woman's nametag — not an assistant, but the Purser herself, Ilea Hamm.

"Was there anything else you required, Maestro?" Ilea Hamm's eyes were focused somewhere lower than Nick's face for a moment, then she glanced up to capture Nick in a clear, blue gaze.

"No, thank you," Nick stuttered and she escaped to her stateroom. Romance writer Carolyn would be having hysterics at Nick playing the part of the stammering ingenue. Nick didn't find it at all amusing.

* * * * *

Conversation stopped when she took her seat at her assigned dinner table that evening. Everyone seemed tongue-tied. There was a moment when Nick could have subsided into the humorless, monosyllabic auteur, but instead she made an effort. "I'm sorry I missed meeting everyone last night. I'm Nick."

There was another awkward silence, then Nick held out her hand to the woman next to her, who said her name was Tammy, shook hands, and around the table they went.

Yet another silence followed. Bloody hell, Nick thought. Do I have to do all the work? "How did everyone spend their day?"

Thankfully, the American tendency to chatter won out, and she was relieved of having to push the conversation along. Still, the others would just start to get excited about something and then curtail their enthusiasm with a glance at Nick, as if they were afraid she would judge them for liking snorkeling or sunbathing. Contrary to popular belief, she did not live in an ivory tower, breathing only the rarified air of the great masters. At least not all the time.

"I've never tried snorkeling," she volunteered. "Is it fun?"

Apparently, it was. Just like that she agreed to go on a snorkeling expedition when they reached their next port the following day. All the equipment was provided and two of the women at the table, Joan and Paula, worked for the lesbian travel agent who had arranged the cruise. They were sure they could find Nick a spot, even at the last minute.

She had skipped the entertainment the previous night, but Joan and Paula's enthusiasm was infectious. She'd never had much time for light entertainment. Even films were a rarity. So she'd never heard of the lesbian comic,

49

but it was apparent almost everyone else, particularly the Americans, had. Nick surprised herself by laughing more than she had in the last decade, then she stayed for the karaoke show that followed. Off-key singing usually made her feel as if she were chewing foil, but the Brandy Alexander recommended by Paula helped her send Maestro Frost to bed while Nick stayed to enjoy herself.

She was surprised to spot Purser Hamm watching the show on the other side of the room, alongside several other female crewmembers. Paula noticed that she kept looking over at them and answered Nick's unasked question. "The lesbians on the crew are always thrilled when we take over the ship — they get hit on all the time. This is the one week where they enjoy it."

So the purser was a lesbian. How . . . interesting. Properly attired in slacks and a silk shirt, Nick allowed that she might be willing to make Ilea Hamm's acquaintance again.

After the show, she thanked the two Americans for their company and drifted into the ebb of traffic that would bring her closer to Purser Hamm. She'd waded through enough crowds to know that a sidestep here and there would bring her seemingly by accident into Ilea Hamm's line of sight.

She had just caught the purser's gaze when a delectable, scantily clad woman brushed by them. Nick could not help but look. The tight red dress left nothing to the imagination. The body it covered did not need anyone's imagination to be considered magnificent. Nick sighed, then remembered Ilea Hamm was next to her.

Their gaze met at about the same time, and Nick recognized the same mute appreciation for the scarlet-clad brunette. They shared a knowing smile and Nick said, "I suppose it's politically incorrect to stare."

Ilea's laugh was both sultry and suggestive. "If she did not want stares she'd wear something else." She nodded with a challenging smile. "This week will be far too short. Excuse me, won't you?"

Befuddled, Nick watched Ilea move toward the voluptuous and apparently unattached brunette and expertly strike up a conversation. The purser was not wasting any time. Great, Nick thought. I just became chopped liver.

Snorkeling was fun, even when one swam as badly as Nick did. She ended up on the same excursion as the two friendly Americans, and they took good care of her as they all floated facedown in the crystalline water. From the surface Paula would point out fish and sea anemones, while Joan dove down to examine creatures that lurked in the shadows. Back on board she thanked them again for their care. What some Americans lacked in decorum they more than made up for with their generosity of spirit. Carolyn was an American, after all. *Bella* Carolyn.

The third day her senses seemed to wake up all at once. The food tasted glorious. The air was a delight to inhale. The sea seemed to be a hue of blue-green she'd never seen before. The star-studded night sky left her speechless.

Having taken Joan's advice about excursions for the rest of the cruise, she discovered a true enjoyment of sailing. Although all she did was sit back while someone else did the work, she loved the surge of the catamaran and was intrigued by the way the vessel worked. They skimmed over water she was assured was over twenty feet deep, but the coral and rocks on the bottom were plainly visible. The crew obviously loved their tasks. She found herself wondering how she could go sailing again, given her busy schedule. An interest in something that wasn't musical — another thing that Patricia had said she needed.

She went sailing on a bona fide wind-driven sailboat

the following day and stayed up late for the shows and karaoke. When she woke up the morning of her last full day, she was not at all sure where the week had gone.

Patricia need not know that she had been right, Nick decided. The cruise had been a long-overdue holiday. She'd almost forgotten about her next performance, her next recording contract. The mask of Maestro Frost that usually hid Nick from the world had been blown askew by some clean sea breezes. Patricia's chief complaint had been that the mask had stopped coming off at all, not even when they were alone.

Swimsuit, sunblock and a beach towel — they were no longer unfamiliar. She bounded up to the sundeck that last afternoon and stretched out for a lovely hour as the ship's band played island and steel drum music in the background.

The path back to her cabin went by the lounge where the night's entertainment would be held. The lesbian band for their last night at sea was wrapping up a rehearsal. The final strains of a high-energy rock song sounded well-conceived and Nick was looking forward to the performance. She peeked through the slightly open door, more curious about the instruments they were using than anything else, and was almost knocked down by the exiting performers. They didn't give her a second glance as they hurried away.

She slipped inside the lounge, not sure what drew her. Two guitars rested side by side in standing racks, backed by a full set of drums, keyboards bristling with wiring, and a cello, also wired for the amplification. A cello, Nick thought, that was what had caught her ear. It wasn't an instrument one automatically associated with rock music.

To one side, almost forgotten, was the ship's own grand piano. She stepped up to it, knowing that the rocking motion and the high humidity would have taken a toll on the instrument's voice. She set the top up on its brace and carefully tweaked a few strings with one hand. In tune, but just barely.

It had been a long time since she'd sat down to play just for the fun of it. She was always rehearsing or practicing so she could perform. The last time she'd played something just because she felt like it had been before Oscar had died. He'd asked for the Barber adagio. She'd later undertaken her variations recording because Oscar had said she had the sense of it in her grasp.

She didn't feel like the adagio now. She'd never played in a swimsuit before, that was a certainty. She didn't want to give in to the call of the keys. There was so little of her mask left. Surely she needed to keep hold of that little bit. Playing what her fingers were itching to perform would sweep it all away.

She touched the closest key and the Rachmaninoff seized her. The third movement surged in her hands and she played for her own ear, knowing her tempo was inconsistent, that her fingers were not up to the finer motifs in the cadenzas. She could hear Oscar's tart criticism of her romanticized entrance into the main theme, titled by someone else, "Full Moon and Empty Arms." Oscar wouldn't like it at all, but she played for him because she missed him. She played for Carolyn because that music would always remind her of Carolyn's romantic innocence. At the last, when the themes overlapped into a crescendo of longing, she played for Patricia, because she should never have let her go.

Her tempo allowed the closing bars to ripple from her fingertips. Chords crashed with such energy she came up off the bench. Oscar had always maintained that music was not emotion. The emotion came from the players. She had trumped him with Bernstein, who maintained that the urge to compose was an emotion itself, the urge to communicate so the composer no longer felt alone. She forgot the orchestra was all in her ears as she signaled the last downbeat with a triumphant gesture, the final chord exuberant in found love and dancing happiness.

She caught herself on the music rack, dizzy with spent energy. Applause startled her and she turned with chagrin to see that a small audience had gathered. She was wearing a swimsuit, for God's sake, and so it seemed that her only choice was a humble bow. She quit the stage and was discomfited to notice Ilea Hamm among the listeners. Ilea mimed an elaborate bow and Nick wondered where the lovely and so very tall purser had been keeping herself all week. She'd thought they might have had a chance at what Carolyn would call a shipboard romance, but Ilea had faded from view after walking off with the red-gowned brunette.

No matter, thought Nick. She would not trade the past week for any other, especially the last half-hour lost in Rachmaninoff. Music so dear, played for the love of it — how could she have forgotten how alive playing for herself made her feel?

She dressed for the last dinner in her tuxedo. "Masked Ball" was the theme for the final evening. She had not thought she'd feel like participating in theme evenings to that extent, but the gift shop had a supply of masks for those passengers who forgot to bring one. She selected one that covered her face from the nose up. Just before she put it on she realized the face in the mirror had filled out just a little, and glowed from all the sunshine.

She looked alive, even with the mask on. Ironic, she thought, that she had believed she wouldn't want to wear a mask, and yet tonight the mask would bring her the anonymity she had craved, anonymity she no longer wanted.

Though some had chosen the simple formal attire and

mask solution Nick had taken, many of the couples had invested in full costumes, giving the dining room a festive air that bordered on hysteria. Never shy at showing their approval of the dining room pianist, the assembled women took to singing along. The pianist seemed to love the attention and Nick had an image of the poor fellow playing the same Montovani music week after week to a room full of people who ignored every note.

Misty-eyed, he launched into a spirited rendition of "It's a Small World." Nick choked on her soup when she realized the cruisers had decided to change the lyrics to "it's a gay world after all." It was too infectious to ignore and she joined in on the final chorus and the rousing applause that followed.

Emboldened by the mask and Champagne, she wandered into the tiny disco after the last of the night's entertainment was over. It was too hot and crowded to enjoy, and Nick conceded that perhaps she really ought to pack. Their bags were to be set out in front of their cabins by three a.m. This week hadn't been about finding romance, but uncovering all the layers she'd wrapped herself in since Oscar's death. Oscar had been so good at protecting her. She hadn't realized she no longer needed it.

One last walk above deck, then, she thought. It seemed strange to know her way around so quickly now, recalling with ease which stairs would open to which section of the various decks. She wanted the main deck below the bridge, where the wind was fierce and cool at night and the stars were spread as thick as frosting overhead. She'd found that very few passengers braved the bow area at night, and she liked the solitude.

She stared at the smear of the Milky Way, committing it to memory. She hadn't seen it in years — it was simply not visible from large cities anymore. When she'd looked her fill she turned back to the stairs and discovered she wasn't alone.

She knew immediately who the tuxedoed, masked woman had to be. There was only one woman on board who was as tall as she was.

"I knew who you were before you arrived. VIP tags, you know." Ilea had to shout over the wind. "But I did not *know* until this afternoon. I cannot even put into words how you played. Only that it was marvelous."

Nick intended to flirt when she said, "You must have me confused with someone else."

"Do I?"

Nick shrugged.

Ilea put her back to the railing and leaned a little closer. "I'm on duty in ten minutes — we have the final cashiering to do. It will take the rest of the night."

"How tedious."

Ilea shrugged. "It's the job. It has fringe benefits, sometimes." She looked down at her hands. "I just wish it wasn't the last night. I think I spent my time unwisely."

"I don't know about that," Nick said dryly. "I'm guessing you enjoyed yourself."

"That I did."

They said nothing as the bow rose and fell several more times.

"Nine minutes," Ilea said, her lips inclined toward Nick's ear as she stared at Nick's mouth. "I had a wonderful time, but I still think I chose badly."

Although she'd been half anticipating it, Nick was surprised by the kiss, and doubly surprised by the way her body responded. In a single heartbeat they went from a kiss to a full embrace, body to body.

The kiss aroused Nick to an extent that left her gasping when Ilea finally pulled away. She drew Nick into the shadow from the bridge overhead and pressed her against the cold steel bulkhead where it was a little less noisy from wind and engines.

"Say no if this isn't what you want," Ilea whispered.

Her hands were at Nick's collar, undoing her tie, her buttons, pulling her shirt out of her pants.

"Dear God," Nick breathed as Ilea pulled up her bra. The wind chilled her breasts, then Ilea's mouth was on them, spreading fire with her tongue.

Ilea's mouth came back for kisses while her hands were busy unzipping Nick's slacks. "Say yes if this is what you want."

Fingers slipped down her abdomen. Nails lightly scratched.

"Say yes if this is what you want," Ilea repeated.

Nick surprised herself again by the intensity of her answer. "Yes," she groaned out. "Yes."

It was so fast and so hard and so unexpected that Nick could only arch her back and let the soul-wrenching cacophony of sensation flow through her. The public place, the hurry, even the rise and fall of the deck under her feet brought all of Nick's focus to the abandoned pleasure of her slick, receptive depths. Like noticing the beauty of the dense stars overhead, she was aware, as if for the very first time, of purely physical ecstasy, from the hard press of Ilea's palm to Ilea's teeth on her throat and shoulders.

Two minutes, at the most, of Ilea's delectable assault led to the first ripple of orgasm. Ilea said something in a language Nick couldn't follow but the plea was clear. She clamped down on her desire to cry out, but otherwise held nothing back as her climax left her literally staggering. Had it not been for Ilea's body against hers she would have fallen. She felt post-performance dizziness, expected the call of *encore!*

"I have to go," Ilea whispered. "I chose the wrong woman. I am so sorry. We could have been wonderful together."

Nick found her breath. "I think we made excellent use of the time."

Humor flickered in the pale blue eyes behind the mask.

"I don't know — I had been hoping to find that mysterious Maestro Frost somewhere, though."

"She's not here," Nick answered. "Not tonight."

There was still some life in the cell phone battery. She was about to find out if the service really was worldwide.

The call went through. After five rings, a grumpy voice answered.

"I woke you."

"Nick?"

"I'm sorry I woke you. What time is it?"

"Did you call me at five o'clock in the bloody morning to ask me the time?"

Nick laughed. "No. I'm sorry. I just wanted to tell you that you were right. I've had a wonderful holiday."

Patricia's voice softened and Nick could hear the rustle of bedclothes. She was still reeling from what had happened with Ilea and yet it only made her desire Patricia more. "I'm glad, darling."

"I sent you a postcard. You won't have it yet. It wasn't true, what I said. I was being pissy."

"Okay," Patricia said easily. "I'll ignore it. You do sound . . . different."

"I was an ass, Patri." Nick used her pet name for Patricia deliberately. "You were right about that too. I felt so exposed after Oscar died that I never stopped being the grand maestro, not even with you."

"Oh my," came Patricia's answer. "I am very glad . . . I worried about you for a while, darling. You were so depressed and I couldn't reach you."

The low-battery beep sounded in Nick's ear. "The phone is going to die in a minute. I want to see you when I get back."

"You know where I am," Patricia said.

Nick took a deep breath. "I'm hoping we can start over."

The phone died before Patricia could answer.

It didn't matter.

Who was the romantic one, now, Nick considered. For all her teasing of *bella* Carolyn for her romantic innocence, she felt the allure of a common bond, shared perceptions, like interests. She had had all of that with Patricia. Five minutes in another woman's arms and perhaps the most shattering climax of her life, yet her first thought when she'd gathered her wits was that she wanted Patricia in her life again. She glanced in the mirror and saw that she still wore her mask.

She took it off.

Car Pool

Published: 1992
Characters: Anthea Rossignole, cost accountant
Shay Sumoto, environmental engineer
Adrian and Harold, gay male friends
Setting: Oakland to San Jose, California, and
along highways, side streets and bridges
in between

The Fourth is for Freedom

Mechanics

(10 years)

"You don't look so good," Adrian said to Anthea as he slid into the booth opposite her. "I take it this dinner is not for celebration?"

Anthea shook her head. She knew that Harold and Adrian had been hoping for better news.

Harold settled in, his expression composed, though Anthea knew he had to be crushed. "I'm sorry," he murmured.

"Me, too. For all of us."

Shay gave a philosophical shrug, but continued to stare

at the steakhouse menu. She'd been studying it while they waited for the boys to arrive. Anthea knew Shay was as frustrated as the boys were by the arrival of Anthea's period, but she hid it well.

Adrian heaved a heavy sigh and Anthea felt like a failure. "Six tries," he said. "Knowing what I do now about how this process works, it's amazing anyone gets pregnant."

"We're going to try again, right?" Harold's dark eyes were both sad and sympathetic. Anthea wondered what his eyes would tell her after they discussed the plan she and Shay had decided to propose. She was having a hard time looking at him.

"Yes, we want to." Shay set aside the menu. She stuffed her hands under her thighs, a sign of nervousness that Anthea had learned to recognize over the years. "But we were thinking we might have to change . . . methods."

"Something other than the turkey baster?" Adrian had never been one to mince words. "Harold can't produce a whole lot more than that —"

"The sample is more than adequate," Anthea said quickly, which was the truth. She felt a blush start and was glad they'd picked a restaurant with low lighting. None of the mechanics of getting pregnant were easy topics for her, especially since they all involved her cycle, her ovaries, her uterus, her cervix, her tubes and her eggs.

"You could try my low-count stuff if you wanted," Adrian said. "Even with the bad motility some of those buggers could get through."

Anthea knew him well enough to understand that his dry humor was just a cover for his bruised ego. As a gay man, Adrian had never intended to use his sperm to start a pregnancy, but finding out he had a low sperm count had, he felt, been a cosmic comment on his masculinity. It didn't help that Harold's count had been off the scale. "I don't think Harold's stuff is the problem."

"Thanks," Harold said. "I never knew I had a motility rate, let alone one that would make an OB/GYN so gleeful."

"Your boys and girls swim fast," Shay noted. "That's why we're depressed that it hasn't worked. Six tries in eight months."

"My eggs are old," Anthea said flatly. It was the truth, and no one argued. Three tries ago everyone had assured her that it didn't matter, she wasn't old, but the process made it hard to think positive.

It just was a fact of life she had to face. Forty-one-year-old eggs were not as viable. Shay was six years younger, but her tubes had fibroids and her cycle was all over the place. They'd agreed Anthea would try for a year before Shay undertook the painful testing and flushing to clear out her tubes and started on the drugs that would regular her cycle. The four of them had a single goal: they wanted children, at least two, if not more. Depending on mechanics, the kids' genes would be WASP-African, Japanese-Jew, WASP-Jew or Japanese-African, with four parents to explain it all, too. All of them were prepared to do whatever it took to get a pregnancy started. For more than a year, they'd discussed all the medical interventions, the drugs, the legal agreements. Everything.

They'd talked about everything except what Anthea and Shay were going to propose today. Although it made perfect sense, this particular fertilization technique had not been in their frame of reference. Anthea opened her mouth to start the ball rolling, but the waiter's shadow fell over the table.

They knew one another so well after almost ten years of friendship that they could have placed one another's orders. Anthea and Adrian went back even further, having gotten to know each other in the cost accounting unit at a Bay Area oil refinery. Shay and Anthea had met through the car pool. When field geologist Shay had introduced co-worker Harold to Adrian, the two men had hit it off right from the start. It had taken Anthea and Shay a little longer to recognize the inevitable.

Anthea pointed at Harold and said to the waiter, "You need to hold the cucumbers on his salad."

"Got it," the waiter said, then he zipped off to get their drinks.

"Thanks, I forgot." Harold was grinning. "You realize that the waiter has got us paired up all wrong in his mind."

"Paired up. That's sort of what we wanted to talk about, wasn't it?" Anthea was glad to see that Shay did look a little nervous, but now she also looked like she was going to laugh. It wasn't funny.

Certainly Anthea had undergone the more unpleasant aspect of the inseminations so far. After all, Harold had Adrian — and other aids Anthea wanted to know nothing about — to help him fill the cup for testing at the doctor's and for use by them. The needleless syringe Shay used to inject the sperm wasn't particularly comfortable, and neither was the half-hour on her back afterward. But they were minor inconveniences. Charting her temperature every day and spending two weeks out of four wondering if every twinge in her belly meant something — it was emotionally draining. Getting her period a day late was very hard. But Harold might not be too thrilled with their proposition. Maybe he wouldn't mind at all. As Shay had said this morning, men are different.

Harold sliced into the crusty loaf of bread the waiter had left. "So what did you want to try? Doctor's office? That process where they wash the sperm and then inject it directly into your uterus?"

They'd all become so clinical. Anthea tried to stay with that tone. "No, not that invasive, not yet. Shay and I thought that we should try a couple of times, um, directly introducing, um —"

"Without the syringe," Shay added. "Directly introducing, um . . ."

Harold was obviously puzzled. Adrian figured it out first. "By direct you mean he delivers . . . um . . ." Adrian's violent red hair seemed to quiver with astonishment. He pointed in the general direction of Harold's lap. "The old-fashioned way?"

Anthea's cheeks were hot. Harold's dark cheeks did not show a blush, if in fact he was embarrassed that they were talking about having intercourse. His babies would be so handsome, she thought irrelevantly. "That's what we were thinking about." It had actually been Shay's idea. She glanced at Shay and had to say, "This isn't funny."

Shay let out the laughter she had obviously been bottling up. "It's the look on your face," she choked out.

The salads arrived. After the waiter had left them alone again, Anthea said, "I'm not sure why we picked a public place to discuss this."

"Because Harold and I have mooched enough dinners off you guys. When I said we should just go out I didn't know we'd be talking about you and Harold doing the nasty."

"Adrian!"

He shrugged. "There's no point in being a prude about it, Anthea dearest."

"I'm not being a prude. I just have no experience at this, okay?"

"Don't look at me," Harold said. "I know where all the parts are, but I've never been up close and personal."

They ate their salads in silence. Anthea ignored the fact that Shay and Adrian were barely holding back giggles.

They were onto their entrées when Harold finally ventured, "Okay, I suppose it makes sense to try it."

Adrian chortled and Shay had to cover her mouth with her napkin.

Anthea glared at both of them. It was not funny. "If this doesn't work it could be you two in the bed, you know."

Adrian laughed so hard he had to put his head on Harold's shoulder. Anthea kept her shoulder out of Shay's range. Shay had no right to be having hysterics.

"I'm glad you two think this is amusing." Anthea really didn't want to have sex with Harold. Nine women out of ten would think she was a fool — he was a god. Broad shoulders, cocoa skin, the deepest bedroom eyes. "We all agreed at the very beginning. If any of us doesn't feel comfortable we just stop. If we can't get through this part in harmony, we're not going to be able to handle the stress of four people parenting."

"As I see it," Adrian spluttered, "all we have to get past is the fact that you two are virgins."

Harold choked on his water.

"I'm not a complete virgin," Anthea said haughtily. "I dated men in college. For a while. And it's not like you two aren't in the same boat!"

"Oh yes," Adrian said thoughtfully. "You are certainly an impetuous creature, especially when it comes to sex. I think I can count the women you had before Shay on my thumbs."

"What exactly is your point?" Adrian knew nothing about her sex life. She glanced at Shay, which was a mistake. Shay's eyes were dancing with laughter.

"If I know you, dating men was a handshake proposition. Maybe a handjob proposition —"

"Adrian, for God's sake!"

"I love it when you get mad." He speared a slice of grilled squash and contemplated it before popping it in his mouth. "You only get mad when I'm right."

Anthea glowered at him. "Fine. Okay, I never actually had sex with any of them. I was a lesbian. I hadn't figured it out yet. I just thought I had great self-control with men."

Shay dove for her napkin again. Harold had to turn his face away, and he could usually be counted on to be mature.

"This isn't funny," Anthea said again. "At least not to me."

Shay sobered enough to pat Anthea on the thigh. "I know, honey. When the time comes I know we'll all be serious. We want the baby."

Adrian whipped out his Palm Pilot to note the dates for their next try, 13 days in the future. "We did the turkey baster twice each cycle. Do you want to do this twice too?"

"*Want* is the wrong word," Anthea said slowly and clearly.

"Inseminating twice every cycle doubles the chances," Shay said. She seemed a little more in control.

"So Tuesday the thirteenth and Thursday the fifteenth." He jotted with the little stylus and then tucked the PDA back in his jacket.

Afterward, Anthea knew it was the cake that was to blame. Harold and Adrian were splitting a fudge cake with a ganache filling.

"This is almost as good as yours," Harold said.

"Well, thanks," Anthea answered, pleased. Cooking was one of her passions. Ever since Harold and Adrian had moved out of San Francisco and into Oakland's Montclair district she'd been happily making dinner for the four of them at least twice a month. She wished they'd just had dinner at home tonight. Talking about the next insemination with a waiter hovering had not been at all easy.

"I do have a concern," Harold said slowly. Anthea ought to have been suspicious of the tiny quirk in his lips.

"Yeah?"

"Well, I don't want to seem egotistical. I don't want to perpetuate stereotypes."

Adrian dropped his fork. "Oh my God. Oh. My. God. I didn't even think of that."

Harold went on, now obviously suppressing laughter. "But since you're not used to, um, you know, well, it might be a little bit —"

"Nothing little about it," Adrian gasped.

"A little bit uncomfortable for you unless you've been, um . . ." Harold's eyes were gleaming with laughter.

Adrian coughed to clear his throat. "If you've been using a dil —"

"Adrian!" Anthea slammed her hand on the table. Everyone in the vicinity turned to stare at their booth.

Shay did not help things by saying, "You don't need to worry about that."

"Shay!" Anthea felt completely out of control.

"I only meant that the female body is designed to expand, given the proper hormonal response." Shay's clinical detachment was completely undermined by her wide grin.

Adrian tried and failed to look concerned. "All I'm saying is that something expansive for practice would be helpful."

Anthea gave him a glare that ought to have set his Art Garfunkel hair on fire.

Harold had more success at assuming an air of innocence. "I was just worried, for your sake."

Adrian made a point of examining Shay's hands. "If you've done any fist —"

"That is it! I'm out of here." Anthea gestured at Shay to let her out of the booth. "I am not talking to this adolescent about my sex life. Move, move."

After a few minutes Shay came to find her in the restroom. "I'm sorry, honey." The quick kiss made Anthea feel a little better. "I'm nervous about it, too. I thought if we just got past the inevitable giggles we'd be better off."

"I suppose. I'm just not in the mood to laugh about it right now."

"The boys have gone home." Shay added sympathetically, "It's just as well you missed Adrian's discussion of which male porn star to tape to your back."

The pharmacy had been out of the pee-in-the-cup, dip-the-stick ovulation tests. Anthea stared blearily at the instructions and the test tube. Her arm was not long enough to read the tiny print and she wasn't going to put her contacts in yet. "Honey, I need help."

Shay yawned her way into the bathroom. "What the hell is that?"

"My ovulation kit. I peed in this cup and now I'm suppose to use this itsy bitsy dropper to combine exactly three drops of urine with the stuff in the tube."

"What do you need me for?"

"There's more." Anthea gestured at the instructions, printed in five-point type on thin, crumpled paper. "It's too early in the morning for this. You're the scientist."

Shay took the cup and dropper. "Okay, three drops. One, two, three. Thirty seconds — one Mississippi, two Mississippi . . ."

Anthea squeezed paste onto her toothbrush and fought a yawn while she attacked her molars.

"Fifteen Mississippi, sixteen Mississippi . . ."

Anthea paused with the brush in her mouth, struck by the fact that not many women had a partner who would, first thing in the morning, cope with someone else's urine and a junior chemistry set.

"Thirty Mississippi. Now in goes this capsule and in five minutes we find out if you're going to ovulate in the next twenty-four hours." Shay dumped the contents of the cup in the toilet, then tossed cup and dropper into the wastebasket.

"Thank you. It was the counting and the capsule that did me in." Anthea put her arms around Shay, loving as always the way their bodies nestled together. Shay was so warm. "I love you, you know."

"I know. I want to brush my teeth now."

Anthea wandered back to the bedroom. She was bending over to get her book off the floor next to the bed when Shay tackled her. They ended up tangled on the carpet.

"I've always liked that view," Shay said. "Makes me crazy." Her hands were busy untying Anthea's robe.

"Good thing, because it's not getting any smaller."

"I don't want it smaller. I fell in love with all these curves."

Anthea arched her back, abruptly reminded of how hot Shay's hands could feel. Her robe was open and Shay was nuzzling at her breasts. It felt quite . . . good. Very good. Excellently good.

"We don't have time for this," Anthea murmured. She wanted to spend the next couple of hours at it.

"Neither of us will get fired if we're fifteen minutes late to work."

"Fifteen minutes? Is that all I'm going to get?" Shay's fingertips flowed over Anthea's thighs.

"We'll skip breakfast, too."

"Now you're talking. Can we use the bed, please?"

Shay laughed as she pulled Anthea from the floor to the bed. "You know, we could avoid the ovulation kit altogether. I can tell when you're ready."

"You can? How?"

"Well, there's the Spinnbarkeit factor, of course. All that wonderful stretchy mucous." Shay bit Anthea's earlobe while her fingers went exploring. "Mm-hmm. Looking good on that count."

Shay's fingers were sliding around so easily, Anthea abruptly felt engorged. Her hips tipped up by themselves. Lord, that felt good.

Shay was whispering in Anthea's ear. "If we hadn't been charting your cycle for the past year, I might not have realized that you feel different at different times of the month. Like you do now — you feel like this when you're ovulating." One slender finger dipped inward, then withdrew.

Anthea gulped. "How long are you going to tease me?"

"I haven't completed my scientific examination."

"How long will that take?"

"Just one last thing." Shay bit softly on Anthea's shoulder, then trailed her tongue lightly over Anthea's breasts. "You taste different."

Anthea had not forgotten about Harold and wanting a baby and the chemistry set and Adrian's jokes and her endless worry that she couldn't conceive at her age. She didn't forget any of it until Shay's mouth was on her — then it all went away for a while. There was just Shay and her hands and tongue and the love behind every movement. Glorious minutes of feeling alive and female and loved.

None of the other worries crowded back until Shay wrapped her arms around Anthea's shoulders. "Sweeter, definitely sweeter. You're ovulating, baby. I guarantee it."

The test tube confirmed Shay's diagnosis.

What do you wear to have sex with a man? The question had plagued Anthea all day, where she gave less than her best attention to her work as a chief financial officer for a large charitable foundation. After the drudgery and idiotic management at the oil refinery, she loved that her practical accounting skills were doing good for somebody. But financial projections just didn't rank high on her list of priorities this day.

She tried to be clinical about it. Sperm can pass the cervix in less than ninety seconds. The desired result was that Harold ejaculate while inside her. She did not care how he managed that. She did not want to distract from his effort. So what would not distract him? She didn't want to wear anything sexy. She thought that would either remind him she wasn't a guy or he'd laugh or, a secret fear, it might work. They weren't supposed to enjoy it. She was a lesbian and she wasn't supposed to enjoy it, if only on principle. Harold wasn't supposed to enjoy it either, though it was, well, important that he enjoyed *something* about it, or he wouldn't ejaculate.

Did men ejaculate when they weren't enjoying themselves? She had no idea. She wasn't going to ask Harold either. Certainly not Adrian.

Regardless, she was committed to someone. If either of them enjoyed it she'd feel like she had been unfaithful to Shay. So what should she wear? Pajamas, preferably flannel? A bag over her head? A robe — the thick chenille one, not the short thin one that Shay particularly liked to remove? She didn't want to be naked. She wanted to preserve some sense of dignity.

Dignity. Right. She was going to have intercourse with a man while both of their lovers waited outside. Good lord, she thought. What if he needs help? She did not think she could handle Adrian being in the room. They were too much like brother and sister. She had been relieved, and unable to say so, that Adrian wasn't providing the sperm. It would feel so unbelievably icky.

She flushed hot and cold on the train, and shivered in spite of the broiling heat inside the car. The hot weather was a reason to shower when she got home. She hadn't been able to find the courage to talk to Shay about how she felt because she hadn't wanted Shay to think she wasn't willing to do it. She was willing. But she was scared.

By the time Shay got home Anthea had chosen an old T-shirt and a pair of shorts. The boys were due in about an hour and a half.

Anthea went about making dinner. It kept her mind off the impending encounter with Harold. Even after the chicken breasts were in the oven, she busied herself with the oranges, making spirals with the peel of one and zesting the other for the rice.

"That smells delectable." Shay stood on tiptoe to kiss the back of Anthea's neck. "How long before it's ready?"

"About thirty minutes."

"Good." Shay's hands slipped under Anthea's T-shirt. "You owe me."

"I'm not sure that . . ."

Shay rested her head on Anthea's back. "I was just thinking about how long it'll be before you want to."

It was the quaver at the end of Shay's comment that made Anthea turn around. She looked into Shay's kind, usually humor-filled eyes and saw uncertainty there. Time for some honesty, before tonight. "I'm scared," she said simply.

"Me too." Shay put her arms around Anthea's waist.

"I'm afraid I'll feel like a baby machine."

"I've been afraid you'd feel violated somehow. Very selfish — that you wouldn't want me to touch you for a while."

Anthea took a deep breath. "I'm afraid I might like it."

Shay stiffened. "Seriously?"

"Seriously."

Shay rocked Anthea slightly. "You probably will. It's okay if you do. I'd rather you did, frankly."

"You do?"

"I don't want you to feel forced. That's what I'm scared most of."

"I don't feel that at all. Truly. I want to have a baby. I'm perfectly willing to do this. It's just a natural sex act, after all."

"Sex for procreation purposes only — the religious right ought to approve."

Anthea smiled into Shay's hair. "Okay, I'm less scared."

"I know what you like, sweetie," Shay said into her shoulder. "Charting your cycle has been an eye-opener for me. I'm thinking of doing mine just so we can learn all these interesting things about my body. I mean, you didn't realize you get heartburn frequently after you ovulate and hardly at all after you get your period."

"That's true. I find it harder to wake up between the end of my period and ovulation, too. But I'm not sure knowing that was worth the fear that I'd fall asleep with the basal thermometer in my mouth every morning."

Shay's fingertips massaged Anthea's ribs through her T-shirt. "Well, I've realized that when you're ovulating you like some things more than others. And I don't think you're going to have any problems . . . accommodating Harold. But I think they're exaggerating just to tease you."

"I'll be thinking of you."

"I'm glad to hear that. And you still owe me." Shay arched her pelvis against Anthea's hip. "Please?"

Anthea glanced at the clock. "Let me just wash my hands, madam."

"Please do — though I'm sure orange juice wouldn't have the same effect as the chili pepper oil."

Lights off. Anthea sat on the toilet wearing only the T-shirt and waited.

Harold said it was performance anxiety, plain and simple. It had nothing to do with his commitment to the process. She had turned on the radio in the shower just to make sure she didn't overhear anything from the bedroom where Adrian and Harold were doing something about the situation.

She felt cold in the pit of her stomach. She was no longer afraid of the act itself. It had helped to talk to Shay about it and helped to make love to Shay for those breathless minutes earlier in the evening. The difference between that and what she was going to do with Harold was crystalline in her mind. The former was to celebrate love and their bodies, to revel in curves of hips and pleasures of breasts. To taste and touch, to know it was Shay.

It simply bore no resemblance to the mechanics of making a baby with Harold.

There was a knock on the bathroom door. "I think we can go ahead now," Harold said.

Anthea opened the door, glad of the darkness. "Did Adrian —"

"He went back to the living room with Shay."

As if to confirm this, the television blared suddenly. "Okay, then," Anthea said, trying to sound good-humored and hopeful. She stepped past him into the bedroom, carefully looking nowhere south of his shoulders. "This is all up to you. Just tell me where."

"Well, I guess on the bed."

Anthea sat down, not knowing if he could see her encouraging smile in the dark. "Let's make a baby, okay?"

"Okay," he murmured shyly.

She had to reach out for his hand and pull him on top of her. He was so much heavier than Shay. For a moment she felt smothered, then he seemed to come to life a little bit. She felt something hard and very warm on her thigh — good lord, she thought, this is it. She stifled a giggle. This was a ludicrous situation. What had they been thinking?

"Please tell me if I hurt you and it's not right,"

Harold said suddenly. "I've been scared that I'll do it wrong."

"We'll figure it out as we go," Anthea said. The angle was off. She didn't want to touch it. Okay, that was better, Harold was taking charge of it.

"I have to move my legs," Anthea suddenly gasped. They were spread far wider than she was used to. She squirmed. He lost contact. "Maybe if I —"

"Let me get off you —"

"Damn, I'm getting a cramp in my thigh. I'm sorry!" The last because she burst out laughing and rolled over.

"Damn," Harold echoed. He sat down on the bed next to her.

Anthea got the laughter out of her system, then said again, "I'm sorry. I see now why you were all hysterical. It is pretty funny that neither of us has a clue."

"Could you go back in the bathroom for a minute or two?"

"Sure." She leaned against the vanity and waited, still stifling a giggle. Well, one thing was for sure. It wasn't passion that was motivating either of them to do this.

"You can come back now," Harold said.

Anthea peeked out the door. "Maybe we should try something different."

Harold seemed more focused. "Well, we don't know diddly about the missionary position. So maybe you could ... on the bed — "

"Hands and knees, would that help?"

"I think so."

It would be less personal in some ways. Anthea didn't mind. Anything that helped Harold's aim was an improvement. She wouldn't have to touch anything, either.

His hand on her hip startled her and she took a deep breath. After a minute, she heard him mutter, "Damn."

"What's wrong?"

"You're up too high. The bed's too high."

"Oh, it must be the pillowtop thingies." Shay usually

had to half jump to get in at night. "Okay, what about both of us on the bed? Let me scoot over."

"I — that's not going to work for me. I won't . . . Adrian —"

"Enough said. Really, you don't have to tell me more." Anthea slid off the bed. "Is the floor okay?"

"Yes," he said with obvious relief. "That will work for me."

Again, his hand on her hip startled her, but she no longer felt giddy or frightened. Noise from the movie Shay and Adrian had put on covered the sound of her uneven breathing and any low noise that Harold might have made.

Anthea suddenly yelped and jerked away. "Harold, honey!"

"What did I do?"

Anthea hoped that Shay hadn't heard her. "That's not the right place to get me pregnant."

There was a stunned silence, then Harold guffawed loud enough to rattle the pictures on the wall. "Force of habit," he managed to splutter.

Anthea laughed into the carpet. Suddenly there was knocking at the bedroom door. "We're fine," she called. "Go away!"

"Okay," came Shay's uncertain reply.

Harold was still laughing when he put his hand on her hip again. "Let's make a baby," he said gently.

"Okay." Anthea took a deep breath.

The boys had been exaggerating, but not a lot. Shay had been right that it wouldn't be a problem. It wasn't. It was different. Anthea thought suddenly of the way Shay felt inside her and was awash with wanting her, but this would have to do for now. She could now understand that most women liked this, but they didn't have Shay to touch the right places, to use her mouth and fingertips so knowingly.

"Is this okay?" Anthea arched her back to help the angle. That was definitely better. "Is it okay?"

"Andy, just shut up for a minute."

She shut up. *One Mississippi, two Mississippi* ... There was no reason this wouldn't work. Her eggs were young enough.

Twenty-four Mississippi, twenty-five Mississippi ... Mother Nature had done everything she could to make this pleasant and needed. Having babies perpetuated the species. Harold had wonderful genes. Shay wanted the babies to have Anthea's red-gold hair. They would all make such good parents. *Forty-six Mississippi, forty-seven Mississippi.*

Harold suddenly put both hands on her waist and caught his breath. Anthea stilled. She could feel what was happening but was detached from that. Far stronger was a rush of tenderness for Harold and his willingness to do this. The moment — all the ingredients in the right place, all the mechanics worked out for this moment.

He helped her onto the bed as if she was made of porcelain, then he collapsed next to her. His head was against her shoulder.

"Thank you," she said. "It was fine. I mean that."

"You have no idea how relieved I am."

Anthea let the affection she had always felt for him show in her voice. "I understand. When it comes down to it, the man only has to be present for a minute —"

"But that minute can be intense. I have never had that problem before."

"You've never been thinking about creating a life before."

He raised up on one elbow. "It did make a difference. Almost as much as you not being Adrian. I kept thinking I could be making a son or a daughter and you could have a horrible pregnancy and it would be my fault —"

She kissed him on the tip of his nose. "You're going to make a good father."

"Adrian didn't want to tell you guys, but he's been

buying books for the kids, all the books he had when he was growing up. He can't wait to read them to the kids."

"Shay has been reading about Japanese culture. She feels like she doesn't know enough about that part of her heritage."

"You realize we're going to have awesome Kwanzaa-Chanukah-Solstice-Christmas celebrations."

"It will be wonderful." She twisted on the bed and pulled her knees up to her chest. "I almost forgot to do this."

"I'll go get them." He scrambled into his boxer shorts before going in search of Shay and Adrian.

Anthea pulled the covers over herself, glad of the T-shirt as well. She no longer cared much about what Harold saw, but Adrian was still like a big brother.

Shay looked a little hesitant. "Everything okay?"

"Yes," Anthea answered. She crooked her finger and Shay scrambled up onto the bed for a kiss. She whispered into Shay's ear, "He's got a lot going for him, but he's not you."

Shay laughed, her cheeks going pink. "You feel fine, then?"

"Just fine."

Adrian and Harold sat down on the chest at the foot of the bed. "So what did you think of my stud?"

Anthea rolled her eyes. "He's just fine." She added wickedly, "You keep your hands off of him, though. We have to do a repeat the night after next."

Harold laughed. "I'm willing to make that sacrifice."

"It's just the first sacrifice in a long, long line," Shay added. "As obnoxious as this entire process is, it's just a training ground for being a parent."

* * * * *

Shay handed Anthea a bagel slathered with cream cheese and topped with lox. "Made especially for you."

81

Anthea took one look and ran for the bathroom.

When she had wiped her mouth and flushed the toilet she realized Shay had followed her. "It's probably the flu," she muttered. "It's only been ten days since we inseminated."

"Pee on one of the sticks anyway."

"It'll just waste it."

Shay went right ahead getting one of the pregnancy tests out of the box.

"It's the flu, I'm telling you." Anthea dropped her toothbrush and felt suddenly as if she was going to cry.

Shay picked up the toothbrush and handed it over with one of the test sticks. "Can you pee right now?"

"I suppose," Anthea said grumpily.

Shay looked everywhere but at Anthea while Anthea took care of the business at hand. Anthea recapped the stick and set it down so the little minus-or-plus window was visible. "How long?"

"Two minutes. One Mississippi, two Mississippi . . ."

Anthea finished brushing her teeth and peered at the stick. "See, it's a minus sign. It's too soon for the pregnancy hormone to have developed — that is, if I am pregnant, which I'm probably not. It's just the flu." Yeah, but how come you feel just fine now?

"Seventy-seven Mississippi, seventy-eight Mississippi . . ."

"It says right here on the box that day ten is too soon to tell. Right there." Anthea pointed out the relevant text on the box, but Shay kept counting. She peered at the stick again. Still a minus sign.

"One-hundred-nineteen Mississippi, one-hundred-twenty." Shay picked up the stick and held it up to the light. "Go get your reading glasses."

"It's a minus."

"Just go get the glasses."

Anthea got them off the bedside table. Shay held out the stick.

A big red minus sign. "So?"

"Look closer." Shay was beaming.

"Those are there just because it's been more than two minutes." The pale pink lines that made the minus into a plus were very, very faint.

"The box says it can take as long as five minutes for the plus sign to show up."

Anthea read the text and looked back to the stick. The pink lines were no darker. She would not let herself hope. Not yet. "Maybe . . . maybe I'm just a little bit pregnant."

"Honey, pregnancy is a binary proposition. On or off. One or zero. You are or you aren't."

"I can be a little pregnant. Tomorrow I'll be more pregnant."

"Okay," Shay said indulgently. She murmured as if to herself, "Yes, honey, you look beautiful to me, honey, of course you're not fat, honey."

Anthea pulled Shay against her, loving the way they fit. "Hold me close while you can."

"Whatever you want, honey."

She kissed Shay's eyes and felt overwhelmed with love. "I suppose we should tell the boys. They said they wanted to go through all the uncertainty and the questions and the heartbreak if — if it doesn't last. I could still get my period in a couple of days."

"If you do, we'll try again. You and Harold didn't seem to have much trouble the second time around."

"None at all. We figured out the mechanics of it and compared to what's coming, it was simple. The hard part comes next."

What had been so scary? Anthea wondered. It had seemed such a monumental thing. Now she was facing squeezing a bowling ball out through a quarter-sized portal in her body. Getting pregnant was definitely the easy part.

She tipped Shay's face up so she could kiss her, but was struck by the change she saw there. Shay was all she had ever been, but now there was something more. Anthea knew it must show in her own eyes, too. They had both abruptly taken on new dimensions as mothers. She had not expected it to happen so quickly.

She tenderly kissed Shay's mouth and wondered how to put into words the changes she felt coursing through both of them.

"It's strange," Shay whispered. "I know how close we are and how strong our relationship is, but I just had the most striking thought."

"What?"

"That we're a family now."

Of course, Anthea thought, that was it exactly. "We've got nine months to get used to it."

"We have to finish fighting with the boys about names."

Anthea stifled a laugh. "Let the name games begin." Everyone had had very decided opinions, but they had tabled the discussion until there was a need. Now, Anthea prayed, there could be a need. She felt a twinge low in her abdomen. Baby? Indigestion? Compared to waiting for the next few days, few weeks, for nine whole months, picking names should be easy.

Shay squeezed her. "Relax, honey. Stress isn't good for the baby."

"Are you going to start that already?"

"It's my job, remember? Take your vitamins, they're good for the baby."

"Shut up," Anthea said fondly. "You can nag me when the doctor says it's official. Think about names, instead."

Shay laughed and let go of her. "Come and eat something. It's good for the baby."

"Shay!" Anthea watched her lover turned mother-to-be walk toward the kitchen and the tup-tuppity of tiny feet was loud in her ears. She had to ask Shay to repeat what she had just said.

Shay paused in the kitchen door. Her smile melted Anthea's fears. "I said that you can tell Adrian that Barbra and Judy are not options, but Bette is open to negotiation."

Painted Moon

Published: 1993
Characters: Jackie Frakes, architect
              Leah Beck, artist
Setting: Mammoth Lakes area of Sierra Nevada
              Mountains and Bay Area, California

The Fifth is for Vision

Smudges

(8 years)

Ocher smeared in alabaster. Broad strokes across her stomach radiate upward and outward. A new brush, smaller, to blend azure with phosphine for her ribs.

"That tickles," Jackie says.

I already know this. Her skin has changed texture, showing more apricot with the goosebumps that prickle after my brush has passed. I outline the swell of her fourth rib with goldenrod and let the line trail over her hip to the small of her back. Goldenrod with ocher here, where the cool of her side yields to the heat I so often feel against my belly when we settle to sleep.

She is the canvas today, and must stay still, so I crouch, huddle and stretch around her as she lounges on her side across a sheet-covered chaise. Colors on her skin are glorious. Malachite swirled with amethyst on her legs, torso, arms. My application of the base coat had settled her nerves as she took on the unfamiliar task of posing, but my ardor to paint her only grows. A different brush for smoke at her ankles. I discover new colors as her skin adds to the bodypaint pigments I have chosen. The ocher of Jackie, the smoke of her, the blue and silver of her neck, all new to me.

Annatto and burnt rose for her shoulders. They are strong enough for the hues and delicate enough for the fine tracing that leads from the hollow of her throat to the uppermost swell of her breast.

She sighs and closes her eyes. Skin has changed texture again, her aureoles puckering from apricot to ripe peach. She was a work of art before I began and is soon to be *Painted Woman* as photographed by a friend for *Vanity Fair*. No photograph would capture the quickness of her breath as I brush each nipple with cadmium smeared in the last of the lilac. She sighs again and my mouth waters. Her swallow is as hard as mine.

I examine her from every angle, brushes small and large modifying or adding color. Light hues for the grace of her curves, saturated colors for the points and edges of bone. Muted, deeper shades for the hollows of her, where I know shadows hide her real heat. Jaw yields to throat, hip to thigh shadowed by light and dusky topaz. From my angle at her back, her malachite and sapphire hand obscures the feminine swell of her pelvis. Her long, dark braid coils over her hip. In a photograph its plaited beauty will obscure the silk of her pubic hair. I straddle her to move the braid, wanting to see all of her. Her art and sex are fusing in my mind, mystery and passion.

"Lee," she breathes.

I have smudged the paint on her ribs with my parted thighs. Retracing my work I can tell her breasts have tightened. Her hips have shifted forward and the prickle of gooseflesh has spread to her thighs and forearms. I dust the crook of her elbow with lapis and consider all I have done. Hours of labor to create the modulating swirl of hot and cold, dark and light that is Jackie.

She is hungry and thirsty and so am I. I fast with her because it seems unfair to appease my own appetites when she will be on this chaise for another four hours. Her eyes are open and she gazes boldly at me, clearly desirous.

One brush left, and only saffron to use. Ethereal lines from toe to forehead, balancing the yellows, browns and reds against the chromatic sharpness of the malachite and purple. I will paint her lips when my friend arrives, in another hour, but for now they are all that remains of the everyday Jackie, that and what lies shadowed by braid and thighs.

"You're beautiful," I tell her, kissing her unpainted lips.

Her mouth opens eagerly. Her arms move to hold me.

"Don't do that," I tell her. "You have to be still or everything will smudge." My throat is tight with wanting her. "When the paint is completely dry you can relax a little."

"Ann will be here by then," she says softly. Her lips beckon and I want to paint this image on canvas, capturing the moment of her knowing she will have me soon, of her loving me.

Her mouth and tongue torment mine, make me ache for her. I repay her with the lightest touches of my fingertips at her jaw, her hips, tracing the long curve of her braid up from her hips, across her ribs, over her arm, along her shoulder. Hardly more than a whisper of touch at the sides of her breasts.

She moans and for a moment I forget the present. The taste of paint in my mouth startles me. Lilac and cadmium smear my lips. The taut red point of her nipple is wet from my tongue.

"The damage is done, Lee, please," she whispers.

I tease the aching point with my teeth as she gasps. Her hand reaches for mine and I stop long enough to say, "Don't move."

"God," she breathes and then holds herself rigidly as my hand carefully slips into the shadow of her braid, between her thighs. She pants my name and paints herself on my fingers with a repressed cry that soon changes to a hiss of pleasure.

"It's not enough," she whispers a few minutes later.

I already know this. Her muscles have all tightened, while her hips seem like liquid. She is satisfied and hungry, both pleased and frustrated.

Her gaze follows me as I wash my hands. I mix more lilac and choose a new brush.

"Lee," she pleads, and I want to give in. I want to stretch her out and feast on her, to paint myself with her. For now it's my eyes that caress her body, my eyes and my brush, tinting her nipple lilac again.

Ann's arrival does nothing for my composure. The fans and lights she sets up make my workshop unfamiliar, but Jackie pulsates at the center of it, the swirl of color, the glint of her eyes. I know she is watching me as I am watching her. Ann is rhapsodic about her subject, darting in for close-ups, backing off with sighs of bliss. I want Jackie's sighs. I want her open for me. I want her to paint my back with her breasts, my face with her thighs.

Ann stops and looks at me, then Jackie. She reposes Jackie so she is on her stomach with her torso arched upward and supported by cadmium and topaz arms. Her long braid coils over her malachite and ocher shoulders and back.

The arch of Jackie's body is too elegant, too cool. Ann leans in and whispers, "Lee is looking at you."

Jackie's arms visibly quiver. Her head tips down, her lips part and her gaze finds me among the lights.

"God, yes," Ann breathes. Her camera whirs and I am dizzy. She circles to Jackie's front. I don't care if the magazine doesn't print these photographs of Jackie's aching body, so obviously aroused, wanting me. I want to preserve the moment. I want to paint the memory, to evoke what it's like between women. I am lost remembering her in my arms the first time.

"Lee, please," she says hoarsely. She is sweating in spite of the fans and the colors begin to run. The blue and silver of her mingles with lilac and goldenrod.

Ann says softly, "I'm done," and she begins snapping off lights while I go to Jackie.

I take her face in my hands and I kiss her with the scent of paint mixing with the scent of her. I want her in my arms but I can't let her paint be wasted on clothing. Naked, then, pulling her hard and close, my thigh between hers.

A light, close and hot, is suddenly on our faces. Our lips part and we turn to face it. Ann's camera clicks several times, then the light is off again. Jackie moves against me with a soft but piercing moan.

From the darkness, Ann says, "I needed a picture of you, Lee. It will be perfect. Art and the artist, entwined."

Jackie gasps her desire, and I hear Ann take an unsteady breath. "Thank you. I'll come back for my equipment tomorrow."

I am beyond answering, then we are alone. Jackie's mouth makes me alive. Her hands make me real. Her voice begs out my name. Ocher smeared in alabaster, radiating upward and outward. I am smeared with her paint and become her work of art.

Wild Things

Published: 1995
Characters: Faith Fitzgerald, professor and historical
                 biographer
              Sydney Van Allen, lawyer and politician
Setting: Chicago, Illinois

The Sixth is Serendipity

Wild Things Are Free

(5 years)

Another awards dinner. I had been to a lot of them, more since Sydney won her bid to become a senator in the Illinois statehouse.

I had a head cold and almost backed out at the last moment. If I had stayed home in Chicago, there was no telling how long I would have gone on innocently believing that nothing would ever change the way Sydney felt about me.

Instead I was in a Springfield hotel ballroom, feigning attention and fighting sniffles. The speeches were mostly tedious but the recipient was one of Sydney's political protégés, a young lesbian attorney who idolized Sydney and our relationship. The young woman delivered her thanks in a style distinctly reminiscent of Sydney's and afterward there were hugs and congratulations all around.

It was then that another senator, Alitza Malm, stepped up to greet Sydney.

I had seen Alitza's picture, of course, and Sydney had long been effusive about Alitza's politics — though she was a Republican — and style. They had spent a lot of time together over the last few months, working tirelessly on a massive, politically charged, bipartisan conference committee bill to reform child welfare services.

I had not given Sydney's unvarnished admiration and respect for Alitza a second thought. But then I saw the way Sydney looked at her.

It was enough. The following morning I had to leave Springfield for Chicago, where I was committed to a two-week graduate seminar. Then I left for Boston to conduct another seminar. I was behind on my deadline on a new manuscript, so when I returned to Chicago I would be deep in my research books and computer until it was done. Our schedules being what they were — hers was simply horrendous with session recess coming up in seven weeks — I would probably not see her again for nearly two months. Senator Alitza Malm — competent, vivacious, charming, committed and intelligent — would see Sydney almost every day.

Sydney's brown eyes, velvet with affection, were what I loved most about her face. But she was not looking at me.

"If I work a few more days, I'll be done," I promised. I was lying. I had never lied to Sydney before.

"Take the time you need, of course. The reading public has high expectations of Faith Fitzgerald." There was disappointment in her voice. Was there also a note of relief? "I'm missing you, that's all."

"I miss you, too," I assured her, and we went on to discuss the more banal topics of our lives for a few minutes. Then the conversation turned to the subject that had lately seemed inevitable.

"If the bill comes out of conference committee before August recess I'll be able to relax a little. It's been a wonderful experience. A true bipartisan meeting of the minds." Alitza's was among the minds Sydney admired, of course.

"I'm glad that one of your efforts is finally bearing fruit." It had been a difficult four years in the statehouse for a woman not used to being stymied at every turn.

"Alitza has really made things happen on the other side of the aisle. She's as determined as I am to get this bill onto the floor before the recess."

"It will be quite an accomplishment," I agreed.

"So, do you think you'll be able to drive down by next week?" Her voice grew huskier. "I really do miss you."

"Yes," I said, hating my lie. "Tuesday, if not sooner." My latest historical biography was done. There was no reason for me to linger in Chicago. Sydney was working almost around the clock in Springfield and I knew that she was giving up sleep just to talk to me. I wanted to be next to her tonight, even if all we did was sleep. I wanted to watch her eyelids flutter as she dreamed.

"Okay. Please work fast. I can hardly wait for the recess. I want to sleep for twenty-four hours and then go on a picnic where there are no cell phones or pagers."

"I'll pack the hamper," I said lightly, even though during these last two months on my own I had almost accepted that Sydney's heart might want someone else on that picnic, even if she didn't yet know it. Rationally, I knew I was probably reading too much into that one, unguarded glance. It was foolish to doubt Sydney's love for me.

Sydney yawned and I told her to get some rest. She promised and was probably asleep before the phone was back in the cradle.

Loving her had remade me. I loved Sydney with a depth that I felt I had never conveyed to her. I knew that she loved me.

What I could not escape was the way she talked about Alitza, the way she had been laughing with Alitza at that awards dinner. I had heard the lighthearted tone in her voice and seen the unguarded smile she usually reserved for her closest family. And for me.

Until now, I had thought her happiness and mine were the same thing. I have always believed that all I have ever wanted, loving her, is for her to be happy. She has always been a wildly dangerous woman to me, brutally honest about herself and her past, and fiercely passionate about her dreams. I love all of her and want her to see her dreams become reality. But what if I am not in that dream? Is my love so shallow that I would ruin her dreams and stymie her desires because they have diverged from mine?

With deliberate awareness, I had decided to put off joining her in Springfield now that my primary task of the summer was done. And so I had lied about not being yet finished. If she was falling in love with Alitza then that was going to happen without my attempting possessive ploys. They were together every day and would be until the coming recess. If she was going to realize and act on an attraction that was so obvious to me then it would be perhaps this weekend when the legislative session recessed for five weeks. I didn't want to be there to weigh the scales of her actions one way or the other. To try to short-circuit something her nature drove her toward would be a betrayal. She is a wild thing and free. I am not made of the same stuff.

* * * * *

My intention to leave her to her own devices, without my interference, lasted a mere three days. I didn't think I could stand watching her fall in love with someone else, but not knowing if it was really happening was unbearable. So I chose the hard place that at least let me be near her. So much for my lofty notions of selfless love.

Chicago to Springfield is a three-hour drive. I was used to long stretches of free time after the harried schedule of teaching and writing deadlines. As I measured time, three hours was nothing. To Sydney, devoting three hours to anything was a schedule-breaker.

I stopped in Bloomington along the way to have lunch with my sister, Meg. She had new pictures of her family to share. I was glad to see her so happy — she deserved it after being widowed at twenty with an infant to raise on her own. She also had pictures of their trip to Hawaii where she and her new husband had visited with our brother, Michael. He'd finally recovered from burns sustained in an engine room fire, and returned to active duty in the Navy. Neither of us mentioned our parents. As an unrepentant lesbian, I was dead to them and their conservative Catholic diocese. Their narrow-minded viewpoints had ultimately driven Meg and Michael away as well.

Meg invited me to stay over, and I almost agreed. She wasn't all that serious about the offer, however, believing that I was in a hurry to see Sydney after a separation of nearly two months. Truthfully, I was in a hurry. But I dreaded what her eyes would tell me when I steeled myself to look into them.

I let myself into the house Sydney had bought in a gated enclave on the outskirts of Springfield. It was our house, in fact, with my name on the deed as well. On a professor's salary and with steady royalties I could certainly afford to own a modestly priced home, but never one like this. She had selected it for its amenities, security and location — the heart-stopping price had never factored into it for her. Van Allen money was legendary, and she had more of it than I could fathom, even after becoming somewhat used to the ease it brought to daily life.

As I crossed the floor the nearest intercom went live with Jacob's voice. General factotum, light duty chef and caretaker, he had released the driveway gate when I buzzed from the street.

"Welcome back, Professor. Would you like anything?"

"No, but thank you, Jacob," I answered, without breaking my stride. I had finally stopped asking Jacob to call me by my first name. "I had lunch with my sister."

"As you wish, madam. You have only to ask. The Senator has meetings until midnight, but she phoned to say she would try to visit at home briefly."

"Thank you for letting me know. Perhaps I could have a salad or some such around seven?" The contents of the icebox in the upstairs sanctum would take care of any munchies until then.

"Certainly. Just ring me when you would like it served upstairs."

"Thank you. Oh, Jacob?" He answered and I went on, "I heard a kind of clanking bump from the brakes as I came in the driveway." It hadn't sounded serious, but I knew as much about how cars worked as I knew about superstring theory, which was nothing. I had only learned to drive after Sydney had presented me with both a stolid, safe Mercedes and an instructor as a birthday gift.

"I'll have a mechanic examine your car right away, Professor. Don't give it another thought."

From the top of the curved staircase, I looked down at the main rooms of the split-level structure. They were large and airy, designed for entertaining and flawlessly decorated. We'd provided some general color schemes and ideas on textures to a professional. They were a stage for Senator Van Allen, ready to gather groups of people from time to time, designed for parties and conferences and the ease of caterers. I passed through the hallway that led to several similarly sterile guest rooms. Even the master bedroom, at the end of the hallway, was part of the public space in the house, though here there were finally signs of her. I was moved by the sight of her hairbrush on the vanity. I had missed her.

I didn't linger in our bedroom. I needed the solace of the place where we were alone together. The master bedroom was the only way into our inner sanctum, a huge room along the north side of the house, which was where we really lived. Its very distance from the rest of the building made it an intimate room in spite of its size. It was a place where only family was allowed, and the closest of friends. Meetings at home were conducted in the formally decorated downstairs office. Even John and Mary, longtime employees of both Sydney's law practice and now her political staff, met with her downstairs. This room was private.

A few weeks ago, Sydney had mentioned in passing that Alitza and she had worked out the final language of their bill in our sanctum. Alitza had been allowed into the warmth of the room and into the closest circle of Sydney's affection.

I could not help but remember that I had first realized my fatal attraction to Sydney when she had invited her brother, whom I had been dating, and me to dinner. The flawless chill of Sydney's Chicago apartment initially intimidated me, but then we went into her study. I glimpsed the real woman behind the ambition and the money. Her warmth and spirit had at that moment begun to lure me to her side.

Alitza had been allowed into our inner sanctum here in Springfield. I gazed at the oversized chairs we'd picked out together, the intimate table for two where we would eat breakfast sometimes, the desk where she worked until all hours, a match to the one on the other side of the fireplace that I used when I was here. Every piece of art, including the original Cassat, had been chosen together as we crafted the room for just the two of us.

I loved this room as I loved its mate in Chicago. We were just Faith and Sydney here and it was where we loved one another. It was a part of her, not a façade.

All I have ever wanted was for her to be happy. It was easy to think so when I had never dreamed some day she might stop loving me.

A door slammed somewhere else in the house. It was only four-thirty. Knowing it was probably not her, I still felt slightly faint with hope that it was.

"Faith? Darling, where are you?"

I stood trembling in the doorway between our bedroom and our hideaway from the world, unable to speak.

She burst into the bedroom, dropping her heavy briefcase and other paraphernalia along the way. "There you are! God!"

Her embrace was at once hungry and arousing. "I have a dinner meeting, but I couldn't bear the thought of not seeing you for another minute," she breathed against my cheek. Her hands were pulling my shirt out of my slacks. "I've missed you so much."

I mewled against her mouth, wanting her with a painful ache. We hardly made it to the bed before she was inside me, her fingers deep and sure, her breath coming in gasps as I clung to her shoulders with one arm and used my other hand to stroke her face, her breasts, her stomach. My own need slaked by her insistent attention, I took what I wanted most from her. The silk of her thighs drew me into the inflamed taste of her. She tangled her wet fingers into my hair and held me there, her body taut with pleasure and anticipation. In the next moment she was limp and her hand dropped back to the sheets. The only muscles in her body that moved were those that clutched at my fingers and tongue. We were suspended in

104

the moment, when all that mattered were the sensations we shared where our bodies fused.

Her breathing was shallow and fast. I was utterly focused on the next transformation, when the rest of her body caught up to the pleasure. It happened quickly. She was a sensuous river of motion, asking for more. Her hands were back in my hair and I didn't want it to end yet. I kept her on the edge as long as my own shuddering desire could manage, then we were soaring and falling, both crying. I rested my head on her thigh and let my fingers tell me what she wanted.

"Faith, oh God, Faith . . ."

All I have ever wanted was for her to be happy. Her hips shifted and I stayed inside her where she wanted me.

"You have a meeting, don't you?" I could hardly find the strength to speak. How long, I wondered, until she realized that I was not the one who made her this aroused, this fevered? I should have cared, but right then I did not. All I could think about was how she made me feel. I wanted that forever.

"Yes," she murmured. "I don't want to go." Her lips were at my throat as we lay tangled in the sheets.

It was bittersweet to hear. I wanted her to stay, not to be able to leave me. But she never had trouble leaving me before when her work called. This day I could not help but wonder at the cause of her extreme desire for me, and her unprecedented readiness when she pulled me into her arms. Even at the first, she had not been like this. "Then stay," I said selfishly. It was a test and either way I lost.

She did stay, her mouth finding me still slick and eager. I lay gasping for breath when she had finished, and I let her go, then. She showered quickly and donned fresh clothes.

"I probably won't be home until two A.M., perhaps later. Then I have a breakfast meeting at six-thirty and I'm hoping to have a staff meeting before that. Some of my poor staffers are sleeping at the office."

"It'll be a tough twenty-four hours."

"I'll be back as soon as I can." Her gaze swept over my sheet-covered body. Her mouth quirked in a suggestive smile. "Don't go anywhere."

She was almost at the door, all her papers back in hand, when she pirouetted to face me. "Come here for a moment," she said softly.

Aware of my nakedness and her devouring gaze on me, I went to her for a last kiss. Her briefcase slipped out of her grasp and we broke apart at the resounding thud.

"Damn," she said, not referring to the fallen case. "I have to go. I really do."

"I understand." I had always understood the limits of her time. I didn't want to understand why, after five years, she could not get her fill of me.

Fear that I was losing her had an unexpected effect on me. Sadness — I had anticipated that. Jealousy, too, was no stranger. She slept next to me for three exhausted hours early Saturday morning. Her alarm woke me as well, then her casual hand on my back instantly aroused me.

"I'm glad you're here," she murmured, still drowsy.

"Me too," was all I could say without betraying that I was a mess of physical desire. She was out of bed a moment later for a shower.

"Don't you need a shower, too," she called, her head covered in suds.

I stood there with my toothbrush in hand, swamped by the memory of the first time we had really been together, in a San Francisco hotel. She'd joined me in the shower, still dressed.

The shower door swung open. "Come on in, the water's fine."

She had a meeting and she was going to be late. I let my robe fall to the floor and joined her under the soapy spray. "This is an efficient use of time."

"Mmm," she agreed. She shampooed my hair and kissed my upturned face. I shivered despite the hot water, and she kissed my mouth this time. I could not help the sounds I made. When her hand searched between my legs she drew back in surprise at my wetness, then pushed forward, pressing me to the cold, damp wall with her body. I was open for her, absolutely unable to hide my panting need.

She groaned, loud in my ear. "After yesterday, I didn't think you would —"

"More," I whimpered. My feet were slipping but she held me there, answering the sharp jerks of my hips.

I had never been like this, either, not even at the very first when the thought of her crumbled the lies I'd told myself about not wanting women. I was pleading with her when there was no need. I begged even when it was clear she would give me what I desired. I used words that had never been easy for me. Her breathy answers were lost in the roar in my ears.

"I didn't want to seem like an animal," she said much later, when I was finally able to stand on my own. "I thought I'd have to convince you to let me do that again."

"I seem to be . . . in the mood." How could I say that part of me was thinking that every time might be the last? Sydney would break with me before she began anything with Alitza. I stood there with the memory of her inside me still sending shivers down my legs and I realized that I had not considered how Sydney would leave me, logistically. Her life was too public and too complicated for her to simply break with me and take up with Alitza.

There was a time in her distant past when she had been, in her unsparing words, a drunk and a slut. Her drinking had nearly killed her and her epic promiscuity with other women had distanced her from her otherwise loving family. Since gaining hard-won sobriety, she had held herself in rigorous check, never compromising the moral code she continued to live by. When she fell in love with me she was on the verge of running for her senate seat. She promised her supporters that she had no secrets for the press to discover, and that she would not flaunt an affair in front of a wary electorate. She had kept that promise by marrying me, as publicly and legally as a same-sex couple could.

Perhaps that was why she was unaware of her growing attraction to Alitza. Perhaps that was why she channeled that unrecognized need into passion with me. The cost of leaving me, for her own happiness, was very high, and in the kind of coin her personal wealth didn't cover.

I considered this, the specter of Alitza in my mind, as I stumbled onto the molded seat and drew her down to straddle my lap. Kisses wet with shower spray made me feel as if I was on fire from within. She rocked against me, silent and focused on my touch.

"I love you," I gasped.

"Faith . . . Faith . . . Faith . . ."

I didn't see her again for almost twenty-four hours. The frenzy at the statehouse in the final hours before the recess was even on the news. Sometime after midnight, I cuddled up in one of the too-comfortable oversized chairs and watched *Casablanca*. It turned out to be a poor choice because I could not decide which part I was playing. I had thought I was Bogart, ready to give up the woman I loved for the good of her life. But I considered that even if Sydney realized how she felt about Alitza she might not ever act on it. That made me Paul Henreid, accepting the continued fidelity of a woman who loved another. I only wanted her to be happy. It had not occurred to me that her happiness was such a complicated question. I did not know what she would do and what I could bear to accept.

I thought of her against me in the shower and told myself that I had no reason other than a few glances and a laugh to think that Sydney was indeed falling in love with someone else. I scolded myself that it was all in my head and fell asleep as Ingrid's plane taxied down the runway.

I woke up with a crick in my neck and the feel of Sydney's lips on mine.

"I'm sorry to wake you," she said, "but you seemed so uncomfortable."

I struggled upright. "You look absolutely exhausted."

"I feel worse than that. I was so looking forward to spending a lazy Sunday with you, now that everything calms down for a few weeks, but all I want to do is sleep."

"Go to bed, then," I said. "We'll do something tonight. Maybe just eat popcorn and watch movies downstairs on the big TV."

"I like it better up here," she said, after a prolonged yawn. The home theater downstairs had been primarily used for Bulls' playoff parties and the State of the Union address.

"Did everything go as you wanted?"

Her smile was instantaneous. "Some things got stalled in committee and died there that I wish hadn't. But the child welfare bill made it out of conference in time to be on the floor schedule after recess."

"Congratulations," I said heartily. "All your hard work ain't been in vain for nothing."

She dropped into the chair across from me. "Lena Lamont from *Singin' in the Rain*," she said, having caught my reference. "Actually, the way it happened was pretty funny. The speaker's desk was getting buried and it was pretty clear that some of the business on it was never going to surface before midnight." She shook her head for a moment, clearly annoyed. "It's no way to run a railroad, you know? Seven months to get the work done and there were hundreds of bills being lined up. At least Litzy and I never let our bill sit — it was the committee chairs who blockaded everything."

Litzy. Not even Alitza anymore. "I have to admit as a taxpayer, I'm appalled at what they described on the news."

"It's so dysfunctional I wonder why I do it."

"I don't. It's in your blood, I think."

She smiled tiredly, but her eyes were sparkling. "Anyway, the desk is deep in paper and it was getting closer to midnight. Our bill was on the bottom because we'd gotten it in early in the day. So Litzy grabs another copy as the speaker was distracted and it was like watching Sheryl Swoops doing a lay-up — she literally slammed the new copy on top of the stack from the floor. She's five-seven and the top of the stack was at least seven feet. People were laughing and when the speaker turned around he picked it up because it was right on top and brought it onto the floor for recording during the recess. It was . . . an amazing moment in an insane day."

Her velvet eyes were bright with amusement and her lips curved in the smile that had first made me uneasy. Litzy.

Where did her happiness lie? What could I do to help her? I didn't know, couldn't know.

She was just about to fall asleep, though. That much I could help with.

"Stop that," I said firmly.

Her head jerked up.

"Go to bed and get some proper rest."

She nodded agreement and went back to the bedroom. I followed after to gather some fresh clothing for myself so I wouldn't disturb her later. The sun was just peeking through the blinds.

She was stretched on her side of the bed. I was almost through the door to the sanctum when she stirred. "Don't I get a goodnight kiss at least?"

Her mouth was warm and eager. I tried to extricate myself only because she needed her sleep. "Night-night."

"Uh-uh. Not yet." Another kiss, this time leaving me dizzy. "You're not the only one in a mood."

Stunned by how wet she was, I felt selfish in my enjoyment of it. Did it matter what stirred her passion if she shared it only with me? I wanted her to be happy — why did that have to be with someone else? I wouldn't be jealous of a fantasy. How could I be jealous of something Sydney wasn't even consciously doing?

Her climax left me gasping, close to my own. Her mouth . . . her fingers, I came so quickly she didn't seem to realize it and I eagerly accepted her continued caresses. We had never been like this, even at the first.

Later, her sleep was deep and restful. For a long time I watched her eyelids flutter as she dreamed.

Jacob's voice seemed to come from far away. "Senator, I'm sorry to disturb you. Senator Malm is here to see you."

Sydney raised her mouth from mine and cleared her throat. "Litzy? Yes, um, tell her to come up."

I hurriedly pulled down my shirt as Sydney straightened her clothes. Sydney had slept until nearly three in the afternoon, then devoured the late lunch Jacob provided. We'd talked about family news and my latest book for hours as we shared the Sunday *Tribune*. My suspicions and worries about Alitza had faded since her desire to reconnect with what was happening in my world was obvious.

After dinner, we settled down to watch an old favorite, *What's Up Doc*. Streisand's musical comment that a kiss was just a kiss made Sydney suggest we see for ourselves. The kiss had led to her hands under my clothes and an undeniable realization between us that we were ready — yet again — to go to bed.

Jacob's voice on the intercom interrupted her mouth's almost bruising exploration of my earlobes and jaw. My intention had been for us to retire to the bedroom the moment I caught my breath.

Sydney seemed slightly annoyed. "We promised no work today, so I can't imagine what she wants."

She left to greet Alitza in the hallway and escort her through the thankfully tidy bedroom. I braced myself to watch Sydney with her, again, and a deeply felt prayer resounded within me, a prayer that I would see nothing because there was nothing to see.

Alitza halted just inside the door, obviously surprised by the sight of me. "I'm so sorry — can you tell I'm single? I completely forgot you have a life, Syd." We murmured appropriate pleasantries to each other.

"We were just watching a movie," Sydney said, with an indulgent smile. "What's up?"

"Just this. The final print copy was delivered as I left tonight —"

"You said you were taking the day off, like I did."

"I lied," she said glibly. "So sue me. Anyway, I thought you would want to see it."

Sydney took the thickly bound newsprint pages, according them some reverence. "It's hard to believe that all those hours came down to this."

She handed the tome to me. It was her conference committee bill, the product of an entire legislative year's negotiations. "How wonderful," I said, meaning it. "Something substantive after all."

"Thanks, Litzy. I almost want to frame it. I was trying to describe your layup last night to Faith. I don't think I did you justice." Sydney was gazing at Alitza with her

deep brown eyes, her velvet eyes, a look I remembered so
well when I had been trying hard not to fall in love with
her.

"I played college b-ball," Alitza explained to me. "It
was nice to find that I still had the moves."

I asked about her college career, all the while watching
Sydney's eyes. They varied between shadowed and bright,
and as the next few minutes went by there was hunger
dwelling in them, as present when she looked at Alitza as
when her gaze would shift to me. She offered Alitza
something from the small icebox hidden in the entertainment center. Returning with a diet soda, she met my
gaze over Alitza's head. It was a look so hungry that for a
moment I could not breathe.

Alitza seemed unaware of the undercurrent I could feel
emanating from Sydney. She sipped the soda and talked
only a little bit of shop, then skillfully drew me out on my
own work. "I only recently realized who you were," she
said, sounding chagrined. "I'd even read two of your books,
but never connected that you were also Sydney's Faith. I
loved *Eleanor*, by the way. It wasn't hard to see your
inspiration."

It was then that Alitza looked up at Sydney with her
feelings plain on her face, an unconsciously offered
intimacy. I knew abruptly that Sydney read it as part hero
worship and put her own feelings — emotions that swam
unveiled in her own eyes — in that category. The two of
them deeply admired each other, and had found surprising
support and encouragement in spite of their conflicting
party affiliations. But there was more than that. I felt it.
Neither of them yet seemed aware of it, but it was only a
matter of time.

Alitza left soon after. "I know you've got more pleasant
things to do than rehash the last year," she said to
Sydney. "We can always do that Wednesday night."

I looked a question at Sydney and she explained. "I'm

hosting a thank-you party for the conference committee members. I hope we'll be able to continue the bipartisan feeling even though our work is done."

I nodded, understanding it as part of Sydney's dream of building cross-aisle relationships as a way to conquer the legislative logjams that helped no one.

"My apologies again for dropping by without warning," Alitza said to me. "If I'd realized you were down from Chicago I'd have left it for tomorrow. I should know how short time is for relationships — that's why I don't have one." Sydney had told me Alitza was divorced, having left an abusive husband almost a decade earlier. I had no idea if she'd also left heterosexuality behind. I only knew that the way she looked at Sydney was beyond intellectual.

I assured her it was not a problem and Sydney saw her out to the hallway. They continued to talk for a few minutes, then Sydney returned to the sanctum. Without pausing she came directly to me, straddled my lap and took my face in her hands. The hunger in her eyes was piercing. I answered her breathless kiss with one of my own.

"Syd, I forgot about the time — oh God, I'm sorry!"

Alitza stood in the doorway, and I was certain my face was as red as hers was.

Sydney, amazingly, seemed only amused. She got off my lap with a grin. "It's a good thing you didn't wait five minutes. Then we'd really be blushing."

"I just — the time for the women's caucus was shifted back," Alitza stammered. "I thought I'd pass it on since I only just found out about it myself."

"I'll tell Mary to double-check it, then," Sydney said.

"I am so embarrassed," she said unnecessarily. "I'm going home now. I will not be coming back for any reason." She glanced at me as she spoke and I saw the transformation that had taken place. She had known Sydney was a lesbian, but it had been an academic understanding. Suddenly Sydney was a sexual being to her. Her face was full of trepidation and an unwilling fascination. Her gaze flicked not to Sydney's eyes but to her body. In that brief heartbeat of time, I saw Alitza's entire world tilt out from under her.

Sydney must have seen it too. She must have. How could she not see that Alitza was retreating not in embarrassment, but fear? Sydney said good-bye with a laughing remark about closing the door this time and Alitza was running for her life. I had not wanted to love Sydney either, so I understood her terror.

I understood, too, why Sydney immediately came back to me, murmuring, "It's been a long time since I've made love to you in this chair."

Steeped in her body, in her sex and her hands. I didn't want to recover from my delirium. I didn't care why, only that she take me again, yet again, and that she let me inside her, body and soul, bathe me in the sweat of her desire and hold me tight in her dreams.

She satisfied me again and again and yet there was no moment I wasn't craving more. For the next two days it seemed as if every minute she was not working she was in bed with me. When, I worried, would she wonder at the cause of my sudden sexual addiction, equal to her own. Eventually she would ask herself why she arrived home already wanting me, and found me again unexpectedly eager for continued coupling that should have, at some point, been enough.

I wiped my mouth on her thigh and released my hold on her leg. She slipped off the bathroom vanity where I'd pushed her. I had tried not to look at her as she got ready for a luncheon, knowing what would happen if our gaze locked. A sharp exclamation of distress had made me turn to see her rubbing her scalp and glaring at her hairbrush. She wore only her thin, silk robe. It was more arousing to me than any negligee.

"Dang snarl," she had explained.

I stood staring because I was helpless to do anything else. The hairbrush clattered out of her hand. She said, "What's gotten into us," and untied her robe, turning as I went to my knees.

"I don't know what it is, but I like it," she was saying now as she pulled me to my feet to kiss me. "It almost makes me want to spend two months apart again if this is the result." She tasted herself on my mouth and murmured, "I love you."

"I feel bad — I'm not letting you get any rest." Truly, she looked as tired as she had after the all-nighter at the statehouse.

"I'd rather do this than sleep." She caressed my shoulders and the planes of my back. "I'd certainly rather do this than go to a rubber-chicken luncheon, even if it is for a good cause."

"I'll come with you and pass you notes under the table, if you like." We'd whiled away many tedious evenings with me providing her quotes and her writing back the source. We played the game frequently.

"Now that's starting to sound like a good deal. Yes, come with me. I'll have Mary phone a head's-up on the seating change."

The luncheon turned out to be sponsored by a women's civic group to provide funding for neonatal care for homeless and at-risk newborns. Although I wholeheartedly supported the cause — I couldn't imagine a child beginning life without a home — it was impossible not to grow weary of the similar speeches of thanks. I surreptitiously scrawled "I could peel you like a pear" in the small notebook I'd brought with me and set it on her knee, which was just a few inches from my own.

She jotted something down and passed it back.

I expected her to have written *The Lion in Winter*, and to have perhaps added the rest of the line, "and God himself would call it justice," but she had not. Instead she had written, "Please do, but not here."

I glanced at her profile. The corner of her mouth quirked with amusement. I fought back a blush, having not realized how bald the words on the page would appear. I set my mind to work, then wrote, "Dare I eat a peach?" I knew she had read T.S. Eliot.

If I hoped to discomfit her further, it didn't work. Instead I was the one who squirmed when she simply wrote, "This morning."

My lips were still raw with the memory. "Where the apple reddens, never pry," I scrawled.

"The breakfast table," she answered.

I gave it up. She appeared to be at least following the speeches, but I was lost in the memory of last night before we'd moved to the bedroom. Alitza simply did not exist for me at that moment and I could only think that nothing else mattered except that she wanted my body, even after five years of having it, and that my mind still intrigued her. My parents had survived in their marriage on so much less.

She sat like a complete innocent in the back of the hired car that took us home after the thanks and well wishes. No one, not even the driver, could see that her hand was up my skirt, stroking the high inside of my thigh. She was grinning as I tried to squirm away. I was raised a good Catholic girl. I had overcome much of the indoctrination, but not all of it.

"Bad girl," I hissed.

"I've done worse," she answered, which I knew was true. She rarely alluded to her drinking days. I was never jealous of anything Sydney had done in that life before me. She had been another person.

The driver turned in at the gate only to find it open — caterers were unloading trays of food for the evening's party. I had forgotten all about it.

So, apparently, had Sydney. "Damn," she said. "Jacob will want to go over details and I . . ." Her fingers squeezed my thigh.

I leaned across the car to whisper in her ear, "Perhaps we could also have a brief meeting in the office."

I had the satisfaction of seeing her blush.

I didn't mind the party, not at all. Though some politicians could be deadly dull, and others lacking in any ambitions that weren't completely self-centered, Sydney had assured me that only the interesting people had accepted her invitation. The conversation would be diverting, and I looked forward to learning more about the bill to which Sydney had devoted a year of her life.

Feeling nostalgic, I slipped on the medieval gold band that Sydney's brother had given me even after I'd told him the truth about my sexuality and what that obviously meant for our future. Eric remained brotherly with me, and I had never seen a flicker of any other emotion from him. Around my neck I hung a closely matching locket, a gift from Sydney. There had been a time when wearing more than a year's salary as mere accessories had made me nervous. When the value of the platinum and diamond wedding band I wore was added, the total was frightening. I was used to it now, but I valued the photo of Sydney inside the locket more. We had taken it in one of those four-poses instant photo booths. She was just Sydney in the picture. No Senator. No Van Allen.

I opened the bedroom door to join the bustle downstairs, and I heard Sydney's laugh as she greeted someone. Light, enthusiastic, open, warm, all Sydney. She sounded like she had the day we'd squeezed into the little booth for the pictures.

Alitza had arrived and in the space of that moment I lost all my certainty that the passionate, brief encounter behind the closed door of the office downstairs had been engendered by thoughts of me.

Why did it matter so? Why could I not just let it go? Perhaps because nothing — not even a casual infidelity — seemed more brutally unforgivable to me than "I don't love you anymore."

Sick at heart, I joined the party.

I felt I was watching the middle act of a play. Two remarkable women, equals in drive and ambition, honor and charm, fell in love. The principal players had such skill that it seemed unconscious. In the final scene, if the play ran true to course, they would find themselves in a promising clinch. When the curtain rose on the final act, I would have my own part to play, but I couldn't stomach it.

Sydney, of course, had had nothing to drink. Alitza had had just enough Champagne to sparkle herself. True, everyone was in the relaxed, gregarious mood I likened to end-of-term relief in academics. At times the mood was so infectious I could almost forget what was unfolding before my eyes. But as midnight approached I escaped to the backyard, where the humid, late summer air was as oppressive as my apprehensions.

I instinctively went to the deep shade that sheltered the gazebo, cursing myself for a fool to read so much into Sydney's friendship for another woman. I sat in the dark with my closed lids acting as a movie screen that would not stop replaying the depth of Sydney's smile, and the awakening, uncertain response in Alitza. Sydney had no idea, I knew, of her own allure and the profound effect she was having on Alitza. To my eyes, Alitza still didn't know what had hit her.

Sydney would come to me tonight, later, as wanting and aroused as she had ever been in her life, and I would be with her, equally hungry and eager. Could I live this way? I did not know. When I went back to Chicago in a few weeks for the new term, would I have dreams of Sydney with me or nightmares of Sydney with Alitza? She would not cheat on me but I could hear the pre-echo of the words that would destroy me.

I don't love you anymore . . . anymore . . .

"Faith?"

I dashed the tears off my cheeks, grateful for the darkness. "I'm in here."

"Needed a break?" She sat down on the bench next to me.

"For just a few minutes."

"Me, too. It's a great party, though."

"Everyone seems to be enjoying themselves." I didn't know how much more I could take. I wanted to scream something, but I didn't know what. I wanted her to put her arms around me, but I dreaded it, too. I would succumb to desire and hate my weakness.

The silence between us was at first companionable but grew awkward as it stretched. I could not see her face and did not know if she wanted to go back to the party, or kiss me, or to talk. I knew her better than she knew herself and yet her heart was suddenly a stranger.

In that extremity, she proved to have more courage than I did.

"What's wrong?"

Her voice was calm, but not cool. She did not touch me; perhaps she knew it would lead down a road that accomplished nothing.

Hot with desire, sick with dread, I couldn't speak. I had wondered about her state of mind and believed her to be so wrapped in her work and Alitza that she had no time to spare thinking about me. I was wrong.

"I know there's something," she said. When I remained silent I felt her take a deep breath. "Tell me. Is there someone else?"

Of all that she might have said, this was completely unexpected. "No," I gasped. "No, of course not." Not for me, I should have added.

"Then what is it? You're — it's like you're desperate to forget something. By being with me. You know what I mean."

"That's not it," I said. So she had wondered at *my* unprecedented sexual demands.

"Then there is something wrong."

Lawyer-like, she had trapped me into that admission and I groped for a way out. There had to be another explanation besides the truth. My mind was a swirl of indecision. "Why do you think so?"

"I didn't, not until tonight."

"I can't —" My throat closed.

Gently, and with fear, she asked, "Are you sick?"

I shook my head violently enough that she could tell in the dark.

"Can I help?"

Again, I shook my head.

She lost patience with me then, and I could not blame her. "I can't play twenty questions," she snapped.

"I'm sorry," I whispered.

"If I leave you alone will it get better?"

I nodded. A lie.

"All right, then." She was angry and worried, but after a deep breath she said, "I'll try to stay out of it."

Her footsteps rustled over the grass as she went back to the house. I wished, not for the first time, that there were back stairs of some sort to our sanctum. I would have to stay out here until I was composed. Composure

121

was not in the cards, however. I broke down every time I realized that she had thought I was the one falling out of love and using sex to deny it.

I did not know how much time had passed, but there had been car doors slamming out front and the babble from the house was dying down. Finally I left the gazebo for the patio and watched her moving between the groups of guests who remained. Her public face was firmly in place. Genuine, certainly, and poised, but always more the senator than the woman. Until she spoke with Alitza. With Alitza it was the woman who spoke, who smiled, who unconsciously charmed and seduced.

I went around to the kitchen and sprinted up the stairs, thankfully meeting no one along the way. Though the night was warm I was shivering, and a scalding shower did not help. I was wide awake when she finally came upstairs to our darkened bedroom after the guests were gone and the caterers all packed up.

She sat on the edge of the bed for a while, then said, "I know you're not asleep."

I rolled over to face her, but there were no words that made sense. In the dim illumination from the clock, she looked remote. The hand that stroked my cheek seemed cool. Then her thumb brushed my lower lip.

"At least this hasn't changed," she said, and her lips feathered the line of my jaw. "God, you're delicious."

I had made no resolve to resist her, so the quickness with which she conquered me held no sting. But I was still caught between selfish desire and what was left of my dignity. Kiss for kiss, touch for touch. We had never been like this, not even at the first. We shuddered with completion that led to longing, moaned as release became torment for more. We wore ourselves out on each other late into the night, finally stopping because tears made kisses impossible.

"Tell me you love me," she demanded, her voice choked with emotion. "Say that you still love me."

"I haven't changed," I managed. "I'll always love you."

"Then tell me. I can't bear to see you in this kind of distress. Let me help."

I found some glimmer of courage. "Do you love me?"

"You know I do."

I looked at her wanly in the faint light.

"Faith?" She turned on the bedside lamp and I turned my face away. "You know I love you." The silence was filled with her disbelief. "Don't you?"

I think that it was then that she understood at least the nature of my distress, but the cause was still a mystery. "What have I done to make you doubt that?" More sternly, "Has someone been telling you lies? Because there's no truth to anything you could have been told —"

"I know that."

"Then what have I done?" She was angry now, earnestly convinced my doubts were groundless and upset that I gave them credence.

"It's what you will do," I said, choosing the wrong words and unthinkingly giving a profound insult to her integrity.

She paled. "You think I'm going to fall off the wagon? That I'm going to get a seven-year itch? I thought you knew me well enough —"

"That's not it." Before she could demand, again, that I tell her exactly what it was, I just said, "Alitza."

She was stunned. She stared at me for perhaps a half-minute before she said numbly, "That's ridiculous."

"I have eyes and ears. I know nothing has happened, but you spend time with her and then you come to me —"

"Good God! Do you think I'd bring her into our bed?"

It was exactly what I thought, but I had run out of courage.

She told me things I longed to hear, but she was in a rage and meant to hurt me. "I'm in bed with you because you're the woman I love. I've been all over you because I missed you. I fucked you because that was what you wanted and it turned me on to think you wanted me that bad. I didn't bring anyone else into our bed, you did that. You have nothing to be jealous of because I will always love you, though right now it's kind of hard." She scooped up the comforter and made a dignified exit, leaving me with tangled sheets. The quiet click of the bedroom door across the hall reduced me again to tears.

I was going back to Chicago. I had no other plan in mind than that. I thought no further ahead than getting to the place I had called home for five years. Sydney had left before I woke up and I was going to run. Run away from her, I suppose that was what I was thinking. I had nothing to run toward.

For nearly an hour I dithered about how to leave. I didn't know what to put in a note. I didn't know how to explain myself. I loved her, but I didn't have the cynicism to be Bogart, nor the distant nobility to be Paul Henreid. I wanted my Ingrid and I didn't care that the world was bigger than the problems of two people.

Finally, I decided to ask Jacob to let Sydney know where I had gone. It was my first setback.

"But madam, I didn't know you would need your car. The mechanic towed it to the garage. Let me check on its readiness."

I had forgotten about the brakes. I gathered the few things I had brought with me and then put on the ring and necklace I'd worn last night. They were pieces of my life I didn't want to leave behind.

It was at least fifteen minutes before Jacob knocked on the bedroom door. "I'm afraid there is a difficulty with your car, Professor. Something called a boot ruptured and the Mercedes-certified parts have only arrived today. The mechanic said it would be a lucky thing if it was ready by this evening, even though I did stress that it was inconvenient."

"That's okay," I said automatically, though it was not.

"Is there an emergency I can help with?" Jacob looked concerned and I suppose I must have seemed to be behaving oddly.

"No, I just wanted to go home today, that's all."

"Then let me call for a car and driver from the service the Senator uses. I'm sure they will be able to accommodate you."

"I could just get an ordinary rental car," I said. "People do that, all the time."

He looked shocked at the thought of someone connected with the Van Allen family in a rental car. "As you wish, madam, but allow me to speculate that the Senator would prefer to know you were safe."

"All right, okay," I said, unable to focus on anything but putting distance between Sydney and me. I'd made such a fool of myself.

I waited for Jacob to let me know when the car arrived, not doing anything but twisting my hands and feeling completely out of control. I did not like the sensation or myself much at that moment. I hadn't felt this mired in an emotional pit since my first, disastrous college affair with another woman. That affair had so destroyed my confidence that I'd spent many years afterward being a dutiful Catholic daughter. I had prayed for strength to resist temptation.

Then I met Sydney and wanted her, though she was my boyfriend's sister, was wealthier than the Almighty, and boldly setting out in a political career as an open lesbian.

I sat reliving our first kiss, the first time she had made love to me, the first time I'd watched her eyelids flutter as she dreamed. Jacob's voice on the intercom announcing the car's arrival jerked me out of my stupor. It was already half-past noon.

I truly had no desire except to run, and I didn't really care how I did it. But when I saw the long limousine that waited in the driveway I wanted to send it away. I didn't want to get out of Sydney's life with this kind of extravagant statement.

Jacob knew me fairly well. He said apologetically, "It was the first vehicle that came available with a driver we've used before."

I did recognize the driver, which only reinforced the need for security checks that surrounded the Senator and the Van Allens. All I had ever wanted was for my Sydney, the woman, to be happy, but I had no idea what to do with myself to make it so.

"Damn," I muttered, near tears.

"Are you all right, madam?"

"Yes," I lied, and I let the driver usher me into the back of the limousine.

Just as the long car was inching toward the gate, the driveway was blocked by a speeding taxicab. The ordinary yellow cab screeched to a halt and Sydney scrambled out of the back seat, shouting at Jacob, "Pay him whatever he wants. We made it!"

I shot a betrayed look at the obviously relieved Jacob and had a moment to wonder if my car was indeed out of service. Then I locked the doors.

"Faith, open the door. You have to open the door."

I wondered how good the privacy glass was as I huddled on the floor.

"I know you're in there. Open the door."

I'm not a child, I wanted to answer, though I knew I was behaving like one.

"Please, Faith." She leaned her forehead on the glass, looking tired and stressed and so unhappy. "Don't make me beg. I will if I have to. Please."

I was creating exactly the kind of scene that she hated. If I was going to leave her I could at least keep the details of the situation private. I unlocked the doors.

Before she joined me she said to Jacob, "Tell Mary everything is as we discussed." She shrugged. "Just earlier."

The limousine left the Springfield residence of Senator Van Allen at a stately pace. I had no idea where we were going.

"Look at me, Faith." I didn't until she added, "I went to see Litzy this morning."

I could only stare, not wanting to listen.

Her velvet eyes were clouded. "You were right. Half right," she added quickly. "I should have seen it and I didn't."

I don't love you anymore. I braced myself to hear it.

"I didn't talk to her about this, of course. But if you hadn't said something I would never have seen that she . . . that we were in dangerous waters."

I don't love you anymore. I couldn't breathe.

"I have never been anything but honest with you." It was true. "Do you at least believe that?"

I don't love you anymore. I nodded and thought I would faint.

"I could love her."

I don't love you anymore. Her eyes swam with tears and I could not look away from the pain in them.

"Why wouldn't I love her? You saw it before I did — I like everything about the way she works, about her dreams, about who she is. She's vivacious and committed and intelligent."

I don't love you anymore. All there was of life for me was her eyes and her voice.

"There's really only one flaw to my loving her. I don't have any love to give her. In another place and time, in another life or some parallel universe maybe I do love her. But right here, right now, in this life, for the rest of my life," she said passionately as tears spilled down her cheeks, "I love you. There is no one but you. If I did anything wrong it was looking for something of you in her because I missed you."

I had no reply because I couldn't take it in.

"You must believe me. Last night — last night when I suddenly thought you couldn't find a way to tell me you didn't love me anymore..." Her voice broke and she had to swallow hard to continue. "It was *awful*. Horrible. It all seemed so empty without you. And this morning, when I realized that you'd been feeling that for days, weeks, maybe longer... I'm so sorry..."

I had never seen Sydney cry like this. Something between us had broken and seemed gone past reclaiming.

"You didn't do anything wrong," I finally managed to say.

"Then how did we get here? Why are you leaving me? When Jacob called — Mary hauled me out of a meeting with the Lieutenant Governor. I told her wherever you were going I was going with you."

I tasted the salt of her tears on her lips. I kissed her not with desire, but tenderness. "I felt like such a fool. I didn't need to say anything and I think deep down I always knew you'd never leave me. I just couldn't stand thinking that your heart would go even if your body stayed."

"My heart was never in danger — please say you believe me."

"I do." Part of me knew I had no choice but to believe her, trusting in her honesty and integrity. But I also knew she wasn't lying to herself and therefore to me. What I saw in her velvet eyes was for me, all of me.

"What do you want to do now?" She kissed me sweetly, without any other suggestion in her mouth but to comfort me.

"I don't want to go to Chicago. Not until I have to."

"How does a picnic sound?"

I felt like an ocean after a storm. The tide of my

happiness was familiar again, gently rolling toward the inevitable shore of her love. Though my nerves still trembled with the emotional turmoil of the last few days, the last few minutes, I could both remember and antici- pate the return of that calm, loved feeling that had swept over me the moment she had first said she wanted me in her life forever.

"A picnic sounds fine," I said.

"You have to button up," she murmured.

I realized the limousine had just passed through a security gate to what appeared to be Springfield's small- craft airport. I rebuttoned my blouse with shaking fingers and watched with regret as Sydney pulled down her suit skirt. A slender Lear jet waited for us. I'd been in it once before, courtesy of one of Sydney's uncles, on the way to a family funeral.

"Where exactly are we going?" All she had said to the driver was that we were, as she'd said, going on a picnic. Apparently she had had a Plan B.

She wouldn't tell me and didn't seem overly concerned that we had packed nothing. The pilot greeted us with charming efficiency and the next thing I knew we were taxiing, then rising into the air. I thought we were turning west, then Sydney unfastened her seat belt and pulled me into her arms.

"When we get wherever it is we're going, are we going to be alone?" I kissed the shoulder I had managed to bare, wishing it were her breast.

"Very alone, I promise."

We necked liked giggling teenagers and snacked from the icebox. I had not eaten anything since the previous night and the can of peanuts we shared reminded me of our first night together when we'd had to raid the hotel mini-bar for something to keep up our strength. Our descent was so gradual I didn't notice until the pilot radioed that we should put on seat belts if we weren't already wearing them. A private airstrip was fenced off from rolling hills covered with low, golden grass. The mid-afternoon sun was hot, but the air was thin. We were in high country where the temperatures would soon turn cool.

In a matter of minutes the jet had retaken the sky and we were alone on the deserted landing strip with a dented and dinged Jeep. Sydney hopped in and revved the engine with a grin. I had barely settled into my seat before she floored it. We shot down the airstrip at a breathtaking speed.

She screeched us to a halt at an exceedingly heavy gate, which I managed to swing open, then we tore off again down a potted dirt road. "I haven't been here since I was a teenager," she yelled over the roar of the engine. "Screw politics. Screw teaching. Screw living in two separate houses. We'll figure out something else because I don't ever want to go through that again."

I could only agree.

After about ten minutes, I saw a large house and outlying buildings in the distance. We didn't turn onto the road that would have taken us toward them. Instead, we headed toward the notch between two hills. The dirt track bounced us along the back of one of the hills and we began to climb toward a knot of quaking aspens at the top. The thin air made me feel a little lightheaded, but I didn't mind. The golden grasses swirled as we passed. I felt far away from teaching, books, politics, the media, from everything.

We were halfway to the trees when four pickups emerged from their shadows, moving at a clip more reckless than our own. Sydney pulled over to let them go by, merely waving at the drivers. They faded into the distance as we went under the shelter of the aspens.

A red-and-white checkered blanket had been staked out on the ground with a picnic basket at one corner. A cooler promised something cold to drink. Beyond the blanket was a large tent. I'd seen circuses with less room. The flap blew open in the crisp breeze and I spied chairs and a bed complete with pillows and a thick comforter.

"This is a picnic?"

"It was the best I could do on short notice." She killed the engine and it seemed so quiet. The wind rose from the valley below us, rippling over the fields of gold at our feet. It fluttered the aspens' fanlike leaves and I thought fancifully of angels' wings.

"Faith." I tore my gaze from the vista. She was looking at me with wonder. "We're alone."

"I hear it," I said. "There's no one here but us." Alitza was not here, and my self-doubt was not here either.

We feasted on the contents of the picnic basket — cold chicken, tossed salad, bread that still felt warm and brownies washed down with lemonade.

Finally sated — for food at least — I gestured at her business suit with the last of my brownie. "You look more incongruous than I do."

"Do I?" She'd taken her jacket off even though the temperature dropped with the sun's progress toward the horizon. She now surprised me by unfastening the cuffs of her blouse. "Good-bye Senator Van Allen. For a few days, at least."

I swallowed hard when she unbuttoned the blouse front as well and shrugged it off her shoulders. "Is this better?"

"Yes," I whispered.

She peeled off her pantyhose, her skirt, everything. Obviously cold, she was glorious as her hair lifted in the wind. I hoped she could feel the heat of my gaze on her. "It's just me, Faith. You and me."

We were alone. I covered her with my warm body, loving the soft curves of her and the way her legs wrapped around me. "Would you like to go inside?"

"Not yet." She sighed, her body relaxing under me. "I

love the way you feel. I don't think I've been this happy in a while. If I was, I was too busy to notice."

She was pliant and responsive, and though we were both eager, we took our time. I learned her mouth again, the curves of her face, the tender flesh of her earlobes, her chin, her throat. We moved slower and slower, treasuring every gesture, every nuance of touch.

We moved to the bed, eventually, and she removed my clothes to learn my body again. She wanted me, but there was no fever, not this night.

The wind sighed with me as she spread me over the sheets. Slowly, deliberately, desiring me, savoring the moments before she had me, we stepped out of time and were alone. We had been like this at the first.

Embrace in Motion

Published: 1997
Characters: Sarah MacNeil, patent attorney
             Leslie Stuart, software startup company
                vice president
             `Melissa Hartley, documentary filmmaker
Setting: Washington state's Seattle and Cascade
             Mountains, California's Silicon Valley and
             San Francisco Bay Area

The Seventh is Up, Up and Away

The Singing Heart

(3 months)

It had taken nearly an hour for Matt's plane to push back from the gate at SFO, taxi, and disappear in the direction of Connecticut, but Leslie wouldn't leave the airport until it did. As eager as Leslie was for breathing space from her teenager, she would miss him every minute Matt was at his father's. Sarah waited patiently. She was used to waiting. To date their courtship had had plenty of waiting.

First they'd spent a pointless six months denying the attraction. All the while Sarah had been foolishly involved with someone else. It wasn't until she had been unceremoniously dumped by Melissa that Sarah had really appreciated the friendship Leslie offered. They had spent last Christmas together, platonically, but Sarah had glimpsed behind Leslie's affection and seen passion waiting for her, when she was ready.

She was ready. Man, oh man, she was ready.

After fiddling about for a couple of months having "get-togethers" (never dates), not saying what needed to be said, they came to an understanding. Part of the delay had been Leslie's need to know that Matt, her son, liked Sarah and wouldn't mind her being a part of their lives.

"What did Matt say?" Leslie turned from the window with a smile that unsuccessfully hid her sadness at Matt's departure.

"Oh." Matt had beckoned to Sarah just as he went up the jetway. "He said he wanted me to be here when he got back. I still have to teach him to use the longbow. He keeps growing like he has been and he'll be able to use mine." It was scary how quickly Matt had shot up.

They walked through the terminal with their shoulders just brushing. Sarah could smell Leslie's shampoo.

She'd never dated a woman with a kid before. It really put the skids on renting a U-Haul. Maybe that wasn't so bad. Leslie's need to protect Matt's welfare was natural, but his presence also added a logistical hurdle.

"He's at that age," Leslie had finally managed to say one day over coffee in her office, "where he's ready to start fooling around. If we, well, if it's noticeable, well, I'd think he would think it was permission. I mean, I've told him sex is okay as long as he's safe, but I'm not ready for him . . ." She had blushed beet red. "Do you get this at all?"

Sarah had said yes, she did get it. At thirteen, Matt was old enough to know exactly what was going on if Sarah was there when he woke up in the morning. And Leslie would not leave him alone at night to come to

Sarah's. They didn't talk about it very often, only enough to assure each other of their understanding — when Matt went to his dad's for his next visit, they'd get to know each other very, very thoroughly.

When they reached the parking lot Leslie started the car, then turned to Sarah. "So where is this surprise dinner?"

The fragrance of Leslie's fabric softener teased Sarah's nose. "The Fairmont. I made reservations."

Leslie oohed. "That sounds delicious. And romantic." She half backed out of the space, then pulled in again. "Only . . ."

"Only?" Sarah watched Leslie's fingers move nervously through her short, curly hair.

"Well, a heavy meal puts me to sleep."

Sarah blinked, then laughed. "Come to think of it, it does me, too." She felt her cheeks stain with color.

"Maybe we could go tomorrow night."

"Maybe that would be best."

"Do you have a Plan B?"

"No, I hadn't really . . . except for, well, after — you know." *A babbling idiot, I'm a babbling idiot.* She didn't look at Leslie. If she did she'd scream, "I want to have sex! Lots and lots! Now!"

"Sarah?"

"Mm-hmm?" She studied the door lock.

"Sarah, you know I lived in a commune once upon a time."

"Yes." Leslie's colorful past was very dear to Sarah. She'd never met anyone like her.

"We don't have to wait until after dark, you know. I learned that in my free love days."

Leslie was laughing at her. She did that a lot. "I've had sex during the day," Sarah said peevishly.

"So what are we waiting for?"

"Well, here and now is okay by me, but I'm going to wipe out my knee on the gear shift."

Leslie chuckled. "Let's just go home. My place. Okay?"

"Okay. No, wait." Sarah lifted Leslie's hand before she could put the car in gear. "I just want to do this."

She heard Leslie's breath catch as she kissed Leslie's palm. She nuzzled her lips against Leslie's fingers. Blood pounded in her ears as she flicked the tip of her tongue on Leslie's index finger, then blew softly on it.

Leslie had the hands of a mother/executive. Rough in a few places, but mostly soft. Not manicured, nails short for convenience. The brush of Leslie's fingertips against her mouth made Sarah ache; her entire body began to throb.

She closed her eyes as she rubbed Leslie's hand against her throat. Her own fingertips brushed Leslie's as they stroked her neck, a confusion of sensations that increased her pulse further.

"Sarah, give me my hand back so I can drive us home."

She blushed and let go. "Sorry."

"I'm not sorry. I just want to get home. Very soon."

They emerged from the parking lot into the brilliance of an early spring Silicon Valley afternoon. Yesterday's rain had left the sky electric blue and the hills shimmering green. "Let's go to the beach tomorrow," Sarah said. "That would a great way to spend the first day of our vacation."

"Maybe in the afternoon," Leslie answered.

Sarah looked at her inquiringly.

"I don't plan on getting up early. I'm going to keep you in bed as long as I can."

Sarah swallowed. "You'll have no objections from me."

Leslie maneuvered to the fast lane, and then stroked Sarah's knee. "I'm out of practice, you know. Really." She kept her eyes on the road.

Sarah watched Leslie's hand slowly move from her knee to her thigh. She could feel the heat of it through her jeans. She shifted in her seat, trying not to be obvious about parting her thighs. "Bicycle," she managed to say.

"Hmm, probably. I think it may all be coming back to

me," Leslie murmured. Her hand rubbed Sarah's inner thigh.

Sarah's lower lip trembled. She couldn't breathe. She raised her hips slightly, her legs opening farther.

The car swerved slightly and Leslie took her hand away. "Sorry. I think I should just concentrate on driving."

Sarah watched Leslie's hands as she drove. It was so easy now to imagine those hands on her body. She didn't dare look at Leslie's mouth — that would be the end of any ability to think.

She realized that Leslie was wearing the soft chambray shirt she'd had on when she had comforted Sarah after Melissa's abrupt departure. Sarah had cried her eyes out on that shirt. She remembered the way it had felt against her cheek.

Careful to not interfere with Leslie's driving, Sarah reached over to undo the top button on Leslie's shirt.

"What are you doing?"

"You're still decent," Sarah said. She continued for two more buttons. "I just wanted to . . ." Her fingertip found its way under the shirt, encountering soft voluptuousness that made her dizzy.

"Sarah, we're gonna die if you don't stop."

I'll die if I stop, Sarah thought. She settled back in her seat and turned so she could look at the curves she had uncovered. It was sexier than if Leslie had been naked. Her mouth watered.

"New Year's Eve," Leslie said.

Sarah blinked. "What about it?"

"In my misspent youth we would make a big deal out of New Year's Eve. We were too holistic for alcohol, you understand." Her mouth twitched with a smile. "However, we saved our pennies to procure the best pot available. We looked forward to New Year's Eve for weeks, more than any other holiday."

Not sure where this was going, Sarah said, "And?"

"We got loaded by ten, ate all the food by eleven and

fell asleep before midnight. New Year's Eve never lived up to my expectations . . ."

Comprehension dawned. "Oh. Well."

"I'm just saying, well." It was Leslie's turn to blush. She did it quite attractively.

"I've been looking forward to this," Sarah said over the hum of the engine. "But I'm looking forward to waking up with you tomorrow morning almost as much. I'm looking forward to eating ice cream on hot summer nights, going camping with Matt and kissing the tip of your nose."

"Matt likes you."

"I like him. You did good. Look, I am really looking forward to . . . you know. But that's just one of the steps on what I hope is a staircase we build together."

"For a lawyer you can be poetic."

"I'm Welsh," Sarah said. "Being Welsh means you make everything in life into poetry and song. Even coal mining can be poetic if you're Welsh."

"And here I am just a plain ol' American girl."

"I've got enough for both of us," Sarah said. She trailed one finger along Leslie's jean-clad knee. "If mining can be poetry you can imagine what other things will be like."

"My imagination is running overtime." Leslie neatly cut over two lanes for the exit.

On impulse, Sarah reached over to run her finger along the top of Leslie's ear. Soft, slightly fuzzy skin tickled her fingertip. How strange and wonderful that the sensation made her smile, and how quickly the smile changed to longing when she brushed Leslie's cheek.

A touch to Leslie's shoulder and Sarah was content to settle into her seat. Her stomach rumbled, reminding her of her hurried, inadequate lunch.

Leslie was already turning into a drive-thru. "I have to have something to eat, for energy." She grinned.

"Sure this isn't a delaying tactic?"

"My stomach says it's not."

"So does mine."

Sarah hadn't quite finished her chocolate shake when they pulled into Leslie's driveway.

"Want to start in the hot tub?" Sarah drained the last of her shake as Leslie shut the door behind them.

"I want to start right here."

Leslie's voice, suddenly husky and taut, made Sarah turn in surprise. As Leslie advanced on her she felt a rush of terror, like a doe confronted by a tigress. But that was ridiculous — there was no reason to be afraid. Except she was.

Leslie took the empty milkshake cup out of her hand, then unbuttoned Sarah's shirt. "I don't think I've gotten a good night's sleep since I met you." She kissed the hollow of Sarah's throat.

Sarah reeled, but Leslie caught her, pinning her to the wall. She could get lost in Leslie's sudden strength, let Leslie tumble her to the ground ... It would be a welcome surrender after all the months of waiting. Surrendering at this moment would be easy; Leslie's mouth was persuasive. Easy, and familiar and yet she wanted to resist the impulse. She had surrendered to Melissa in the space of minutes and failed their relationship by never finding her strength again. This time needed to be different if her life with Leslie was going to be different.

Leslie's arms were around her waist. Sarah captured Leslie's face in her hands and tried to draw the demanding lips up to her own, but her knees were buckling. Leslie steadied her, but they were both losing their balance.

The floor knocked the air out of Sarah's lungs, but she managed a choked laugh. Leslie groaned next to her, then sat up, rubbing her elbow.

They stared at each other for a few moments, then said at the same time, "So much for —"

"You first," Leslie said.

"No you. I can't breathe."

"I was going to say, so much for my attempt at macho."

Sarah chortled. "That's *exactly* what I was going to say."

"I may have lived in a commune, but I'm really an old-fashioned girl." Leslie got to her feet. "Let's just go to bed, okay? Meet you in the middle. Last one there is a rotten egg!"

Sarah scrambled to her hands and feet, trying to block Leslie's escape, but it was no use. Leslie nimbly danced around her and up the stairs to the master bedroom.

Sarah followed, feeling more lighthearted than she would have thought possible.

Leslie was shimmying out of the last of her clothes when Sarah entered, then she slid between the sheets. "You're a rotten egg."

"Cheater." Sarah disrobed in record time, and with a giggle joined Leslie in the middle of the bed.

The sheets were cool. The press of Leslie's warm skin against Sarah's made her shiver, and laughter fled. "Let's get serious," she murmured, then Leslie kissed her.

It was so sweet that Sarah sighed. It felt like coming home after a long absence, to a warm fire or a good book. She smiled against Leslie's mouth. This felt like a happy ending.

"No laughing," Leslie whispered.

"I'll laugh if I want to."

"Laugh later." Leslie's warm fingers slipped between Sarah's thighs.

Leslie's gasp echoed Sarah's. Answering the pressure of Leslie's hand, Sarah straddled Leslie's waist and rested her forehead on the headboard. Leslie was paying delicious attention to her breasts, and Sarah ground her hips toward the welcome heat of Leslie's fingers.

It was too much to bear in silence. She stuttered,

"There, there, there," then a taut cry of exhilaration escaped her.

Below her Leslie gasped, "Yes!" Then, "Please."

More," Sarah stammered, but she was beyond needing it. Her body shook with release as she crumpled on top of Leslie. Their mouths met again with hunger, but Sarah was startled to taste tears.

She held Leslie tight and whispered in her ear, "I thought I was the one who was supposed to cry."

Leslie sniffled. "I love you, you big dope."

"You tell me this just to insult me?"

"Can I go on?"

"Insulting me?"

"No." Leslie seemed caught between laughter and tears. "Loving you."

Sarah said softly, "There's an old Welsh story about a singing heart. If you search for it you'll never find it, but when you stop looking its music will lead you to your true love. I didn't understand until now what a singing heart was."

"That's so sweet. Kiss me."

"I love you, too."

"Kiss me."

"I'll do more than that." Sarah shinnied under the covers. The sheets were warm now, and Leslie's thighs against her cheeks even hotter. She groaned while Leslie twisted against her, calves tangling arms, knees bumping shoulders, and they rolled in a dizzying coil of silken skin and slick passion.

"So how is New Year's Eve so far?" Sarah reached over Leslie for the carton of ice cream.

"I think I'm staying up until midnight this year. Give that back."

143

"You've had more than half," Sarah protested, but she surrendered the spoon and carton.

"You really do love me," Leslie said in mock surprise.

"Romance is sharing the ice cream." Sarah snuggled into the shelter between Leslie's arm and ribs. She was suddenly sleepy — small wonder. Leslie had no compunctions about asking for more of what she liked. Her freedom made Sarah equally bold.

The downy hair on Leslie's arm tickled Sarah's eyelashes. She smiled on her way to sleep, aware that Leslie's breathing had slowed, as aware as if it were her own. She felt Leslie's pulse under her cheek, and the rhythm was a lullaby to her singing heart.

Hot Flash

(4 years)

I'm not making her breakfast today. Leslie yanked her hairbrush through the snarl at the nape of her neck so hard it brought tears to her eyes. *She can get her own damned breakfast.*

One look at Melissa in her skimpy muscle shirt and second-skin biking shorts made Leslie feel like a Class One Frump. Melissa was reading the paper. There was no coffee made.

It was hard to keep a rein on her temper as she ground beans, but Leslie greeted Melissa civilly enough. So she was rail-thin and young and out almost every night with a different woman. Leslie was hardly jealous of that. Okay, she was a lot jealous of the thin, young part. But she had Sarah in her bed every night. Once upon a time Melissa had been so lucky, but not anymore. In the battle for Sarah's heart, the patient almost-crone had won.

"Morning," Sarah murmured a few minutes later, her hair still damp from the shower. She poured herself a cup of the steaming coffee and scrabbled in the cupboard for cereal.

"I've already done five miles," Melissa shared as she also got some coffee.

"I'm exhausted just to know that," Sarah answered. "Nice blend, Les."

Leslie spread jam on her toast and sipped the steaming, caffeine-loaded brew. "Mmm, hits the spot."

Melissa did not say anything about the coffee. No thanks for Leslie having made it, again, for the twenty-second day in a row. Day 22 of Melissa's prolonged stay was so far exactly like every day before it, that is, when Melissa was actually at their house in the morning. Leslie was used to being taken for granted by her son, but even Matt knew the phrase *thank you*. Thoroughly vexed, Leslie watched Sarah pour a second bowl of cereal, this one for Melissa, who of course would like some since Sarah already had it out.

She was so out of sorts she missed the warning signs of an impending hot flash. Given enough time, she usually shucked her outer layer of clothes to save washing them, but there was no way she was showing that much of her body to the taut, toned Melissa. She fanned herself surreptitiously as her stomach turned into a supernova, sending a wave of fire from the inside out. In a matter of seconds she was drenched from head to toe.

Sarah was chatting with Melissa about her ride when Leslie left the kitchen. She tried not to stomp up the stairs, but hot flashes left her temporarily drained of energy and her footsteps were heavy. She tossed her wet clothes in the hamper, then scrubbed her face and the back of her neck. In the flat morning light the gray streaks in her black hair looked as if they were lit by neon. A blast of cool air surprised her and she turned to see Sarah opening the window.

"Why couldn't it happen before you took your shower — but I guess hot flashes have the same inconvenient rules as periods. You know, they start when you're wearing new white pants." Sarah leaned against the bathroom doorjamb looking sympathetic. She even had a fresh polo shirt over one arm.

"Thanks," Leslie murmured, trying not to cry. Damned estrogen. Too much, too little, too much, too little. No more kids, not that she wanted any more. Matt was plenty. She was getting old and fat. She had hair in surprising new places, but was losing hair in spots porn stars had to shave. She reached for the shirt.

"Hey, not so fast," Sarah said. She snaked an arm around Leslie's naked waist. Her kiss was brief, but thorough.

"I'm all sweaty," Leslie muttered.

"When has that ever stopped me?" Sarah kissed her again, one hand lazily appreciating Leslie's bare back. Her teeth nipped at Leslie's throat. "I'm enjoying the side effect of your perimenopause and you know it."

The side effect of Leslie's hot flashes was what the gynecologist unromantically called vaginal mucus, but she hadn't disagreed when Leslie had summed it up with, "I get horny."

Sarah was on her knees now, making Leslie lightheaded with anticipation. She wondered if her body was making up for all the years she hadn't had intimate relationships. After her early life in a commune she'd had a prolonged dry spell as a single mom. Then Sarah, wearing an uptight attorney's suit and spouting patent law, had become a surprisingly close friend. Sarah's only flaw had been her choice of the shallow, too thin, too attractive and too young Melissa for a girlfriend.

Sarah had left a settled life in Seattle to join Melissa in San Francisco. She'd set aside an excellent career with a huge software manufacturer to become inside counsel for the software company Leslie co-owned. Melissa had soon departed for fast living in L.A.'s Hollywood, leaving an uprooted and devastated Sarah in tatters. It was while Leslie helped Sarah over her broken heart that their comfortable workplace friendship had solidified into something more. Under the suit and dusty law books Sarah had an enthusiasm for life that made her a good friend. Months later, Leslie discovered Sarah also had an energy for sex that made her a great lover.

"God, you're beautiful," Sarah breathed. She peeled Leslie's panties downward, tongue following fabric.

Like the bedroom door beyond, the bathroom door was open, and it was entirely possible that's Sarah's earthy groan would carry downstairs. If Matt weren't at his father's, Leslie would have made Sarah stop long enough to shut the doors. She didn't care what Melissa might overhear.

Legs trembling, Leslie leaned hard against the counter. Sarah did not seem to care that they were going to be late to the office. Did not seem to care that Leslie's legs were still damp with perspiration. Did not seem to care about anything but the copious wetness her tongue was swirling through, that she thirstily reveled in.

Sarah was greedy at first, but Leslie knew that Sarah never began anything she didn't intend to finish. An Olympic medallist in archery, Sarah always had a goal. Always having the target in mind whenever you nocked an arrow was one of the life values Sarah had passed on to Matt after coming into their lives. Already Sarah was slowing, her thirst satisfied for now. Her tongue teased and attacked with purpose. She wrapped her arms hard around Leslie's legs. After four years together, Leslie could almost hear Sarah's mantra: focus, sight, fly.

Sarah made Leslie fly. Leslie had not thought there was any mystery left to sex for her, not after her years of Free Love. But Sarah's concentration and stamina had taught Leslie a new awareness about her own body's needs and abilities.

"There, right there," Leslie panted. She tangled one hand in Sarah's hair and crooned her name.

"Maybe we should just take another shower." Sarah laughed into Leslie's ear.

"You *are* wearing Eau de Leslie." Leslie kissed Sarah's nose, trying to hide how Sarah's jean-clad thigh was making her feel.

"Maybe we could call in sick —"

"Right, as if everyone would believe we're both sick on the same day —"

"And stay in bed all day." Sarah punctuated her suggestion by shifting her thigh as Leslie arched herself against it. "You'd like that, wouldn't you?"

"Oh, yeah," Leslie answered, chagrined. "We don't have the house to ourselves, though."

Sarah's vexed sigh was gratifying. "Don't I know it. Well, just stop having hot flashes at work, okay? I wanted to do what I just did yesterday, right in the meeting."

Leslie had to laugh. "Stop that. It's hard enough for me to cope with one in public without having to worry about you jumping the table to ravage me."

Sarah took her warm, hard thigh away. "You go right on worrying about it." Her laugh was evil.

Leslie showered for the second time but felt definitely

less frumpy when she went back downstairs. It was impossible to feel unattractive after Sarah's thorough demonstration of how desirable she found Leslie.

Melissa's voice reminded Leslie of her continued presence, but it didn't have the same sting as before. Between projects and cash flow, Melissa was waiting for both housing and a guest lecturer spot at the university to open at the end of the month. Nine days, Leslie thought. I can make it nine days.

"... did live in a commune, you know," Sarah was saying.

"I know, I'm just surprised. You — I mean, I know how you can get." Melissa's tone was both knowing and smug.

"She keeps me on my toes," Sarah said lightly.

"Sure she does." Melissa's smirking tone made Leslie want to smack her.

Sarah's laugh surprised Leslie, though. It was genuinely amused. "Oh Mel, you only wish you knew." Sarah's laughter suddenly died. "Mel — don't."

"Sorry, I couldn't help myself. You look so alive this morning."

"Thanks, but no thanks."

"Sure?"

"Yes, of course." Sarah was snappish now.

"I seem to have upset you." Did Melissa sound hopeful?

"You've made it awkward. If you can't keep your hands to yourself then you'll need to find someplace else to stay." Sarah did sound upset.

"Have I actually gotten under your skin? I haven't forgotten the way we were together, you know."

Sarah's voice was low and firm. "I am not on your menu."

"Then why are you so bugged by a little flirtation?"

Sarah was angry. Leslie could tell because she itemized her points. "A, it was more than that. B, I am very married, and you know it. C, as the queen of politically correct lesbian thinking, you should know you're being ageist when you assume that an older woman is *de facto* sexually dysfunctional. That's what pisses me off the most, if you must know." Sarah said something more, but it was lost in the whir of the garbage disposal.

"Okay, I'm sorry. Pax." Melissa did sound chagrined.

Leslie crept halfway up the stairs, counted slowly to ten as she took several calming breaths, then clattered back down to the kitchen.

Sarah was jingling her keys. "There you are. Ready?"

Leslie didn't give Melissa a glance. "For anything," she answered.

Sarah handed her a fresh mug of coffee for the car. "Promises, promises," she said teasingly.

Leslie didn't know what to think or feel. Sarah had obviously rebuffed Melissa's advance, but she'd been unnerved by it. Loyalty and fidelity — they were qualities Leslie loved about Sarah. If those impulses were what kept Sarah free of Melissa's all-too-eager clutches, then Leslie was twice as glad of them. Sarah always admitted she and Melissa had been great together — at least in bed. It didn't matter if, for just a moment, Sarah had been reminded of that. She'd still said no, and emphatically.

"I'm sorry," Sarah said abruptly. She changed lanes at a snail's pace, easing between an 18-wheeler and a laboring Volvo.

"For what?"

"I don't know what it is about her — maybe it's the audacity. I thought we didn't exactly part on good terms, and she calls me out of the blue, all pals."

Leslie thought it best to make a noncommittal noise. They'd discussed this before, several times.

"It just caught me so off-guard. I said yes before I even realized what she wanted."

151

That reflexive impulse to give Melissa what she wanted was what had Leslie just the tiniest amount worried. "It's just another week or so."

"I know. I completely forgot she was there this morning, even." Sarah patted Leslie's knee as she merged off the freeway into the Silicon Valley office park where MagicWorks was threatening to split its warehouse offices at the seams.

Sarah had opened her door and turned back for her coffee mug when Leslie seized her by the collar of her shirt. "Just to tide me over," she said with a grin, and then she kissed Sarah all the way to her wisdom teeth.

Sarah's eyes were dancing with humor and she looked as if she might blush. "You have my permission to do that again, any ol' time you want to."

"You guys have to stop necking in the parking lot." Richard toddled in the door to the conference room, Fritos in one hand and a Surge soda in the other, prepared as usual for their weekly pipeline meeting.

Leslie smirked. For a day that had begun with being treated like furniture by Melissa, she felt . . . perky. "You only wish."

Sarah, who still regarded cuddly, anarchist Richard as an authority figure, said, "Okay, Richard." She sipped her fresh cup of coffee. "We'll park on the street next time." She gave Leslie a laughing look, her color high.

Gene, the programming manager, drained the last of his Jolt. "I'm just an ordinary straight guy and I don't care if you make out —"

"Christ," Leslie snapped. "It's not like it's an everyday thing."

"Can we change the subject?" Sarah really was blushing now.

Richard and Gene were enjoying themselves far too

much. Leslie echoed Sarah's request. "We're supposed to be reviewing timetables, remember?"

Gene launched into the new timetable for their latest software innovation. Having established themselves as the premiere software design group for video applications, the core group of programmers was taking a break by working on a project for the Children's Television Workshop, completely customizing a software program to aid in their production of parts of *Sesame Street*. Motion, their video/animation merging software, had made all of them a ton of stock market Monopoly money. Doing something for nothing was refreshing.

Leslie caught Sarah looking at her, still with the faintest hint of the blush that had started after Leslie grabbed her in the car. What was that about? Sarah was not — repeat, was not — shy about sex. But she was suddenly acting that way.

Life must be damned good, she pondered, if all you have to worry about is why your sex life has gone from great to fantastic.

"Absolutely not." Leslie waved her hand at the printout she'd removed from the wall of the programmers' cave. "You might think it's funny, and I might have a giggle or two, but it could easily be taken the wrong way. We are not a warm and fuzzy little startup anymore."

"Ah, Les." Greg, who was known for his two-word sentences, looked exactly like her son when she'd made him scrape the "Shit Happens" bumper sticker off her car.

"Blonde jokes are always about women, and that makes this list demeaning to women, okay? Look, I think number eight is hilarious, but I'm dead certain that there are women with blond hair who won't. It's just a matter of sensitivity and being a warm and fuzzy bigger startup company."

"Okay," Greg said sullenly.

"I don't think you're a pig or anything like that," Leslie added. "I don't want anyone else to get that idea, though."

Greg slouched back to the cave and Leslie tossed the "Top Fifteen Reasons Why Blondes Prefer Rich Men" into the recycling. She had just returned to her backlog of e-mail when Sarah rapped on the doorjamb.

"It's lunchtime — you have time to grab a bite or should I bring you something back?"

"I'll grab a bite, all right." Leslie waggled her eyebrows for emphasis.

Sarah burst out laughing, and that adorable, shy little blush came back. Leslie liked it, though she had no idea yet what was causing it. They flirted all the time. Now that Matt was nearing high school graduation, they even flirted in front of him. Usually they did it just to make him beg them to stop because it was "be-scusting, Mom!" Payback as a parent was fun.

Still looking discomfited, Sarah said, "Okay — I was thinking the salad bar."

"I'll drive," Leslie offered as they approached the car. She pulled out of the parking lot and then immediately to the side of the road. She lunged across the car to assault Sarah's mouth with a breathless kiss. "You promised Richard we'd neck on the street, remember?" She went back for more.

Sarah gave a startled squeak and then responded by sliding her hands up to Leslie's breasts. They stayed like that, exploring each other's mouths, until Leslie had to give it up.

"The gear shift," she explained. Tomorrow she was going to regret the bruise, but today she felt no pain.

Sarah's face was very red. She fanned herself with a map from the glovebox.

"Are you having a hot flash?" Leslie just didn't know what was making Sarah so embarrassed.

"Not the kind you mean," Sarah said with a laugh.

Driving toward their favorite salad bar, Leslie turned the situation over in her mind. Sex between them was great. Whenever she wanted anything, Sarah was right there with her. The oral sex was incredible and the hot flashes had only made that better and better. She'd never had such good oral sex in her life, and that included her Free Love days when several people had considered themselves experts.

They waited at a particularly long stoplight and Leslie continued to think. This morning, for example. Sarah had gotten right down to business. If there had been time she would have certainly returned the pleasure. Maybe Sarah was still turned on from that. No — there was something else.

A kiss goodnight that changed to something more. That was how sex usually began when a hot flash wasn't involved. Sarah would tease Leslie's body, her fingers light but sure. Inside they were like fire, knowing exactly where to stroke. Sarah's mouth was equally persistent and Leslie usually had to rest for a few minutes before she could repay Sarah for the attention.

You idiot, she suddenly thought. That's it.

Instead of a left turn, she made a U, then swerved into a motel parking lot with a vacancy sign.

"What's up?" Sarah looked at her as if she'd lost her mind.

"Nooners."

"Les, there's no need —"

"Oh yes, there is."

She left Sarah in the car while she got them a room. It was hardly the Ritz, but all she required was clean sheets.

Sarah was still looking at her like she'd grown a new head. "Are you going to have another hot flash?"

"Not the kind you mean."

She held the motel room door for Sarah, then stood

behind it, looking at the woman she loved. A pale peach mouth and blue eyes just turning to violet. Sarah was looking at her with unmistakable desire as she pressed Leslie into the door. Her hard, warm thigh was between Leslie's legs.

For a moment, when Sarah's mouth nuzzled at the hollow below Leslie's ear, Leslie forgot her inspiration in the car. She rocked herself on Sarah's thigh because it felt damned good. It was hard to push her away.

Sarah was startled for a moment, then she pulled Leslie toward the bed. "Let's get comfortable."

She pulled Leslie down on top of her for a long, languid kiss while she pulled up Leslie's shirt. Leslie almost yielded to the delight of Sarah's warm fingertips, but she remembered her plan just in time. She trapped Sarah's hands with her arms. "We're going to do things a little different today."

There was uncertainty on Sarah's face, but it faded as Leslie slowly unbuttoned Sarah's blouse. The zipper to Sarah's slacks opened next and Leslie rolled over, pulling Sarah astride her. She slid the blouse off and pulled down Sarah's bra straps so she could massage Sarah's shoulders.

Sarah's face was tinted with shy pinks as Leslie pulled her bra down farther. Stretching upward to kiss the bare breasts, Leslie marveled at Sarah's faint trembling. Sarah, always so strong, always taking care of Leslie first.

"Take the rest of your clothes off," Leslie said, knowing her voice was barely audible. "I want you naked against me."

Sarah shuddered under Leslie's touch. She was breathing hard as she stood up long enough to strip. Leslie kicked off her own shoes and socks and stretched out on the bed, arms open.

Sarah was flushed and shivering as she came back to Leslie, knee to knee, breast to breast. Leslie insinuated her jean-clad thigh between Sarah's naked legs while her tongue tasted the faint perfume on Sarah's arms and throat. Sarah was moaning against her.

Her hands in Sarah's hair, kissing Sarah's eyes, her temples, Leslie murmured, "You first this time."

Sarah gasped, "Please," as Leslie kissed her again.

She rolled Sarah tummy up, her knees between Sarah's. Skin against her tongue, her lips, then an eager welcoming *oh* of pleasure. Leslie reveled and drank, being selfish at first because there was so much to enjoy and it was what made loving a woman such ecstasy.

Gradually the sound of Sarah's rapture pierced her own desires and she concentrated on making the next few minutes all that Sarah could want. Her fingers pushed inward, causing new tremors in Sarah's thighs. She did exactly what Sarah was begging her to do and for as long as Sarah wanted. Her hand, her shirt, her face — they were all drenched by Sarah's climax.

Idiot, she told herself fondly. It took you way too long to figure out that sometimes she likes to go first.

Her shirt and pants were not fit for a return to the office. Sarah averted her eyes from the stains, and her face was a delight of pinks and peaches. They grabbed some quick burgers as they drove home, having been gone from the office far too long already.

Leslie dashed inside and encountered Melissa pouring herself a glass of soda. "I need fresh clothes," Leslie explained as she passed through the kitchen.

"Another hot flash?"

She heard the condescension in Melissa's voice and did not care one whit. She stopped just long enough to say, "Not the kind you mean," before she ran upstairs.

Making Up for Lost Time

Published: 1998
Characters: Jamie Onassis, master chef
              Valkyrie Valentine, home repair expert
              Sheila Thintowski, media executive
              Kathy Smitt, Jamie's childhood friend
Setting: San Francisco and Mendocino, California

The Eighth is for Eternity

Mendo Chili

This is a moderately spicy meat-lover's chili. Any kind of bread is a great accompaniment. I like carrot sticks alongside to kill the fire and provide a veneer of virture to this rich dish.

4 slices bacon, cut up or crumbled after cooking
an onion and a clove of garlic, coarsely chopped
1 tablespoon or more to taste of hot red chile pepper
1-1/2 teaspoons each ground cumin, oregano (preferably Mexican)
1/4 pound pork sausage
1/2 pound ground beef
1 pound beef round cut into mouth-sized chunks
small can of diced green chiles
2 6-ounce cans tomato paste
3 cups water, maybe more
16-ounce can pinto beans, drained

With a little care, you can make this entire dish in a single non-stick Dutch oven or other non-stick 5-quart pot. Begin by frying the bacon in the Dutch oven until it's very crisp. Drain on paper towels. Discard bacon grease, but don't wipe the pan. In the same pan, sauté the onion and garlic in the pan until translucent. Toss the cumin and oregano on top at the very end and stir in. Dump the resulting mix on top of the bacon to cool. Now you can wipe out the pan and proceed.

Fry the sausage and ground beef until browned, then add the beef round until browned. Drain off as much of the fat as possible. Crumble the bacon if it's not already in pieces, then add back in the bacon-onion mixture, chiles, tomato paste and water. Stir thoroughly. Simmer uncovered for 2 hours, stirring every so often.

Taste and season to your liking. Stir in the beans and simmer for another 1/2 hour. Serves 4 very hungry people.

Hacksaw Pastry

(3 years)

"Good God almighty!" Jamie Onassis twisted her fists hard into her ribs to keep from heaving her largest stainless steel bowl out the nearest window. A half-hour ago it had been filled to the brim with baby-tushy-soft dough, fragrant with basil and yeast and dusted with Parmesan and Romano.

Now it was just glop. Unfit for pigs. All the delicate air that made the mixture pliant was gone. The flour gluten that gave the dough resilience had overcome the yeast's bubble factory. Not enough sugar or salt? Not enough heat? Too much olive oil?

It was the third time this week. The second time today. It was not even noon. Aunt Emily was no doubt looking down from heaven and wondering where Jamie's deft touch with bread had gone.

"What happened?" Dar peered through the dining room pass-through into the kitchen. "You okay?"

"Yes," Jamie said shortly. Thank goodness Dar recognized the tone and said no more. She apparently warned off the other server, who didn't know Jamie's moods as well, because both of them left her alone as she prepared for lunchtime's quick and easy menu and the evening's more elaborate fare. Jamie seriously wanted to pummel something.

The Waterview's own special beef stew was the main event for dinner, and the meat still needed to be tenderized. She attacked the mound of top grade round steak with her heavy steel mallet until her arm ached.

She felt better.

It was an unwelcome task to turn out the spoiled dough and start over, but Jamie was determined to have fresh Italian rolls to accompany the cacciatore special for lunch. It was pouring rain outside and nothing shook off a chill like hot bread.

Her kitchen helper, Marco, stomped his way in the back door. Marco had wandered into Mendocino looking for chef's training at one of the world-famous restaurants. Unlike Café Beaujolais, the Waterview was not famous the world over, but he liked Jamie's approach to food: simple, unembellished, hearty, but gourmet delicious. He'd also stayed because he'd taken pointed note of the gregariously attractive — and perpetually hungry — Jeff O'Rhuan in Jamie's kitchen most mornings.

"Let me do that," he said as soon as he'd donned his apron.

Jamie relinquished the dough bowl with a muttered, "Another batch fell on me."

"It's this atrocious weather," Marco muttered back.

"Why don't you give it a go? I've got the chicken breasts to grill or we won't be ready for lunch."

"No lunch pie today?" Marco had leaned out to scan the menu board. Jamie's sour look silenced him and he went about measuring the dough ingredients.

No, Jamie wanted to snap, there was no lunch pie today, just like there had been no breakfast pie this morning and no apple pie last night. No pie at all yesterday and not the day before. One could not make pie without pie dough. The flat, tasteless, cardboard-textured shingle she'd been rolling out lately did not resemble pie dough. So no pies.

She hadn't been able to make a decent pie or bread since she'd gotten back from New York. Not that that had anything to do with it.

Jamie tried to hide how peeved she was when she congratulated Marco later on the beautifully fluffy, succulent rolls he produced. He had used the same ingredients she had. Her pride would not let him make the pie dough as well — at least not yet. She wondered how she had offended the baking gods and went back to work.

At the end of the long, frustrating day, Jamie clumped up the stairs to the third floor where she and Val shared a bedroom and each had separate offices. The rooms had the slight echo they always did when Val was away. The charm of the master bedroom that Val had so carefully renovated failed to lift Jamie's spirits. Even a long soak in the large clawfoot tub didn't revive her much.

Her own days were usually so busy she rarely had time to miss Val, but everything about the inn made her think of Val tonight. Val was often gone for one- to two-month stints, taping her cable show in Los Angeles studios and making personal appearances around the country as Valkyrie Valentine, "VV," home improvement expert and chef. The months would usually fly by and then Val would be back for a couple of months to work on the inn or a book or whatever project she had taken into her head.

Val was definitely making a name for herself, which was why three weeks' taping for a special series had been arranged in New York. Jamie had had a good time visiting New York and watching Val do her thing live. The brief vacation coincided with the slowest tourist time of year in Mendocino — early February. Back at home she'd been greeted by rain and the worst case of the doldrums she'd ever experienced.

She punched a pillow viciously and closed her eyes. Just as she fell asleep she remembered Val sparkling in front of the live audience, doing a guest cooking spot on a very popular talk show. The host, widely reputed to be a lesbian, seemed enchanted with Val, praising her high-protein-low-fat burritos to the skies. Who didn't love Val? The leather tool belt, the chef's apron, the luscious lips, the silky hair . . .

A creaking floorboard startled Jamie awake. She fumbled for the bedside light but couldn't find the switch.

"It's only me."

"Val!" Jamie bolted out of bed and bodily tackled the dark figure approaching the bed. They thudded to the floor and Jamie straddled Val's waist. "A day early! God I've missed you!"

"Same here — take that off. Let me —"

"I got it — the zipper's stuck, there it goes . . . oh . . ."

Val's hands on her body had never felt so good. Jamie surrendered her T-shirt in spite of the cold and savored Val's warm fingers as they raised goosebumps on her back. Her own fingers seemed stiff and frozen as she fumbled with Val's shirt buttons. The shock of her bare breasts against Val's was satisfyingly arousing and Jamie buried her lips in the hollow below Val's ear.

Val's throaty laugh was a symphony to Jamie. "You did miss me, didn't you?"

"You know I did," Jamie answered. She cupped Val's face in the dark. "It feels wonderful just to touch you."

Val drew Jamie's hands down to her breasts. "You'll get no arguments here."

After a thorough exploration of Val's shoulders and breasts with her fingers and mouth, Jamie let Val persuade her that the bed would be more comfortable.

"Let me," she whispered, when Val would have rolled on top of her. Val trembled as Jamie's teasing fingers found their way between her legs.

"I don't think so — not tonight." Val leveraged one leg under Jamie's thighs and tumbled Jamie onto her back. "I've missed you — you don't know how much."

"Yes I do." Jamie all at once felt free as the wind. "I've been cursed by bad weather and bad yeast, but now you're home."

Val kissed her quickly and said, "Stay right there." She scrambled off the bed and began rustling through her traveling knapsack.

"What are you doing? Come back to bed." Jamie sat up. "You got me on my back. Promises were made."

"Yeah, yeah, yeah," Val muttered. "Where . . . here it is. Okay, back on your back, missy."

"Make me," Jamie challenged.

She did not mind Val's demonstration that she was taller and stronger, but was quite surprised when Val picked something up off the floor. She heard the sound of a jar being opened. "What *are* you doing?"

"Special recipe." Val knelt astride Jamie's hips and raised the jar.

Something cold plopped onto Jamie's stomach and she let out a startled shriek. "Val!"

"Breathe in," Val whispered.

Summertime and peaches filled Jamie's nostrils and lungs. She inhaled the scent of honeysuckle, and the dreary February rain was gone.

Val's hands were spreading the aromatic concoction over Jamie's stomach and breasts. Jamie put her hands on top of Val's and encountered something not quite sticky, not quite oily.

She could see Val dipping her index finger into the jar. She extended a dollop of the contents toward Jamie. Without hesitation Jamie took Val's finger in her mouth, letting her tongue take its time as it tasted Val's creation. Definitely pieces of peach suspended in a slippery substance that melted from the heat of Jamie's body. It was delicious and sensuous. "What is it?"

"Something I worked on while thinking about you." She smeared more across Jamie's cheeks, then down her throat.

"Peaches, obviously. Freestone?"

"Mm-hmm." Val began massaging Jamie's hips and ribs.

"Gelatin, flavored with a noble wine?"

"Mm-hmm." Val's tongue began a lazy journey from Jamie's belly button to her throat.

"Honeysuckle-infused oil?"

"You're good," Val murmured.

"And so good for you," Jamie giggled. "It's making an awful mess."

"Sure is," and Val covered Jamie's body with her own. Val's hands were everywhere and her mouth followed. Everywhere Jamie kissed she found the taste of Val's skin mingling with peaches and wine. They were slick against each other and Jamie felt drunk on the promise of summer.

* * * * *

166

Jamie opened her eyes to bright sunshine. Her first thought was that the rain had stopped, at least. No fog, no clouds. The sun had welcomed Val home. A glance at the bedside clock confirmed that her alarm had not gone off two hours ago as it ought to have done. She found she had to peel the sheets off her now decidedly sticky body. It had been more than effective last night, but was distinctly gross in the morning.

There was no sign of Val, but her bathrobe was damp. Jamie quickly showered as well and stripped the bed. She found the forgotten jar of the peach stuff on the floor. Val had written, "For Jamie" on the jar lid.

She blinked back happy tears and went downstairs to find Val.

She discovered her kitchen bustling with activity. Marco was whisking something in the large copper bowl and flirting outrageously with an oblivious Jeff O'Rhuan. Jeff, general handyman when he wasn't fishing, was devouring what looked like Belgian waffles. Val was rolling out a thick dough that glistened with butter. Using cookie cutters, she pressed out stars and carefully transferred them to baking sheets.

"Is that your very own Starbread?" Jamie went on tiptoe to kiss the back of Val's neck.

"You betcha. I felt like making it."

The dough was perfect: pliant, puffed and fragrant with rosemary and salt. "And what are you making for lunch, oh lovely chef? It might be February, but we still get customers." She glanced through the kitchen pass-through. Dar was filling salt shakers and chatting with a couple of regulars who stopped in for coffee and breakfast pie every now and again.

Breakfast pie — they were eating breakfast pie. "Did you make pie?"

"Yeah," Val said. "You were zonked out. I went with

167

the bacon-cheddar combo and used half eggs and egg substitute."

Jamie examined the half-eaten slice sitting in front of Jeff. The crust looked . . . perfect.

"It's awesome," Jeff offered.

"Of course it is," Val said tartly. "It came from the kitchen of the Waterview Inn." She slid the baking sheets into the oven and set the timer. From there Val went to the walk-in refrigerator and returned with two different ground meats and several large sirloins. "We're having Mendo chili on the lunch menu, with Starbread, of course.

Jamie watched Val move about, setting out frying pans and the chili pot. She'd accurately gauged the amount of food they'd need for the off-season lunch demands. Three years ago Val hadn't known the difference between salt and sugar, and now she could run the kitchen as well as Jamie had ever done.

Marco handed over the whipped egg whites in the copper bowl and took over dicing the sirloin. Val spooned some of the contents of the large mixing bowl into the egg whites, stirred gently, then folded the rest back into the mixer. "Spice cream cake — Em's recipe," she announced.

Jamie had nothing to do and it was a very strange sensation. "I'll watch the meats," she said quickly, and she took over frying the bacon until it crumbled, then browning the ground pork and beef for the chili.

Jeff went off to mend nets with his father and Marco sighed. "That boy will never notice me."

"Keep feeding him," Jamie said. "I've never known Jeff to respond to anything else. Well, food and fishing."

"I hate boats," Marco bemoaned.

"You may be star-crossed, in that case," Val pronounced. "What about the guy who always orders whatever it is you made?"

"He hasn't been in for three weeks," Jamie said.

"How depressing."

"Tell me about it." Marco dumped the last of the sirloin into one of the frying pans Jamie was tending.

Their friend Liesel dropped in a few minutes later, greeting Val with enthusiasm and an invitation for evening snacks to catch up on her travels and adventures. She kissed Jamie almost as an afterthought, but then, she saw Jamie every day. "I really stopped in because Jeff O'Rhuan just asked me the most interesting question, Marco."

"Oh yeah?" Marco paused in the midst of washing his hands. "About me?"

"It seems that Jeff isn't quite sure that you're interested in him."

"What?"

Jamie chortled. "He only drapes himself on Jeff every morning, scurrying about with fresh coffee and fresh cream and reheating his breakfast if it gets cold."

"I do not. It's not *that* bad."

"He's just not sure you're gay."

"What!"

They were all laughing now. "Jeff is not a subtle person," Jamie finally said. "Perhaps he's just missed the signs."

They all looked at Marco. Marco shrugged. Just standing still he screamed, *Gay, gay, gay!*

It was a mystery.

Val lowered her voice so as not to be heard in the dining room. "Perhaps you need to wear an Assmaster T-shirt."

Marco flicked his wet fingers at her.

Jamie smelled something burning and with horror turned back to the stove. "Good God almighty!" The bacon was beyond crisp: it was carbonized. "I don't believe this."

Val went to the freezer for more bacon while Jamie dumped the contents of the pan. "Want me to do the next batch?"

"I can do it," Jamie muttered. She kept her eye on the

169

bacon every minute, even when Liesel left and two women who ran a shop down the street came in because they'd heard there was breakfast pie again. Val's breakfast pie. They raved.

With one hundred percent of her attention, the bacon was fine. Val stirred it into the chili, and the savory aroma seemed to drag people in from the street. The Starbread was melt-in-your-mouth perfect. The spice cream cake was gone in the first half-hour, so Val made more.

That afternoon, when Jamie's roasted tomato and red pepper ragout scorched, Val quickly made Welsh meatloaf while Jamie rewrote the menu board. Jamie's crackerbread had no crunch for some reason, though Val's came out crisp and golden. By the end of the night Jamie wanted to cry while Val looked more and more like the goddess of cuisine. The chef's apron, the sparkling eyes, the tall, slender physique. Val looked just as lovely and charming and talented as she had on that talk show, where the wildly popular, often-rumored lesbian host loved everything Val had made.

When the dinner crowd noticeably thinned Jamie gave up all pretense at cooking. She scrubbed pots — the ones she had personally burnt, scorched and bent were the hardest.

Liesel, Aunt Emily's lover for most of Jamie's growing up years, loved hearing about Val's travels and tapings. They shared Liesel's light-as-air savory cheese dumplings floating in a simple onion broth as Val described the celebrities she'd rubbed shoulders with, no matter how briefly, and the food she'd sampled and concocted in the course of taping her television show.

The VV brand, which was how Warnell Communications referred to Val, was catching on. Her combination home repair, decorating and cookery books had strong sales, and Warnell was running numbers around launching a VV magazine. VV's unique demographics appealed strongly to younger single women with no children. Disposable income was what the advertisers were after.

"It does intrude," Val said, in response to Liesel's question. "I just want to do what I do — I don't want to worry about who is watching the show or not, and if they have babies or not. That's Sheila's job. But she thinks I should care passionately about all that, and I don't."

"Are she and Kathy still together?"

"If you can call it together. They have a different kind of relationship, that's for sure. Kathy loves being Sheila's hostess, that's obvious. But they hardly sleep together."

"How do you know?" Jamie sipped the soup and watched Val's face. Jamie had wasted years of her life wishing Kathy would stop being a spoiled brat and realize that Jamie was offering her real love. It had been the outrageous Sheila Thintowski who had finally broken through Kathy's denial.

"Sheila told me. Sheila tells me everything about her private life. Who she sleeps with, who she just has quickies with, who she wants —"

"That includes you, of course," Jamie said. She hadn't meant to sound so bitter about it.

"Of course." Val was smiling understandingly at her. "That's never going to change, but believe me, every year Sheila gets less and less appealing."

"I'm glad to hear that," Jamie said tartly.

Val's response was an indulgent wink. "I'll mention it more often, if you like."

Liesel patted Jamie's hand as if comforting a child. "The rules are different in Los Angeles and New York. Fortunately, Val only commutes there."

Four or five months out of the year, Jamie wanted to add.

"Sheila's in New York most of the time, anyway. We do conference calls for the most part."

"Jamie, I almost forgot," Liesel said. "I was cleaning out the old dresser and found this. I don't think you ever saw it."

Liesel laid a photograph on the table. The edges were yellow, but the central figures were bright and clear.

Jamie caught her breath. Aunt Em's beloved face was one of the three pictured. "I don't think I ever saw it. When was it taken?"

"Near as I can tell, I took that the summer I met Em. It was just after you came to live with her, too."

Jamie looked at her eight-year-old face and then Kathy's. They'd been happy together as children.

"You look adorable," Val said. "You all do. I don't think I've ever seen Emily this young in a picture before."

Liesel touched Aunt Em's face gently. "She was so handsome."

Jamie nodded. "I so wanted to be just like her."

"You're more like her than you realize," Liesel said. "More than you give yourself credit for."

"Even Kathy looks happy," Val observed. "Was that before she turned into a bitch?"

Jamie laughed. "Yes, definitely before that. She was just a bitch because she was scared. Every time she turned around I was there, puppy-eyed and wanting to be loved. It must have been excruciating for her at times, especially in high school. She wasn't strong enough to come out to herself."

"Hardly an excuse to be a bitch in your thirties," Val said dryly. "She wouldn't let Liesel live with you guys, after all."

"That's all old water under the bridge," Liesel said gently. "Em was just trying to be a good mother."

"She was a great mother to me," Jamie said. Her own mother had left her with Emily, a virtual stranger, and hadn't returned for over twenty-five years. Jamie had found all the love and stability she craved in Aunt Em's house.

Val coiled one hand around Jamie's. "You turned out wonderfully."

Jamie rolled her eyes. "Flattery? What exactly are you after?"

Val waggled her eyebrows promisingly. "I was away a long time."

"Then get yourselves home." Liesel shooed them away from the table. "I've kept you up late enough as it is."

"Morning at the Waterview does come early," Val said. "Though I love it. It felt so good to get busy in there this morning."

"She let me sleep in," Jamie volunteered, though she was still bothered by how useless she had felt. Burning the bacon — how clumsy was that?

"Now that's good for you. You should just close for February, like some of the other places do. Go someplace warm." Liesel was still offering similar advice when they waved good-bye and walked up the wooden sidewalk toward home.

The night air was rich with the scent of eucalyptus and the sea. Jamie was encouraging when Val stopped to kiss her, and they quickly became lost in the warmth of each other's bodies.

"You're a good kisser," Jamie mumbled into Val's mouth.

"I'm out of practice," Val answered. "Honey, I want to talk seriously about something. Really. I was going to wait, but I'm just completely fed up with us being apart so much. I know it's my fault — I'm the one who has to do the traveling. But I miss you so much. When you came to New York it was like heaven."

Jamie had been unsettled ever since, and still didn't want to think about why. "So what are you proposing?"

"I make a lot of money, you know that. We haven't talked about mingling our assets and that's just stupid. Let me contribute to the bottom line, if that's what it takes, so that you can travel with me just a little. Hire another chef — Marco's really good. Let him run things during the slow months and hire him an assistant. Jeff O'Rhuan would make a great official caretaker and he could handle the boarders. I'm sure I could rearrange my shooting schedule so I'm filming now and free during the summer when you need me here."

It made sense. It all made perfect sense. "No," said Jamie. She started walking.

"No?" Val wasn't moving yet and her voice followed Jamie. "That's it?"

"My life doesn't need fixing," Jamie said, not sure Val could hear her.

"I'm not saying it does." Val was hurrying after her, but Jamie did not slacken her pace. "I'm the one who misses you like crazy. I'm trying to figure out a way to be together more."

"By taking me away from all this."

"That's not what I meant, and you know it. I'm not Julia Child — yet. I can't film the cooking segments from my own house. I have to go to a studio. I have to do promotional appearances in studios. I have to do the renovations we film on location. Do you think I wanted to spend last summer in Alabama? I wanted to be here. I wanted to be in your beautiful kitchen and your bed."

I don't believe her, Jamie thought, though she knew Val was telling the truth. I don't want to believe her. God, what's wrong with me? My bread won't rise, my piecrust is crap and she has all the solutions. "I'm sorry Mendocino is so far off the beaten track." She picked up the pace, but Val had no trouble keeping up.

"What is with you?"

"Nothing is with me."

"You're mad about something, I can tell."

"I am not."

"Yes, you are. You're mad at me because I have to go away."

"I am not." Jamie snatched open the back door to the

inn and marched inside. She hurriedly shed her heavy coat and boots on the mud porch. It was useless. Val matched her move for move and was right behind her on the stairs.

"Then what are you running for?"

"I'm cold."

"You can say that again."

Jamie spun around on the second-floor landing. "If you don't like the temperature in here, you have choices."

Val looked stricken. "What are you saying?"

Jamie burst into tears and dashed for the top floor.

Damn Val and her long legs, shapely and muscled and too damn fast. She passed Jamie on the stairs and opened the door to their private suite. "After you," she said stiffly, hardly out of breath.

Jamie threw herself on the bed not so much for melodramatic purposes but because she could not bear to look at Val. She was making a fool of herself for reasons she could hardly put into words. How could she complain that Val was . . . was too perfect?

"Maybe you don't want to talk about it right now, but I'm not sleeping anywhere else," Val announced from the doorway. "Maybe in the morning you can tell me what I've done wrong."

"You haven't done anything wrong." Jamie sobbed into the pillow.

"That makes sense, then."

"It's me. I'm the one who is messed up." Jamie rolled over to find the tissues. She hiccuped. "It's me."

"What have you done wrong?"

"I'm jealous and petty and envious and stupid." Jamie mopped her eyes, then twisted the tissue until it shredded.

"That does not describe the Jamie Onassis I know and love," Val said slowly. She closed the door, then crossed slowly toward Jamie. "Come on, Jamie. Do you really think so little of me that I'd love the person you described?"

"You just don't know me." Good God, I'm a basket case, Jamie thought.

"What is it?" Val sat down on the bed close enough to stroke Jamie's hair.

Jamie shied away from any contact. "Don't be so damned patient and understanding."

"Would you rather I yelled and stormed out?"

"Yes, I think I would."

"Well, I'm not going to. You can't make me."

"I could if I tried." Jamie sniffed.

"What the hell are we arguing about?"

"Me. And you."

"Well that certainly turns on the light bulb."

"Did anyone tell you I can't cook?"

"No. Why would they? It's not true."

"It is so true. Yesterday alone two batches of dough fell and today I burnt the bacon. Bacon! Do you know what it takes to burn bacon to the point of its being unusable?"

"Is this really about cooking?"

"Of course not," Jamie snapped.

"At some point this conversation will make sense. I know it will." Val abruptly stretched out next to Jamie. Her nearness made Jamie want to cuddle and cry.

"I want to do what you said," Jamie said. "If you still want to try it."

"You mean about coming with me sometimes?" Val was obviously surprised by Jamie's change of heart, but she didn't argue. "I would so love it. You have no idea."

"I do."

"What are you jealous of?"

"Everybody. All of them," Jamie said in a rush.

"I mean — do you think I'm having an affair? Or something?" Val's tone indicated she thought this a ridiculous idea.

"No. I'm jealous of all those women who love you because it seems like they have a piece of you I never saw before." Finally, Jamie thought, you're making some sense.

"This morning, you were like that. You were perfect and poised and coiffed and delightful and charming."

"You don't like that?"

"I love it, but I also like you cranky and sarcastic and just a bit childish."

"You're not losing that, you know. I'm sure eventually I'll stop being delighted to be home again and I'll do something cranky. I know — ask me to fix something. That usually does it."

"That second-story window still leaks."

"Shit. Get off my back, woman. I'll fix it when I damn well feel like it."

Jamie went from tears to laughter in a split second. This was the Val she loved. "I guess I felt it the most when I watched you tape that talk show. I mean — that woman adored you. She had huge stars in her eyes."

"She was very sweet, but there was nothing —"

"I know that, but I suddenly saw who she saw. VV, Valkyrie Valentine, The Complete Woman. I just never realized I was sleeping with her."

"You're not, silly."

"I'm sleeping with her and I don't know her."

"There's nothing to know. She's says vapid things sometimes and is quite the social butterfly. You'd hate her."

"And then you came home and you were so perfect — this morning you ran my kitchen better than I do."

"That's ridiculous. I was just having the best time. I miss this place. I miss you."

Jamie rolled over into Val's arms. "You must think I'm an idiot."

"I don't. Unless you think you're a failure because you're not on TV. That would really piss me off."

Jamie shook her head. "No, that's not it at all. I don't feel like you're famous so I should be too. I was glad to write my cookbook, but I have no desire to corner the

177

market. I love my life here, making people feel welcome and warm. It's what Aunt Em did all her life and that's what I want, too. But not at the cost of not knowing who you are."

"Let's tell Marco tomorrow and then plan a vacation. Someplace warm and very, very soon."

"Maybe I was feeling a little bit country mouse. I feel that way when I think about Sheila Thintowski."

"Even a city mouse would feel dowdy next to Sheila. She's gone from retro Sixties to steady Chanel."

"She's good at what she does."

"Oh yeah — she'll be CEO of Warnell when Mark retires, you can bank on that."

"Am I forgiven?"

"I was never mad at you," Val said. She snuggled closer. "I just didn't know what you were thinking, that's all."

"Neither did I. That happens where you're concerned, as you're well aware."

They were quiet for a few minutes. Jamie burrowed her head into Val's side. "I don't suppose you would indulge me for ninety minutes."

"Babe, I'd love to." One of Val's hands crept over Jamie's breast.

"Not that — well, later."

"Hon, it's after eleven."

"I want to make a pie. Breakfast pie."

"Now?"

"You can help. You make up the filling. I'll do the crust."

Val reluctantly followed her down to the cold kitchen. Jamie assembled shortening, flour, salt and ice water while Val beat cream and soft Jack cheese together. She was slicing Pippins by the time Jamie finished cutting the shortening into the flour.

The rolling pin felt like a magic wand in her hands. Jamie dusted the pliant dough with flour and turned the pin this way and that until she had an approximate circle. She fetched her favorite glass pie plate and greased it. Then she slipped the feather-light dough onto the plate, fluted it with precise pinches, trimmed the excess, then pricked it with a fork around the sides and across the bottom.

Unbaked, it looked like perfection.

Val brought her chopped apples and mixing bowl over to the assembling counter. "I almost don't want to ruin that."

"Go ahead," Jamie said.

"I'm honored. You usually won't let me within a foot of your pie crusts." Val quickly combined some crushed apples and simple syrup with the cheese mixture and spread it into the shell. Then sliced apples were layered carefully and topped with crumbled brown sugar.

Jamie moved it to the preheated oven and set the timer. "Now we wait."

Val yawned. "Fifty minutes? Wow — you'll need to think of something to keep me awake."

Jamie pulled Val toward the stairwell. She held up the timer. "It can go with us."

"Now we're getting somewhere," Val said. "No peach delight, no chocolate sauce. Let's just get down to business."

"We will have to come back downstairs, you know. To taste the pie."

"The proof will be in the tasting," Val said philosophically. "That's the business I have in mind right now."

Jamie felt as light as her pie dough as she tickled Val and chased her back up the stairs.

"We have breakfast pie again today," Marco observed. "That looks quite delicious."

"It is," Jamie assured him. "My crust, Val's filling."

Marco grinned. "By the way, I dropped in on Jeff last night. Just to chat. And to take him some of those scones he seemed to really like. Since I had some leftovers."

"Liar."

"Well, when you make a dozen all for yourself, there are leftovers."

Just then Jeff O'Rhuan came through the back door. He beamed at the sight of Jamie filling his favorite coffee mug, then looked sideways at Marco.

Jamie gaped. Jeff was blushing.

"Scones, eh?" That was all she said, but Marco laughed delightedly and Jeff blushed harder.

"Something smells wonderful," Val said from the back stairs. She cinched an apron around her waist. "French bread?"

"Sourdough," Jamie corrected. She had removed the picture-perfect loaves only a few minutes earlier.

Val unceremoniously helped herself to a slice, ooching as the hot bread burned her fingertips. "This is wonderful."

"I know," Jamie said.

"Excuse us for a moment, fellas." Val lifted Jamie onto the counter and kissed her thoroughly. "What do you think of Key West?"

"I've heard it's lovely."

"Good. We leave tomorrow."

Jamie felt a tinge of anxiety, but then she sighed and pulled Val against her again. For quite a while she had thought she was married to the Waterview, but that had been mistaken priorities. "Marco, how would you like to be chef for a while?"

When there was no answer, Jamie looked up from the beauty of Val's eyes. They were alone.

"We'll ask later," Val whispered. She kissed Jamie again.

Watermark

Published: 1999
Characters: Rayann Germaine, advertising executive
             Teresa Mandrell, artist
Setting: San Francisco Bay Area, California

The Ninth is for Never-Never Land

The Tapestry

(1 year)

The door slammed with finality. Teresa fumbled her way to the bed and huddled under the cold blankets.

She was numb with panic, with self-recriminations, with Rayann's white-hot anger.

Thirty minutes ago, Rayann had left Teresa gasping with satisfaction. Thirty seconds ago she had said with deadly calm, "Don't be here when I get back."

* * * * *

At moments of crisis, Rayann tended to run. She knew that much about herself and there had been plenty of crises in the last two years to finely hone the art of running away.

You ought to have stayed and just had it out with her, she told herself. You can't just end it this way.

She asked herself where she was going, but she was just following her feet. Around the building, toward PacBell Park, which was lit up for a night game. She forged through the crowds, calling herself a fool.

She was trying to tell you something. You haven't been listening.

A Muni train was disgorging passengers for the game and she got on after it finally emptied. Where could she go? To the Lace Place, or her mother's? Old habits die hard.

She put her head down in her hands and waited for the train to get going. *Who are you to throw her out? What has she done to deserve you walking out like this? Go back and listen.*

I can't, she thought. I can't.

She had not known she could still hurt like this.

"I brought home Sumi's," she had called out, laden with sushi boxes and her endlessly bulging briefcase.

"Yummy," Teresa had called from the bedroom. "I'll be right there."

Rayann set the food down on the counter and paused, as she always did, to admire the view. She had only lived in this building for eighteen months, and it still felt new. The last of the sun painted the bay orange as it stretched almost from her feet toward Oakland and the East Bay. Lights on Treasure Island were starting to show, but the distant hills were bathed in the golden glow of a glorious fall evening.

"Tell me you got lots of California roll." Teresa bounded out of the bedroom to peck her on the lips.

"Enough for even you," Rayann promised. "How was the day off?"

"Wonderful. I slept until eleven."

"You deserved it." Teresa had been working too many hours. No matter where she worked it was a bad habit. Her current freelance job, creating and producing backdrops and sets for an art program on PBS, was proving to be a real challenge, but Teresa loved every minute of it.

"Then I went for a walk and ended up at MOMA. They have an exhibit of chairs that was killer. Then I had a Jamba Juice and watched soap operas all afternoon. Did you know that Erica Kane's daughter is gay?"

"I'd heard that," Rayann said. She popped the lid on the first container of California roll. "This is spicy. The other one is regular."

"Share." Teresa held out her plate and Rayann dumped four slices of the crab, avocado and cucumber sushi delicacy on it. "So that was cool to find out. I saw the new Beakman's campaign."

"I didn't know they were buying daytime ad space."

Teresa coughed and reached for her water. "There's way too much wasabi on this."

"I'll take it if you don't want it," Rayann said. She loved wasabi. "Wimp," she added fondly.

Teresa was blinking away tears. "That totally cleared my sinuses in a very painful way." She shook her head fiercely.

Rayann was rinsing the dishes when Teresa pinned her against the counter. Her hands cupped Rayann's breasts, and she had to put the plate down before she dropped it. "Oh my," she breathed. "I thought we were going to the movies."

"Maybe later. I love this blouse. You know what a few extra hours of sleep does to my libido."

"I most assuredly do," Rayann said. "You slept in on

Labor Day and we were almost late to the ballgame that night." It had been . . . memorable.

Teresa was unbuttoning her blouse with deliberate intent. Rayann shut off the water and welcomed the familiar rhythm of arousal. Though Louisa had been gone for over two years, she no longer felt guilty about the brief moment when she had to consciously tell herself that it was Teresa who held her. Time would take care of it, as it had the sharper pains of grief.

It wasn't that there were any similarities between the two. Louisa had been in her late fifties. Teresa was in her early thirties. Louisa had been close to Rayann's height, while Teresa sometimes seemed to tower at five-foot nine. Teresa was mercurial and brazen and flashpoint funny while Louisa had rarely done anything without knowing exactly why and how she would do it.

Teresa had her bra loose and Rayann knew it was Teresa's hands cupping and teasing her breasts. It was just a moment that she needed to remind herself that this wasn't infidelity. Louisa herself would be glad that Rayann had recognized Teresa's love and her own tentative, growing feelings for a woman ten years younger than she was. The irony was not lost on her; she had been the younger lover with Louisa, twenty-nine years younger. But the way time marched these days, the ten years between her and Teresa sometimes seemed almost as vast.

It mattered little now, when her body responded so quickly to Teresa's touch. She helped Teresa's hand slide under the waistband of her pants, eager for the caress of Teresa's fingers. Her mouth was suddenly dry and she knew what would quench her thirst. She knew that Teresa would want that; she readily admitted she would never get enough. Another way Louisa and Teresa were different.

Louisa was too much in her head, Rayann suddenly realized. It was Teresa who said, "How nice," at what her fingers quickly reveled in. Teresa who pinned her against the sink and murmured, "I have no intention of going to the movies tonight."

"Let me get my clothes off," Rayann gasped.

"Not right now," Teresa whispered in her ear. "You feel too good right now."

The next few minutes were exquisite torture. As wonderful as Teresa's precise stroking felt, Rayann wasn't sure it was enough, but all at once she knew it was. Her temples throbbed with crimson lightning as Teresa's voice urged her to climax. As if she had a choice, when Teresa knew so clearly how to make it happen.

Teresa looked smug when Rayann caught her breath and turned around. Her expression quickly changed when Rayann shed the rest of her clothes without breaking eye contact. Then she advanced on Teresa, who backed up until she was against the opposite counter.

"This will be easier if you take off your sweatpants," Rayann said. "Or do you want me to do it for you?"

Teresa lost no time shedding her pants. When she would have pulled off her T-shirt as well, Rayann stopped her.

"We'll get there soon enough." She pushed Teresa up onto the counter and slipped her bare shoulders under Teresa's legs. "Right now this is what I want."

What mattered most was the sound of Teresa's moans. Vocal, specific, needy, they told Rayann she was desired and loved. Louisa had not often wanted this yet Rayann loved it so much. How wonderful that Teresa was begging for it not to stop, not yet, for it to go on and on.

Rayann made it last as long as it seemed Teresa could stand it. The sunset gently illuminated Teresa's face when Rayann finally pulled Teresa into her arms. The kiss that followed was full of promise and hunger. Teresa shed her T-shirt as they moved to the darkened bedroom.

Rayann settled on her back and pulled Teresa on top of her, kisses and hands teasing. Eyes closed, she gave herself up to Teresa's mouth on her heaving shoulders, her hardening breasts, her churning hips. Legs open, inviting, she pressed Teresa downward with a throaty plea.

The colors behind her eyelids mutated from white to black, yellow to purple. It had been a long time since it had felt this good to have fingers pressing inside while a demanding tongue left no part of her wanting. Her life might not be even half over and she'd been blessed by incredible lovers who knew what her body craved.

How much longer? She couldn't stand it. It felt too good, so loved. She opened her eyes to interwoven moons and stars. Her sky was outlined by a briar border of golden leaves and red roses.

The body entangled with her legs was too far away to reach. She heard a voice, husky, demanding.

She was coming undone, something was unraveling. *Louisa*. It couldn't be. It had to be. The tapestry was above her, and the last place she had seen it was over the bed she had shared with Louisa for so many years. She had to be in their bed, above the bookstore. They had made love and sold books and made love and cooked and talked and made love. Nine years of profound happiness. It hadn't ended, her body knew it had not.

She cried out because she had no choice. Muscles contracted hard against the fingers that were so sure she wasn't done yet and she wasn't, there was more and she cried out again. Memory collided with the present and left her breathless. Arms were around her. A soft voice cooed that everything was okay.

Where was the hair, the curtain of silver and black that ought to have surrounded her during these grateful kisses? She touched short curls and saw then unexpected eyes and a trembling mouth that curved with a loving smile.

Dear God. Please, God, let me not have called her Lou.

It was all Rayann could think for a moment, that she had called Teresa by the wrong name. But her darling

Reese was smiling so tenderly. She shuddered then, knowing she had not been at this door before, not in the year and more she and Teresa had been lovers. Never once had she thought Reese was Louisa.

She looked up and saw the tapestry again. She had not imagined it. She ought to have listened, ought to have at least held Teresa for a moment, a recognition of the wonderful passion they had just shared.

She had not done any of that. She looked up at the tapestry that vividly reminded her of Louisa and their lovemaking, looked up and knew every color and stitch. She had said, "What the hell were you thinking?"

I only wanted to show her I wasn't jealous of Louisa, Teresa thought. But she wouldn't even listen. The bed had been warm and welcoming, but had been quickly chilled with anger.

She had been fiercely jealous of Louisa at first, anybody would have been. Louisa was a saint, a paragon of virtues, a fabulous lover, a woman of convictions and confidence. She knew that Rayann tried not to talk about her that much, but the phrases "Louisa thought" and "Louisa said" were not unknown to Teresa. Louisa had read every fucking book on the planet, Teresa thought bitterly, and had had opinions about all of them, and why not?

You, on the other hand, haven't read a book in years. She railed at herself for all her flaws, for all the ways she was not the hallowed Louisa and never would be. Her father had tried to tell her that her very difference from Louisa was very likely what attracted Rayann most.

She didn't want to be loved because of who she wasn't.

She stood on the bed and untied the tapestry from the posts. She knew what it represented to Rayann. It had belonged to Louisa and her first lover, Chris. After Chris died, Louisa had kept it and eventually Rayann had slept under it. Rayann had even said that at first she had been uncomfortable to share her bed with something that had to evoke strong memories of another woman in Louisa. But she accepted it because Louisa proved, over and over, that Rayann was the only woman in her mind.

She had only wanted to make that point to Rayann — that she knew Louisa would always be there, but she knew also that Rayann loved her. She didn't mind what the tapestry represented to Rayann. It was a part of her and always would be. That was all.

Rayann had been hysterical. Okay, she should have never touched the thing. But . . . but to tell her to get out?

Teresa folded the heavy fabric gently, fighting the urge to rip it to shreds. Rayann had sealed the tapestry away after having it carefully cleaned and preserved, and certainly the bed didn't need the tapestry to be beautiful. The four tall posts of fired olive wood had been thickly carved by Rayann herself, a twining of vines and roses that were their own art. In quiet moments Rayann would add another leaf or hint of vine so that the work never ended.

She couldn't get the tapestry back in the cleaner's bag, so she just left it on the chair. She began to get dressed, then realized she needed to wash her face and hands.

Her hands were fragrant with Rayann, her mouth and chin raw with the proof of Rayann's need. It had been an incredible climax, unbelievable after the fierce passion that Rayann had always displayed. Rayann had only begged, "Yes, please, please" but every movement of her body had screamed, "More, harder, now."

Teresa went back to dressing, her movements leaden and unfocused. She ought not have touched something that so vividly represented Louisa. She knew that now. It had been a mistake.

But when, her own sense of self asked, when would she matter like that to Rayann?

It was the anniversary of their moving in together, after all. If the answer was never, then it was time to move out. Rayann should not have shouted, should not have thrown her out. But maybe it was still time to go.

How dare you! What were you thinking? It wasn't for you to decide!

Teresa had tried to explain, but Rayann hadn't been able to hear over her anger and pain. Teresa had unilaterally decided it was time to let Louisa's spirit float around their bed. Teresa didn't know anything about what that tapestry meant. The first time Louisa had made love to her Rayann had felt pushed to those stars by Louisa's touch. The next morning she'd felt captured by golden borders of briar roses. Teresa had no right to touch it, no right to decide it was time to test Rayann like that. What had Teresa really wanted?

She wants me to tell her I love her more than Louisa. That won't happen. It's not a case of more or better. She wanted to manipulate me into choosing, Rayann told herself. That's why I'm so angry.

That's why . . .

The Muni train suddenly lurched into motion and Rayann covered her eyes as the streetcar slowly moved through the crowd still streaming toward PacBell Park. There were the usual shouts and thumps and she shut it all out.

The old bitterness was easy to wallow in. She'd held it close for a long time, until Teresa had finally eased the grief. Her therapist friend Judy said it was time to stop hating the drunk driver, but Rayann was a long way from there. If he'd been sober, if Louisa had been ten feet one way or the other crossing the intersection, then Louisa would be alive, and they'd still be loving each other under the tapestry.

There would be no Teresa in her life.

It wasn't fair, that she should have to know this bittersweet agony. Knowing that of course and without hesitation she would give anything to have Louisa alive. Did she want it so because she was safe knowing it would never be? She would never really have to choose because Louisa would not suddenly come back to life.

She asked herself if Teresa really wanted that declaration. Did generous, sympathetic Reese really want Rayann to say, "I'm glad Louisa died so I could find you"?

No. That was not Teresa. That could not be what Teresa wanted.

The train finally eased into Embarcadero station and Rayann got off. She knew she had to go back, and it would only be a matter of minutes before a train would arrive in the right direction. She decided to walk home, even though she felt exhausted. Walking would help her think. Anger led to exhaustion. She remembered that all too well, having spent all those months after Louisa's death being so angry all she could do was sleep and dread the next day.

Who are you really angry with, Ray? Judy would ask that question, and Rayann paused at a pay phone. It was approaching eight o'clock, which was Joyner's bedtime. Judy would be in no mood to talk, not with her bed-resistant daughter clamoring in the background.

She plodded on, certain she knew whom she was angry with, and not wanting to face facts.

How dare you! What were you thinking? It wasn't for you to decide!

Teresa knew Rayann's bad side — that had been the woman she first met. Angry and poisonously sharp-tongued, Rayann lost no time slicing Teresa to emotional ribbons. Later, meeting under fresh circumstances, Rayann had not even remembered. She hadn't been angry anymore, just frozen. Teresa didn't learn about Louisa until after she had fallen in love all over again with the Rayann who finally let go of grieving. Passionate without the anger, patient and understanding. Teresa had accepted that she would never be what Louisa had been to Rayann. But she wanted to be more than what she was.

She wanted to somehow show Rayann that she had done some growing up. She could live with the shadow of Louisa. She accepted that the shadow was there.

She didn't know where she would go, but Teresa knew she didn't want to face another flaying at Rayann's hands. Things would be said that could not be taken back. It wasn't time to leave for good. It couldn't be. They just needed some breathing room and then Rayann would be able to talk about it.

Her dad would be really proud of her. She was usually the one who engaged mouth a full minute ahead of brain.

She would leave a note. Something to indicate that she had not taken Rayann's ultimatum seriously, but she understood that they needed to calm down before they could deal with the problem.

Teresa lost her nerve with the pencil and paper in her hand. She could not bring herself to write a single word of what might end up being the last thing she said to Rayann.

I've gotten even grayer, Rayann thought. She had stopped to see how much it appeared she'd been crying, but the dim reflection in the shop window didn't show much beyond her hair being flecked with yet more gray. She searched for her eyes, but they were lost in shadow.

It was easier to talk to herself when she couldn't see her eyes. "Face facts," she said aloud. "You're a self-indulgent bitch and you'll be lucky if she's still there."

Self-indulgent, she echoed, as she hurried toward the south of Market building where they lived. Maybe the moment and the tapestry carried you away, but you knew Teresa was the one screwing the proverbial daylights out of you. You just thought you'd pretend for a moment, see if you could get away with it. What could be more fun than being in bed with two women at the same time, cheating on both of them and neither knowing?

A bitch to make it all Teresa's fault when the person you're really mad at is yourself. You let this happen. Teresa doesn't want you to choose. You don't know what she was trying to do because all you did was yell and grab clothes and storm out. Running is easier than talking.

It was certainly easier than admitting you'd been thinking about Louisa the entire time Teresa was fucking you. Easier to run away.

She was running now, helter-skelter toward home, hoping Reese was still there and would understand. Reese loves you, she reminded herself. She's put up with a lot of shit from you because she knows you're still hurting. She'll give you one more chance.

The challenge, Rayann told herself, with her lungs aching and muscles in her legs screaming, the challenge was to make this the last chance she would need. It was time to tell Teresa how she felt. A year was too long to avoid the words just because Teresa understood why she had not been able to say them at first.

She swiped her building keycard and dashed to the elevator. It was maddeningly slow but at least she knew that Teresa wasn't using it to leave.

Her lungs ached and her legs protested that she was even standing. Key in the lock. The lights were on. Reese was there. She had a pen in her hand and looked uncertain, chagrined and unhappy all at once.

"I didn't mean it," Rayann gasped, then she collapsed on the floor and focused on breathing.

Teresa's expression mutated to relief mixed with anger, remorse and more than enough pain to bring tears to Rayann's eyes. How had she ever thought Teresa too young to feel like that?

"It was my fault," Teresa said. "I should have left it alone."

Rayann waved her hands, not able to speak coherently. She needed more exercise, obviously. But not running. Her bosoms would eventually knock her unconscious. "Wait."

Teresa seemed on the verge of tears, but she was almost smiling when she handed Rayann an icy bottle of water from the fridge. It felt wonderful going down and Rayann got back to her feet. Teresa was already tall enough without trying to talk to her from the floor.

"I ran halfway from Market Street," she explained.

Teresa arched an eyebrow. She wouldn't think anything of a run that distance. "I think I'm flattered."

"Don't," Rayann said carefully. "Don't make a joke. Don't let me off the hook." She swallowed the last of the water and gave Teresa her full attention. "I've been a bitch."

"Not really —"

"Yes, I have. I've been having it both ways. Loving both of you, as if she's alive."

"I don't want you to stop loving her," Teresa said passionately.

"I can't. But I love you."

Teresa gulped back whatever she had been going to say. "Could you . . . could you say that again?"

In all this time Rayann had never said it. She'd told herself it meant she would lose Louisa for good. But she had already lost Louisa. She could not lose Teresa, too. "I love you, Reese. I have for some time. I mean, I've really known it. But I didn't say so."

"You thought you were betraying her. I understand." Teresa was so willing to forgive.

"It's more complicated than that. I was loving both of you. A paradise with you in bed and her in my mind." Her voice faltered. "It wasn't fair."

"You mean — like today? You were thinking about her?" Teresa looked stunned.

It was hard to go on. "Yes, and I got lost. The tapestry made it so easy to pretend."

"I don't want to be her stand-in." Teresa's eyes turned bitter.

"You're not," Rayann said fiercely. "That's just it. You're not." She put her hands on Teresa's shoulders. "I was just being selfish."

"I understand."

"No, you don't."

"Well, I'm trying!" Teresa shook off her touch. "You finally say you love me and admit you're fantasizing about her while we're in bed. I'm sorry she died, I'm sorry about what you went through when she was in the hospital all those months. But what if she was just an ex-lover? Being with me, thinking about her — you're right, it's not fair, it's been long enough for —"

"Yes, I know. It's been long enough. I was being selfish and indulgent and I want to do better. If you'll let me try."

"Of course I want to try," Teresa said through tears. "What's the other choice?"

"Nothing I can even consider," Rayann said slowly. "I've loved every minute of living with you. Almost a year —"

"A year," Teresa echoed.

"Just about —"

"No, it's been a year."

Good lord, Rayann thought. She didn't need to look at a calendar to confirm. "I'm so sorry. I forgot." Okay, another mark on the selfish record. So it's been crazy at work. It's always crazy at work.

"I was just trying to do something to commemorate it.

I wanted to show you that I'm not jealous of her anymore. Not a lot, anyway."

"I'm an idiot," Rayann admitted.

"No, you're not." Teresa opened her arms and Rayann happily nestled into her body. "Sometimes it hurts and you don't expect it. I didn't expect it either. It's a beautiful tapestry, but I shouldn't have touched it. It was for you to do."

"You live here, too. You're not a guest." Rayann felt Teresa's shoulders unknot and realized she had not made that point often enough.

"I've been afraid that you only cared for me because I wasn't at all like her. She was so . . . perfect. And I'm so not perfect."

Rayann had to laugh. "She wasn't perfect. Nearly, but not perfect. You have your moments."

"But it's different, isn't it? The way you feel about me compared to her. Oh, forget I said that." Teresa had gone stiff again. "I don't want you to answer."

Rayann kept holding Teresa tight. The answer was yes, still yes, might always be yes. But that didn't matter. "I've been asking myself that question. What would I do if she suddenly walked through that door?"

Teresa tried to pull away. "Don't — I don't want to know."

"Why?"

Teresa's voice was thick with tears again. "Because if you say you'd pick me I would know you're lying. If you say you'd pick her I — I don't know what I'll do."

"I don't know the answer. While I was wandering around I realized that the answer just isn't relevant. She isn't going to walk through the door. I'm not secretly biding my time, hoping that she will. I did that after she died, but not anymore." She looked up into Teresa's face. "I'm here with you. My choice isn't you or her. It's you or misery. Because I love you."

"I want to believe you," Teresa whispered.

Rayann was suddenly inspired by something her mother had done when Rayann was a child to demonstrate how love really works. Her mother had been trying to explain that though Rayann's father had died, the love didn't. "Stay right there," she told Teresa.

"Okay." Teresa looked dubious as Rayann dashed into the kitchen.

Junk drawer, in the back — a box of slender birthday candles and a lighter.

"You're going to think this is hokey," she called. "Come on in here."

Teresa definitely looked askance at the candles. "We don't have a cake."

"We don't need one. Okay." She lit one of the candles and set the lighter aside. "This is me. This is my love for myself." She picked up another candle. "This is my dad. You know he died a long time ago." She lit the second candle with her own and dripped enough wax at the far end of the tile counter to hold her father's candle upright.

"I get the metaphor," Teresa said. "Your candle is still lit, and so is his, though it's far away."

"This is my mom. This is Ted and his family." She set two candles close by. "This is Michelle. You've heard about her. She goes way over there. Zoraida —"

"Zoraida gets to be closer than Michelle," Teresa ruled. "I liked her when she dropped by that day."

"Yes, she's much closer. Here's Judy." She lit Judy's candle and set it right in front of her.

"Everyone still has their light, they're just closer or farther away." Teresa almost shrugged. "It makes a pretty display."

"Here's Louisa," Rayann said quietly. She set the candle next to Judy's. "She's close. Her light is still very bright."

Teresa said nothing.

"Look at my candle, Reese. That's the point. My candle

has just as much light as it ever did." She picked up the final candle. "Enough for you."

Teresa wiped away a tear as Rayann dripped wax and set Teresa's candle down just in front of Louisa's. She crouched down to level of the flickering lights. "Her flame is still there. Yours is in between us now," she finished as she lit Teresa's candle.

"I was thinking earlier today that I'm in her shadow."

"Honestly, I was thinking that way too. Not you in her shadow, but our relationship in the shadow of what I had with her. It doesn't have to be that way." Rayann glanced toward her father's distant candle. "I'm just realizing that if I were to light a candle for everyone I loved or who has loved me, I'd burn the place down. I'm so lucky."

As soon as she said it, Rayann realized she'd crossed a threshold into a new beginning. After Louisa's horrible accident and lingering death, Rayann had never thought she would consider herself lucky. All those candles, and she hadn't lit one for everyone. Ted's family was really three candles, because Tucker and Joyce loved her. There was Judy's lover, Dedric, who was a solid friend. Their baby, Joyner — a whole different kind of love. And the people who had loved Louisa and therefore her as well: Danny, Marilyn, Jill and more.

Teresa crouched alongside Rayann to look at the lights. "Okay, this *is* corny," she said. "But I see everything differently. Her light . . . it illuminates me, too."

"I've taken you for granted," Rayann said softly. "Let me start over today."

"I'll start over too. I've just realized that my light illuminates hers in return."

Rayann didn't want to blow out the candles, but her mother's candle abruptly fell over. So she snuffed them all out while Teresa blew her nose. "It's not too late to go to the movies, you know."

"I have no intention of going to the movies," Teresa whispered.

199

* * * * *

Rayann slept soundly, but Teresa didn't want to go to sleep, not yet. She searched her feelings for the shadow of dread she'd been carrying around, expecting any day for Rayann to realize that what they had simply didn't compare and wasn't worth pursuing. The day had taken an unexpected turn instead.

She felt confident now. As far as Teresa was concerned, there was no subject more serious between them than Louisa, and they'd finally been able to talk about it. They'd probably have to talk about it again. Anything else that might come up would seem like child's play by comparison.

Rayann didn't wake up until Teresa accidentally stepped on her hair as she tied the last corner of the tapestry to the post nearest Rayann's head.

"Reese, what are you doing?"

"Sorry, I'm almost done. I didn't want to wake you. But I thought you wouldn't mind this now."

Rayann cleared her throat and said sleepily, "Oh. I don't."

Teresa settled under the covers again. In the dark the moon and stars seem to glow of their own accord. "It's beautiful."

Rayann snuggled closer, her head next to Teresa's. "I always loved looking at it. I'm glad to have it back."

She was soon asleep again. Teresa felt peaceful yet aware of the moment. She'd been in love all this time and had not wanted to accept how incomplete it was, not believing she was loved in return. Roses and vines framed her sky as she realized she stepped into a new beginning.

Unforgettable

Published: 2000
Characters: Rett Jamison, singer
Angel Martinetta, genetic scientist
Lt. Natalie Gifford, retired Army
Cinny Keilor, real estate agent
Setting: Los Angeles, California, and
Woton, Minnesota

Ten Makes a Celebration, Loud, Loud, Loud!

Unforgettable, That's What You Are

(4 weeks)

The heat made me think of her. Even with all the windows down, it was sweltering in the car and there was no nearby shade. When I'd told my mom who I was going to meet she'd given me one of her piercing looks and said, "You get what you deserve when you play with fire, Natalie."

"They taught us that in the Army, mom. It's just business." We both knew I was lying.

I closed my eyes to the September sun and thought about Cinny Keilor, like I always did of late. There had been times in my past when she had popped into my mind, but since the dance we shared at the class reunion a month ago she has never been far from my thoughts. I indulged myself by savoring them again. After twenty years in the Army fantasy was my private luxury and it certainly passed the time.

I spent those twenty years tied to computers in places all over the world. Sometimes I would watch a tall blonde walk by and I'd think about Cinny. Other times a husky voice would put a chill down my back and I'd think about Cinny. It always seemed like wishful thinking. Until 1991, sitting in a cold, dank hangar in Biloxi, waiting for the boarding signal. Looking back, that's when everything changed.

It was very quiet. The faint scratching of pens on postcards or paper was the only steady noise. I had bought extra stamps and even passing them around it seemed like everyone spoke in hushed tones. We were all thinking hard and trying to write positively about the next few days, weeks.

I kept repeating to myself what I knew for a fact. We outgunned them. We had better tech. We had for damned sure better people, even if some of the enemy had been trained by us for a different war. There was no way we weren't going to win. But that didn't mean some of us wouldn't get hurt along the way. Some of us might die. It could be any one of the other seventeen people. It could be me.

I was writing a note to my parents. I told them not to worry, of course. They would, but I wanted to remind them that I would be where the computers were. Later, in Bosnia, I would be closer than I ever told them afterward, but when we got to Kuwait I would be safe in a bunker, keeping the information flowing. I said I was sorry I had to cancel my leave and wouldn't be able to help with the planting. I'd always bitched plenty about loading seed bags and driving the tractor, but at that moment I'd have given just about anything to be at home.

I knew there were things I was willing to die for, but oil wasn't one of them. I wanted to go to the Cokato Corn Festival again, lie out under the summer sky and watch lightning bugs dance, gossip with my mom, and daydream about girls. My ego was not invested in some line in the sand. It would be in Bosnia, but this war it wasn't.

The signal came and the petty officer collected everyone's notes and cards and promised they'd get in the mail out of Biloxi.

We lined up and climbed aboard the cargo-class aircraft. We were the last unit on. The next stop was the Persian Gulf. I know I wasn't the only one thinking I'd written to my loved ones for maybe the last time. I joined the Army because I wanted to serve my country, which I loved for all its history and mistakes. I loved it mostly because our American mentality was founded on the idea that tomorrow can be better than today. Defending my country's interests and obeying the orders of my commander are a link in a very big chain that helps bring better tomorrows.

That's the way I've always looked at it, anyway. That's why I joined up, then went to school to learn encryption and ended up with a degree. That's why when the master sergeant said I had a chance at officer's training, I took it, pretty much deciding I'd do the full twenty years right there.

When I'd stopped going round and round in my head about what I knew and how I felt, there was a flicker of something else.

That was when I thought of her. It was the first time I was going into a war zone and there she was in my head. Cinny Keilor. I was remembering her the way I'd seen her during my last leave back home. She'd been helping with the Christmas Carnival at Hubert H.

Humphrey Elementary, though she had no kids of her own. Everyone was going home and Cinny was smiling and saying 'bye to folks. I'd always liked to look at her, like a jacket that's way too expensive or a car that's way too small and too fast.

That night was different. I caught her in a moment of tiredness, maybe. That was what I was remembering. She looked sincere enough as she shook hands and hugged people, but she also looked like she wanted to be someplace else. Almost as if she wanted to be someone else. I understood the look. I saw it in my own eyes sometimes. I remembered all at once how she smelled and moved and I sat there shivering. Cargo planes are noisy and cold and not usually the place where dreams find fertile ground. I wanted to be snuggled with her someplace sunny and warm.

That was the moment when I told myself that if ever there was a way I could campaign for Cinny Keilor's heart, I'd do it because happiness deserved some sort of effort after all. If I lived through whatever the Army threw at me, that is. If I survived.

So that's what happened. I was going to war and she was in my head. She became more than a fantasy. Cinny Keilor, heart, mind and body, became an objective founded on private desires.

What happened for years after that really doesn't matter much. It was predictable and unexciting — mostly. When my mom wrote a few years ago that Cinny had finally married, I thought that was that. I'd always known my objective was unachievable. The Cinny Keilors of the world, with their leggy unaging beauty, don't go for the Natalie Giffords who lust after them from afar. I didn't have any of Rett Jamison's talent and charm, and if Rett Jamison couldn't get Cinny, I didn't have a chance.

Cinny wasn't the reason I didn't have a romantic life, though. There were times when other women definitely had my interest, but it never went further than that. Don't Ask, Don't Tell sucks as a policy. It was wrong-headed and made things much worse than they were before, but I lived up to and beyond it because I'd taken an oath. I threw all my energy into soldiering, working out and, when I had the chance, dancing. After the first ten years, celibacy is actually easier than dating.

When I retired with my twenty years in, I went home because I'd no roots anywhere else. Celibacy hadn't just kept me from potential lovers, it had robbed me of friends, too. Everyone assumed Natalie Gifford with the short-cropped hair and lean, angular body was a lesbian, so the straight women tended to avoid me unless they wanted to experiment. The lesbians either avoided me because they were afraid they'd be outed by being my friend or they pursued me as a potential affair. Ergo, I made no friends except among some of the men — the gay ones, I suspected, though I never asked and they never told.

Woton, Minnesota, isn't exactly overflowing with lesbians. True, there was a small support group of ex-Army dykes in Minneapolis and I'd enjoyed myself at a couple of potlucks, but they were all in couples, every last one of them. Wait, that's not quite right. One woman was willing but she was also an alcoholic, which made her not my type.

Everything changed at the class reunion last month. I'd always had a crush on Rett Jamison. Who didn't? She was so talented and cared so little about what anyone thought of her. Back in high school she dressed how she liked and didn't take crap off of anyone. I wanted to be like her so much. There was a line ahead of me, though. Angel Martinetta — I was half in love with her, too. The school brain and totally hooked on Rett.

Rett, on the other hand, was completely into Cinny Keilor. Back in high school I'd been out hiking and seen them kissing. At the time it made me weak for Rett, but that might also have been when Cinny Keilor snuck into the back of my mind, waiting for that moment in the plane to the Gulf, when I thought of her.

Cinny came out at the class reunion. She left her husband that week and I think she was hoping to hook up with Rett after all those years of saying no in high school. Rett and Angel had finally gotten their wires uncrossed, though, and Cinny was left on her own. It was like a sign. I had finished my commitment to the Army. I was only forty and I had a lot of life ahead of me. I wanted that life to be as full of love as the first half had been empty.

So a couple of days ago I went for a ramble and had a long talk with myself. I was sitting in the sweltering afternoon sun, waiting for Cinny, because I now had a solid, considered strategy to bring Cinny into my life.

I figured to have a chance with her, I had to do five things. First, I had to show her who I really was. Second, I had to conquer my own damned shyness. Third, she needed to see the person I wanted to be. Fourth, we had to have some time together without me letting her know I wanted to rip her clothes off. Last, I had to prove to her that I knew the meaning of romance.

I had already taken care of the first strategy. I figured that if she danced with me while I was wearing a tuxedo and Florsheims, she understood that I'm butch and there's no other way to cut it.

She danced with me. The whole town was buzzing about her being a lesbian and leaving her husband, and she danced with me. She was wearing a wild red sheath cut up to paradise, showing off a body as firm as it always had been, but more lush in the places where lush is what I spent twenty years dreaming about.

She danced with me, all perfume and scarlet lipstick. It was a crazed salsa dance, her breasts heaving against mine. All those years I'd burned energy dancing and working out let me show her I could pick her up in my arms, hold her and keep up with her wild moves.

She danced with me and the whole town was looking as her body stretched the length of mine. It was the only time she danced all night, and that one time she danced with me.

The second strategy to conquer my shyness was what I was working on today in a roundabout way. See, after that dance, after she stepped away, holding her head up like she didn't care about the stares, well, I hadn't been able to say a word. Not one word. The kind of conquest I had in mind would take at least a little bit of talking. Like "hello" and "nice to see you." I had let her walk away.

Four weeks passed. I'd even seen her on the other side of the street and not crossed over to say something. That made me shit-on-a-shingle and I really needed to work on it. I needed to find a way to talk to her that was logical.

My stroke of genius: she's a realtor and I need a place of my own. When there was business to be done, I was never shy.

While I was having that long talk with myself I'd come to the conclusion that a woman like Cinny isn't going to be permanently attracted to someone who's only thinking about how to get her into bed. That led me to my third strategy. She needs to see that I have dreams. I am thinking about tomorrow and how to make tomorrow include her interests and ideas. I have a nice retirement pension from the Army and when my folks pass away, I'll have a good piece of land that farms well. God willing, that won't be for another fifty years. But neither of those things will really show her who I want to be. I'm 40 and I'm still living with my parents. On the surface, I don't look too promising as mate material.

I needed my own place and it needed to reflect me. I needed to get going on my consulting plans. I was good at data encryption and computer security and I had a number of contacts with people who'd gotten into dot-coms. I was confident of the marketability of my skills. Coasting along for a few months after being discharged was understandable. But it was time to settle into the next phase of my life. I wanted that phase to include Cinny, and I was willing to discuss a variety of conditions for mutually satisfactory armistice.

The only real difficulty here was how I felt about her. It wasn't rational and cool. I wanted her in my life and my bed, real bad. Not scaring her off with my more base impulses was strategy four.

Fortunately, I've always had a lot of self-control. That red dress tested it, to be sure. I wanted her legs wrapped around me. I wanted to kiss her until next year. I wanted to give her what her husband couldn't possibly have understood she needed. I wanted to show her what she had not experienced before: an open, honest love, out of the shadows. I'd never had that either, but I could not consider any other kind of future. She doesn't need to know my feelings yet. She'd just left her husband, after all. She needs time and I am very good at waiting.

My last strategy was a bit sneaky. I wanted to show her I understood romance. Initially, it would seem like innocent friendship — and it would be. But if she finally opened her eyes and saw me as a potential lover, I wanted her to already know I had a romantic soul.

Beautiful, vivacious, charming, perfect Cinny had been showered in chocolate, roses and perfume all her life. Prom Queen tiaras and cheerleader pom poms, citizenship awards and student council accolades had been routine in high school. Her husband had lavished expensive gifts and cars on her, but my mother told me — my mother knows everything about everyone in Woton — she'd already signed or given everything back. Everyone in her life assumed she took big gifts and gestures as her due. I didn't think she was that way at all. That was just part of the role of a beautiful prom queen and country club wife, and I guessed she was real tired of that whole head game. That was why she finally came out.

She was looking for something different. Don't get me wrong, I haven't forgotten that she's used to being worshipped. I intended to go right on doing that. But I planned on worshipping the whole person, especially the lesbian part of her, the part of her that was most like me.

Romance, in my book, isn't roses and chocolate and perfume. It was a cold drink on a hot day. Which was why I had two bottled iced teas, thoroughly chilled, in the cooler next to me. That's romance. Romance is anything that says that for no reason at all, with no thought of what you'd get in return, you thought of someone else and what might make her today a little bit better. Sometimes roses can do that. But on a hot, muggy day like today I was betting on the iced tea. Better todays mean better tomorrows. A whole lot of better tomorrows adds up to Forever. In my considered opinion, yessir, it does, sir.

Our appointment to see the house for sale wasn't for another five minutes and I congratulated myself on the brilliance of having chosen a businesslike way to get to know her better. I wouldn't be as shy as I usually was. Provided I could control myself, she would never know that I had plans for when she started liking me.

It seems true to me that you can't love someone you don't like — love them forever and go on loving them when they annoy you or when something struts by that looks like it might be a better deal for a while. I don't want an affair with the woman. I want a life.

I'm saving for later the picture of her walking toward me in a thin pink blouse and ivory linen skirt. All legs and curves, all honey blond and tan. Later I'll let myself think about her body against mine. Fantasy and I are old friends.

She took the tea and said thanks. She looked at me,

then. Really looked at me. If she was thinking about that dance we had shared, it didn't show in her face, but I didn't think for a second that she had forgotten.

I glanced at the house where we were beginning the search for my perfect home. She didn't realize that what I was looking for was a house she would also like. "So what's the story on this place?"

"Three bedrooms and a newly remodeled kitchen. The sunporch faces south, too. You talked about a garden, and there's a small one out back."

Her cream-colored sandals made her feet look as fragile as glass, but I'd held her in my arms. She was strong under all that soft skin. That was why I didn't feel clunky next to her, why the difference between her strappy sandals and my thickly velcroed Tevas didn't bother me in the least. We were both strong. It just showed differently.

I got past the fantasy of wanting to lick the faint film of perspiration from the back of her neck. It was way harder than I thought it would be.

I didn't like the house right off. The rooms were small and laid out so that there was little chance of remodeling to something more spacious. The garden was nice but a bit small.

"There's way too much zucchini in here," Cinny commented. She'd been carefully noncommittal as I explored, but I had the distinct impression that she didn't like the house either. It did have two acres of privacy, and the master bedroom faced a neighboring farm instead of the road and town. After the close quarters of military housing, the vista was welcome. Still, the poor layout of the sitting and family rooms was insurmountable.

"You don't like it, do you? You didn't like it the moment I unlocked the door." Cinny regarded me thoughtfully. I was surprised that she read me so clearly, even though I'd been trying to hide my almost immediate negative reaction. I hoped she couldn't read anything else I was thinking.

"I like the decorating, but that's beside the point. I can see past the paint and wallpaper. It's the rooms — ideally, I want a great room for the house, not the only-for-guests sitting room separated off. That seems like a waste of space. But this sitting room shares a wall with the bathroom, so I can't knock it down to join it with the family room unless I want to move the plumbing."

"You want to do that? Renovate?"

"I wouldn't mind it. Give me something to do with my free time. When I start doing independent consulting I'll be working a lot of hours, but I'll still have a lot of time on my hands." I laughed at my own expense. "It's not like I've got a life, or anything. Not yet."

She glanced at the thin watch that circled her deceptively delicate wrist. "How much time do you have?"

I shrugged. "All evening." Get the message, I thought. There's no one in my life.

"There's a real fixer-upper available that I've always thought was just waiting for the right buyer. It's been on the market for nine months — incredible bargain at this point. It's between here and Cedar Mills."

I could tell that there was something she liked about the place and that made me eager to see it, too. More time in her company was also welcome. "Then let's go."

She locked up the house and walked briskly to her car. "Mind if I drive?"

"Not at all."

She unlocked the door of her cute little silver Mustang convertible. "I should just have only women clients. It saves a lot of time." In response to my raised eyebrows, she went on, "I always have to convince men to let me drive because I know the way, because the neighbors know my car by now and won't be alarmed if it's after dark. They think I can't handle a car to begin with and haven't realized that as a woman I'm at risk every time I go into a vacant house with a man I don't know very well. It's survival basics — take your own vehicle, for your own sake."

"I can't tell you how many times I had to assert my turn to drive the Humvee. Those things drive like tractors and I could drive a tractor when I was eight."

She accelerated sharply onto the roadway, then said with a laugh, "Are you telling me that men are the same the world over?"

"No," I said seriously. "I've met good men. I've seen men who make the knuckleheads in this part of the world look like saints." I had to turn my face away for a minute as sudden images from Bosnia floated up in front of me. I'd gone to counseling after I'd come home, like just about everyone else, but the disorienting flashbacks had barely started to ease. I'd been told it took years sometimes. Yippee.

"I'll bet," she said quietly. She turned onto the back road that led most directly toward Cedar Mills. "How do you feel about losing some cobwebs?"

Right there I knew I had correctly understood at least a part of her. She didn't want to be the cheerleader driven about by the captain of the football team. She wanted to drive herself, thrill herself, and do something because she had the skills and the power.

"How fast does this thing go?" We were already doing fifty-five on the rarely-traveled country road.

"One-ten's as high as I've had it. This road — eighty is the top."

"Seems a waste if the top isn't down," I said, feigning indifference.

She threw me a laughing conspiratorial glance that left me near breathless. The top retracted smoothly and she stomped on the gas with a shout of glee. "Don't worry — I don't have a death wish. I know this road like the back of my hand."

We were off. She handled the car like a pro, easing up at every intersection. The sun was hot, but the wind was wildly refreshing. She had to slow to a crawl where a creek ran across the road in the winter. It was dry now, but the dip was considerable.

"I love that," she said as we reached the bottom. "Do you feel how it's cooler right here? The trees and the little bit of water make such a difference."

The moist, cool air felt great. "I remember when I was a kid, we'd drive out to our favorite lake. There was no air conditioning in the camper. It would be so hot, and my dad would always slow down for the dips. That five degrees of relief felt like refrigeration."

She eased up the far side of the creek, then punched the gas when we crested into the sun again. "I thought I was the only kid in the world who noticed that. It's just a few minutes more."

Our entrance into the driveway was sedate by contrast. Cinny was already closing the top before we came to a stop.

The first thing I noticed was the privacy. The house was at an angle to the road and faced away from the nearest neighbor, a family farm. "What's the acreage?"

"Five full," she answered. "But there's growth restrictions on this parcel that dates back to when the road was moved and that conglomerate bought out two of the farming neighbors. You can't subdivide and you can't rezone. Neither can they. This plot is residential only; they can farm. You can get away with your own garden, but technically no tractors, et cetera. You know the drill. I guess a lot of people think five acres ought to be farmable, but to my mind, that means no subdivision next door with eighty houses and a hundred plus cars driving past you every day."

"I hear that." She had a point. Two rolling hills cradled the little house. An open field lay behind and the hills were dotted with sturdy Norway Red pines. The house looked like a dump, but houses can be fixed. The surrounding landscape was just perfect. "Let's take a look inside."

Unlike at the last house, she seemed intent on selling me this place. She obviously liked it. "See, the sitting room and the family room are back-to-back, then this odd little storage room, then the kitchen."

"All those walls could come down, then." I'd have the great room I was looking for, from kitchen to front windows. "Take out the ceiling and go up another story for height. That is, if the basement and foundation are sound." I turned in a circle. The current layout was crap, with the shared rooms on one side of a dark hallway and the bedrooms on the other. "Take out this small bedroom for a stairwell and foyer, add a second floor for bedrooms and at least one more bath. Two would be better. This middle bedroom is big enough for an office." I strode down the hallway to the biggest bedroom. "This would make a nice guest bedroom. Just off the bathroom and the kitchen."

"I've always thought this place needed a second story. There's no restriction on height. Put in at least three bedrooms upstairs, though. Don't forget about the eventual resale — everyone wants at least four bedrooms these days."

I nodded. It was practical advice. "I'm thinking an open landing in front of the bedrooms that looks down on the great room."

She was sparkling with enthusiasm. "If I thought I had the energy and the know-how — and the money — I'd have bought this place myself. Come and look at the horrid kitchen."

We waxed rhapsodic about how much work the kitchen needed, including an expanse of wall begging to be knocked out for a sunporch and a larger dining area. The avocado stove and refrigerator were blatant invitations to new, larger built-ins. For a while I forgot I wasn't made of money, but I didn't see how I couldn't have things the way I wanted — which seemed to be the way she wanted as well — in five years. One step at a time.

"I feel like I'm pressuring you," Cinny admitted. "I should just shut up now."

I took another look around. "Let's make an offer," I decided.

"Now I know I said way too much."

I shook my head. "You didn't. You read me right, that's all. I want to dig myself in somewhere. I've got roots here, like you, but I need my own place." I felt it was time for a little bit of plain speaking. "I'm what I am. There's no princess charming going to ride into my life and present me with a stage to play my days out on. I'm one of those women who makes her own stage."

She took my hand, for just a second, squeezing my fingertips before she let go. "I know just what you mean. I've always wanted to make my own stage, but I never had the courage it took to get off the ones everyone else pushed me onto. I wasn't ready for the dark space in between their stages and my own." She turned away and I almost didn't catch the rest of what she said. "I'm still not ready to start over."

"Has it been hard?"

She drew one finger across the dusty surface of a countertop. "Yes — but not as hard as I thought it would be. I thought I'd get hate mail. I thought someone would spray-paint my car. Two people have cut me dead at the market, but that's it. You know how some people get."

"The morons, mostly. Yeah, I know. Can't handle what's different."

"My dad is really uncomfortable around me all the time now. My mom sometimes cries for no reason. My sisters are okay, but my brother just thinks I'm going through yet another Cinny-being-selfish phase." She sighed.

"I found out who my friends are, and the real ones have been fine. But I walk into some place like Denton's and there's a chill in the air. It hurts."

"Would it help to know that the chill has always been there for me? In a way, it's not personal."

She turned back to me, her face a mix of shadows and regrets. "Oh, I know that. It's impersonal and very personal all at the same time. Some of it's because I waited so long to do it, and I told so many lies to hide who I really was. I should never have married Sam and I feel bad about that, really bad." She plastered a smile on her face with an effort. "Let me get my briefcase and we'll write up an offer."

I didn't mind changing the subject. She'd shared some personal stuff though we didn't know each other very well and I was content with that.

She was very methodical, writing up the offer with contingencies spelled out so the seller wouldn't have any reason to counter-offer and perhaps suggest a higher price. There had been several construction reports already done on the property for earlier sales that fell through, and Cinny took the known problems — a roof leak in one corner was the biggest one — into account. "They ought to be glad to get this much, and before winter, too. Apparently, they moved into one of the developments north of Minneapolis. Dot-com money, I think. I would guess any offer that pays off the mortgage here would make them happy. If not, they'll counter."

We talked about whether I could qualify quickly for a loan. The more quickly we promised them their money, the less likely they would want more. I was paying a lot less than I thought I'd have to by way of a mortgage, but there was loads of renovation to do, most of which couldn't be undertaken until next spring. That gave me time to pick a contractor, get permit approvals, plan the garden and landscaping.

The prospect of building my own nest was exciting. My

enthusiasm must have engaged her because she lingered just to chat. We were laughing about something silly when my stomach growled.

Cinny's gaze flicked to her watch. "Goodness, look at the time."

"You must have somewhere to be," I said.

"No, no, I just didn't want to take your whole evening."

Get the message, I thought again. "I'm in no hurry to be anywhere. But you must have plans."

"Laundry," she said drily. "It's not like I'm dating or anything. The dating pool here is nonexistent."

"I noticed," I said, equally dry. "Let's grab something to eat and complain about the lack of babes."

She laughed and gathered her things. We had steaks and a bottle of wine at the dinner house near the interstate, and then she drove me back to my car. We must have talked about everything, because dinner took almost three hours. Books and television I'd missed when I was out of the country, places I'd been, and places she wanted to go. Movies and gossip and even a little bit about women in our past. We both had real short lists.

There was a moment before I got out of the car when I might have hugged her or something, but that wasn't the way it was. Not yet. There was nothing in her manner that I could take for even the remotest invitation. Nevertheless, as I drove toward my parents' home, I considered the day to be a huge success. My strategies were working. She liked me. Spending time with her had only intensified how I felt about her. We had plenty to talk about. She wanted to travel and it's something I love to do, too. That alone could take us a lifetime to do together.

That night I had the nightmare that had plagued me since Bosnia, but I came out of it differently. Every other time I woke up feeling the weight of the rifle in my hands, but tonight I sat up with my hands over my ears, trying to shut out the sound of my own gunfire. For the first time since I'd been home I hadn't woken my mother. Maybe it was getting better. I could certainly see how getting on with my future, having some plans, could make those images fade. My ears were ringing from the memory of the screaming and the noise. I drank some water and thought about Cinny and — also for the first time — I went back to sleep.

The sale of the house went smoothly. I saw Cinny again when she met my folks and me so they could see the place. My dad was as enthused as I was about the renovations, and my mom and Cinny were having a jolly conversation about carpets and wallpaper. My mom would remember everything Cinny said; I'd pick her brain later. When my mom looked at me speculatively, I smiled and shrugged. She looked back at Cinny with appraising eyes, then gave me a little wink. Apparently Cinny was no longer classified as fire. She would be an acceptable daughter-in-law, even with her notorious divorce on the horizon.

I wasn't able to come up with anything other than a flat-out request for a date to see her again, so we didn't meet up until the closing. She gave me a bottle of Champagne when the title officer gave me the keys.

"I can't drink it by myself. We could pick up some dinner and share a toast at the house," I suggested. It was not exactly a request for a date, and I congratulated myself on sounding friendly and not too eager. All my instincts said she was not ready for anything more.

She was amenable and insisted on picking up the dinner. We agreed on burgers and I then had the solitary joy of driving to my new home and unlocking my own door.

First item on the to-do list: oil the lock. I had a lot of work ahead, but work has never daunted me.

I went outside when I heard the Mustang pull into the driveway, and there she was, wearing a turquoise sweater set that outlined curves I'd committed to memory. "There's nowhere to sit," I admitted as I relieved her of the sodas she was juggling in addition to the fast food bag.

She laughed, unfazed. "I forgot about that. The carpet will do."

Her legs seem to stretch out in front of her for miles. I thought about the long journey from ankle to thigh and tried to swallow my burger. After choking down another bite, I drained my soda and wondered how on earth I'd managed to go without sex for so long.

It occurred to me after the last curly fry that there was no reason for her to visit me again. I had failed to establish a routine with her that would continue to bring us into contact without it seeming like a date.

"So what are you going to tackle first?"

She offered me the rest of her fries, but I waved them away. "The office, I think. I can sleep anywhere, though I prefer something soft instead of the floor and a bedroll. Been there, done that."

She laughed and I liked the sound of it. She had always been vivacious and high-spirited, but I honestly did not remember her laughing as much as she seemed to now. "My bones don't appreciate sleeping on the floor anymore, either."

"Forty is a bitch," I acknowledged. "But I can cope for a while. I want to get the office up so I can go online and take up the two contract offers I have pending. The companies are ready to use me if I can sign on to their networks to do my thing."

She asked about my specialty, data encryption and

network security. The sun set while I was explaining it — she seemed genuinely interested — and I got up to turn on the weak but functional overhead lights. "So I think I'll start with a full court press tomorrow," I finished, pointing at the bedroom I was going to turn into an office. "Rip up that carpet and put down durable flooring. I need a boatload of bookshelves. I'll do everything but paint and paper because next year the roof comes off."

"What kind of flooring?"

I already knew her preferences. Wonderfully, they matched mine. "The new tongue-and-groove synthetic for the office because of the chair. I like it because it warms easily, for one thing."

"Easy on the toes in the wintertime."

"You got that right. I like carpet in bedrooms for just that reason, but I won't do anything beyond the floor in the office so I can get the heavy furniture down and put in the bookshelves. After that I guess I'll start tearing up kitchen counters and cabinets. The contractor will start the installs next month after the first inspection. I save a lot doing the demolition work myself."

"Do you need any help? I've done some renovating in my time. It's great therapy, tearing stuff down."

I hid my gulp of enthusiasm. "You bet. If you want to slave on my behalf, I won't stop you. My mama didn't raise no fools."

"How about tomorrow? I'm already experiencing the fall and winter slowdown at work. It started a little early this year. I can only guess why." She was trying not to sound bitter, but I heard the edge.

"It'll get better," I promised, as if I could change people's minds. "Hold your head up."

"I try." She gave me a sideways look that held a measure of affection that I never dreamed I'd see. "If I forget how, I'll just think of how you do it. You and Rett — good role models for me. I just took too long to notice."

I offered a hand as she got to her feet. I forced myself

not to watch her smooth her skirt. "I'm an early riser, so whenever you feel like it, just stop in. I'll have places to sit tomorrow — my mom has scrounged the county for card tables and folding chairs, spare dishes. She even located a coffee maker, as if I couldn't afford to buy one."

"If you're promising coffee, I'll be human by ten." She walked toward the door, then turned suddenly. "We forgot all about the Champagne!"

Yeep. "I bet we really need it tomorrow, 'long about three o'clock."

"You're probably right. Let's save it — don't forget to ice it, though. Warm champagne is disgusting." She lightheartedly waved good-bye, and the house seemed dark and lonely without her.

I gave myself a stern talking to. By no means was any future with Cinny certain. I would have to make this place my own, but leave the door wide open.

We tore up carpet, we carted home boxes of hardwood tile, we bruised our hands spreading paste and cutting odd shapes, and we drained the Champagne when we were too weary to do more. She was methodical and painstaking in every detail and promised to spend her next free day doing what she called therapy.

That was how the fall went. She dropped by about once a week and we'd work companionably, always talking. I prefer Pepsi, but always kept a supply of her preferred Diet Coke chilled. My office looked great, for the moment, and I was also hard at work downloading files and writing encryption routines for two different Web hosting companies. The hourly pay was fabulous and often called for twenty-hour workdays. But I got to pick and choose what I did and could give myself decent breaks along the way.

Cinny shopped for appliances with me, and was there when I picked the countertops and cabinets for the kitchen. She liked those awful pink snowball things as a snack but they're hard to find. I surprised her one day with a large supply because I'd seen them on sale. She was there when I plotted out the garden with the landscaper and approved the designs for the second story so we could get a permit going. There was only so much that could be done while the weather was wet and cold, but we did what we could. She was as organized as I was and as the weeks went by, she seemed to always know what I was thinking. My nightmares eased, which was also a wonderful thing.

I had been lazy about getting my hair cut and unexpectedly, she said she liked it just a little bit longer, with just a hint of curl at the ends. I decided to leave it for a while and see if I could stand it. There was a day when she had been in a hurry and not put on her makeup. The crow's feet and slight imperfections of her skin that makeup usually covered were exquisite to me. I loved the pale pinkness of her bare lips. All I said was that she didn't have to gild the lily on my account. After that she was more often *au naturel* than not. I considered that a major step forward in our friendship. I hoped she understood that I loved her beauty, but my definition of beauty extended deeper than Avon could reach.

She helped me hang Christmas lights all around the house right after Thanksgiving and stayed late enough to see me light them. I didn't realize until then that she always left before dark, even after the time change. The only exceptions were when we went shopping and stopped for dinner. She always left as soon as we got back to the house, though.

I came down the ladder from changing out a dead bulb. It wasn't all that easy to do wearing full winter regalia. The wind chill was ten degrees, and snow was promised overnight. Cinny was huddled on the hood of her car, but when I flipped the lights back on, she applauded and clambered down.

"They look great."

They did. "I'm freezing."

We tromped inside and started the process of shedding coats, boots, hats, gloves, wrappers and earmuffs. My zipper had jammed when I put my coat on, so I tried to take it off over my head. After a minute of struggling, I had to say from the depths of the coat, "I'm stuck."

She tried to get the zipper to cooperate, then yanked on the jacket. "That's my ear," I yelped.

She apparently found it all very funny, because she was laughing quite hard. Her next approach was to try to free my arms from the sleeves so we could work on getting my head through the collar. It seemed to work, but as I got one arm free I realized my shirt had stayed with the coat. I tried to get my shirt back on just as she yanked on the coat. The next thing I knew I was waist-up naked and she had my clothes.

I don't need a bra. Wished real hard right then that I wore one anyway. Even a sports bra.

She stopped laughing for just a moment, then plunked down on the floor, nearly hysterical. I lunged for my coat, but she stuffed it under her and we had quite a tussle — which did nothing for my composure. I ended up with my shirt back on in less than thirty seconds while she just lay there laughing at me.

"You brat," I scolded. "I'm freezing." I wrapped my arms over my rock-hard breasts — cold and her nearness were both culprits — and didn't have to fake shivers.

"I'm sorry," she said, not looking in the least bit contrite. "It was too much fun to see you less than poised for once, Lieutenant."

I rolled my eyes and headed for the kitchen.

"I just want to check the news before I take off," she said, flipping on the portable TV that sat on the card table. It was the only TV I had so far and it was plenty for me. She was a real news hound and never liked to be out of touch for more than half a day.

What happened next was completely unexpected. The volume was very low and she punched the remote. She muttered, "What's wrong with this thing?" Suddenly the volume was way too loud.

I didn't register that it was a news story about continued bloodshed in the Middle East. I heard the gunfire. I head a woman screaming. I was back in Bosnia. We were moving into a new zone and I was along to secure and investigate some enemy computers that had been abandoned so quickly they hadn't been destroyed. I wasn't supposed to be on my own, but I'd heard the screaming. All the reports I'd encoded about what they were doing to the women made me run, made me pull my weapon around for use. I heard my C.O. bawling at me to get my ass back with the unit, but I went through the dark doorway without regard to my own or anyone else's safety. The three lifeless bodies, clothing and bodies mutilated, the woman-girl on the ground screaming, the huddle of men over her, the other three women screaming too, knowing their turns were coming — judge, jury, executioner. It was over in ten seconds. Not even that. Over. Gunshots. Blood. The screaming didn't stop.

"Natalie —"

My C.O. was livid at my recklessness and I was in shock. The women escaped into the warren of abandoned buildings, taking with them the barely alive, barely pubescent girl who had been on the floor. They ran. Maybe they didn't know I was a woman, that I wasn't trying to take them for myself. The C.O. looked down at all the dead bodies — three women, five men — drew his sidearm, and shot each man once in the head. *Bang. Bang. Bang. Bang. Bang.* I was being sick while he searched the women's bodies for some way to identify them. His report didn't mention my failure to obey orders or the danger I had placed my unit and myself in by running off. Instead, he recorded what we had interrupted and that he had carried out summary justice. He made no mention of my bullets in those bodies, sparing me a nightmare of inquiries.

I was on my feet, being sick in the sink. Someone strong, warm, soothing was holding me, trying to help. I panted for breath and used the brick imagery the therapist had suggested to block the images out. One by one.

The roaring in my ears stopped abruptly and I knew I was safe. I'd saved lives and taken lives and had never wanted any of that responsibility.

Cinny was rinsing the sink while she kept one arm around me. My face was a mess. I'd only hinted about not sleeping well sometimes, and that I had some bad memories from overseas, but I hadn't wanted her to know much more than that. I had certainly never wanted her to see me like this.

"Better?" She offered me some water after I scrubbed my face.

"Yeah, thanks."

There was a long silence, which she finally ended by saying, "You don't have to tell me — I don't think I want to know."

I shook my head. "You don't." No one wanted to know. The list of war atrocities hardly hinted at what had been routinely done to captured women. "That's the first time that's happened since I've been home." I was hoping it was a final catharsis. I didn't want to stop caring about what had happened, I just didn't want my horror and regrets to incapacitate me. I drained the water and started a second glass.

"I have to go," she said quietly. "Are you going to be okay?"

"I'm here," I answered firmly, feeling stronger by the minute. "I'm not there. I'm not going back there. That situation doesn't even exist anymore. And I'll be fine."

I followed her to the doorway. Maybe she didn't expect me to be so close behind her, because she turned quickly and was almost in my arms.

"Oh —" She looked startled, then stunned, then I knew she was deeply aware of me. Her breath seemed to quicken, her mouth opened slightly.

We leaned toward each other, the slightest inclination of our heads, and then she backed away. "I can't," she stammered. "I can't."

Rett Jamison had never told me any specifics, but putting two and two together from what both she and Cinny had let slip, Cinny had always been the one to back out of their high-school encounters, only to come back for more. I was too emotional to stop my mouth. "I won't play games. I'm not Rett."

"No, you're not," she agreed. I had no idea if that was an indictment or a compliment, or just a simple statement of truth. She slung on her coat and was out the door before I could think of another thing to do or say. Her footsteps crunched over the hard ground, then the car door slammed.

She was gone, and at high speed.

Christmas and New Year's came and went and I didn't see her. I knew that for two of those lonely weeks she was in Florida with her parents. She and her husband had made those plans back in the early summer. She'd said it seemed ages ago, but she was keeping the promise she'd made. I knew she was probably not having a wonderful time, given her parents' continued reservations about her "sudden" change of lifestyle.

But there were a good ten days when she was most likely home and she didn't come near me. I should have picked up the phone. I should have made an effort, but I didn't know what the problem was and didn't want to fall into the same yes-no scenario Rett had endured. I was old enough to know better.

What bothered me, though, was I knew I hadn't misread her. She accepted who she was now, and I really didn't think she wanted to play the tease anymore.

Except for the situation with Cinny, the holidays were otherwise good to me. I had only two nightmares in nearly three weeks, and the family gathering Christmas Day was the most congenial I could ever remember. Grammie Jean made gingersnaps and I had no problem sitting down with all the littles to have my own snaps and hot cocoa after dinner. The oldest little was seven, and then there was me. It felt great to be a kid again, if only for a half an hour. I didn't know that kids these days are card sharks. I lost nine gingersnaps in a vicious game of Crazy Eights.

I also got a ton of work done — consulting work. With Cinny's help, and the preliminary work by the kitchen cabinet maker, the house had reached a stasis until warmer weather. So I had lots of time to give and raked in a shocking amount of money. Extras I had put on hold for the renovation — remodeling the downstairs bathroom was one — were starting to look doable this year, not next.

The first Friday after New Year's it snowed late in the afternoon, so I was surprised to hear a car in the driveway. I didn't let myself think it was Cinny, but it was definitely her Mustang, with chains on.

She looked bedraggled and miserable in the wan porch light. Of course I let her in.

She peeled off the winter layers without saying anything beyond, "I hate putting on chains."

My office and the kitchen were the only livable rooms — the bedroom was beyond sparse — so I headed for the kitchen as she kicked off her snow boots. "Do you want some coffee?"

"I came to show you this."

I turned from the cupboard to see her holding out a thick sheaf of papers. "What is it? Something related to the house?"

"I went down to the county courthouse this afternoon to get my copy. It was issued today at two p.m." She continued holding them out to me.

The legal papers were topped with a cover page that read "In re. Johnson vs. Keilor." I looked at her. She wore no makeup and for once looked every bit of her forty years. "I don't understand."

"It's my divorce decree. I'm a free woman."

It was probably only a minute that we said nothing. The kitchen was cold and silent like that cargo plane had been, full of uncertainty about the future and awareness that life and happiness were not givens.

I looked my fill at her with a prickling in my stomach, knowing that I was looking at a woman who loved me. A Life. Together. That had been my objective. Now it stared me in the face and still felt unexpected. I had done nothing to deserve this kind of grace.

But that was no reason not to embrace and treasure it. My mama didn't raise no fools, no sir, she did not, sir.

"I think I understand. Everything."

"I lied so much, Nat. So much. I didn't —" She choked back tears. "I felt like I had no honor left, and I didn't want to dirty you with it."

"I didn't care about the technicality." I glanced down at the document that meant so much to her.

"I did. For your sake, if not my own. Don't you think I see the way you deal with the contractors? They hint at ways to get around permits and save money by cutting corners where it supposedly doesn't count — you shut them off before they even get started. You care about technicalities. The Army told you you couldn't have a sex life and you didn't."

I realized she was right. I had simply forgotten she was still married, but at some point I would have realized it. "It might have given me a twinge. Not a very big one. You had left him even before we became friends."

"I didn't want even a twinge, not after the things I've done."

"You were just trying to survive —"

"You don't know it all, you can't." She was wiping away tears now. "It's not just what I did to Sam, marrying him out of fear."

"You were just trying to convince yourself —"

"I wasn't, Nat. Don't make me out to be better than I am." She was angry, but I knew it wasn't at me. "I knew I was a lesbian. I *knew* it. There was someone — a woman. She wanted me to move in with her, get married in her church in St. Paul. I was terrified. *Terrified.* She loved me and wanted to be open about it and I couldn't do it. I told myself I didn't love her enough to do it, but I was just a coward."

"You ended up in the right place," I said soothingly.

She waved my words away. "You don't understand."

"It can't be that bad, Cin."

"It is — good God, Nat, I had sex with her the night before my wedding!" She was shaking all over and I wanted to hold her, but I could tell she didn't want that. She wanted me to love all of her, especially the mistakes.

I could only think to say, "I'm listening, then."

"She didn't know about the wedding, I hid my engagement ring whenever I saw her. She didn't know I was leaving her. We had sex, and I left. I had to take Valium to get through my wedding. Do you know what I did to her? On my wedding night, after I'd — I'd slept with Sam, I took one of the instant photos of the two of us in our wedding finery and I sent it to her. No note, not even a return address." She tangled her hands in her hair and pulled hard. "It was a horrible thing. It's unforgivable. I want you to know what you're getting. I'm a coward, a coward, I don't deserve you —"

"Stop that. Don't hurt yourself." I brushed her hands out of her hair and pulled her into my arms. Her heart was thudding so hard I felt it against me. "You feel bad about it and you should. That's a step in the right direction, you know."

She sobbed into my shirt for another minute, then began to calm down. "I wasted all that love, Nat. I looked her up in the phone book and wrote her a letter a couple of weeks ago. I don't know if she got it. I just wanted to tell her I was sorry and it was all my fault and I don't think I will ever forgive myself. I can't even imagine the pain I caused her."

"I wish I could make it better somehow."

She surprised me with something that passed for a laugh. "Oh, stop. As if you can fix it." She sobered. "I have to fix it. I'm trying."

That's when I kissed her. I just couldn't stand it anymore.

Her lips were like silk over velvet and salty with her tears. I hadn't kissed a woman in at least fourteen years, and I'd never kissed a woman I was completely in love with. And I was, with all of her, mistakes, tiaras and tenacious strength.

She pulled back, turned her face away. "Shit, Natalie, I'm a mess."

"I don't care how you look."

"I know that, but still." She scrubbed her face with a napkin from the holder behind me. "I'd like to have the illusion of seductive powers."

"Okay," I said. "Seduce me."

She looked at me then, really looked at me. My knees went to jelly.

"You're on," she said. Her voice was husky and it sent a chill down my back.

* * * * *

My vision went flat. All I saw was her fingertips as she slowly reached for me, fingertips that glowed golden. They brushed my jaw as she leaned into me and lifted her mouth for my kiss. For a moment I couldn't breathe, then I realized I had been holding my breath as those fingertips mesmerized me. I fell dizzily into her, tasting all that she offered. It was a kiss that gave up everything and yet painted mysteries and fantastic promises. I was suffused with a dazzling array of sensation throughout my hungering body. She was strong under all that soft skin, thank God, because I held her tight and hard and close as I kissed her.

The arms that had circled my shoulders were suddenly gone and I felt her hands under my sweatshirt, moving upward. I shuddered as her nails grazed my back, swayed when they brushed my ribs and found my breasts. She whimpered into my mouth and broke off that incredible kiss.

She had my sweatshirt up. Her mouth was hot on my skin. I was abruptly self-conscious of the uncurtained windows and the lights on. Sex in the kitchen, before dark no less, was simply not done in Woton.

Her palm pressing hard between my legs made me forget about that. She leaned back far enough to yank the snap to my jeans open. One little snap and I felt naked.

Her body was stretched the length of mine as she kissed me again, arms around me, tongue promising. I had the leverage I needed to pick her up in my arms and spin slowly in a circle while she kept on kissing me. Out of the kitchen, flipping the lights off with my shoulder, I carried her to my Spartan bedroom. Someday this bed would be sufficient for guests while she and I coiled on something bigger and more luxurious upstairs. Tonight it was my paradise as I set her down and stretched out over her, liking the dim light and the wonderful softness of her sigh.

233

I unbuttoned her sweater and devoted myself to her skin. She tangled me in my sweatshirt but it was so much better with it off, her skin against mine, her mouth whimpering against mine. Beautiful woman, I thought, strong enough to need me and say so.

"I can't take much more," she whispered. "Whatever you like, want, take me there with you. Show me."

I tugged off her slacks so I could touch her, my hips between her thighs. She bared her breasts, the stuff of my fantasies and dreams, her wetness, her taut nipples, her voice rising. Her thighs crushed my hips as my fingers slipped inside and we moved together, slower, slower, until every stroke was an aching eternity. She held me against her breasts as her hips convulsed under me. She cried out once, then again. I broke her grip on me so that I could taste her sweetness and begin again.

We rocked against each other, knees to shoulders, and there was nothing of her that I did not learn, her hungering, sensuous depths, her unreserved passion. I planned a lifetime of worship. It would take that long to satisfy me.

She lay still as I wrapped my arms around her hips, eager to resume pleasing her, needing only the slightest encouragement.

She surprised me by rolling me onto my stomach, then covering me with her warm, damp body. The room was chilly and the heat of her was healing. Her mouth was on my back, her tongue on my shoulder blades.

"I love your shoulders," she murmured. "Love them." Her warmth was abruptly gone as she knelt behind me, then pulled me up into her arms. Her hands explored my stomach, my breasts, my thighs. My head fell back onto her shoulder as she caressed me gently but thoroughly. She pushed me forward, onto my hands, and her tongue traced my spine.

I wanted to tell her she didn't have to be gentle with

me. She must know that I am as strong as she is and I had been loving, but not particularly gentle, with her.

I felt her fingertips on the backs of my thighs and my arms trembled. Her voice was in my ear, husky and desirous. "Tell me what you like."

None of my strategies had taken me far enough to envision this moment. I had imagined her surrender and never foreseen mine. She heard my answer in my gasp and shudder as her fingers plunged inward and we were moving faster toward a release that would fuse us for much longer than that moment.

I wanted to tell her I loved her, but I didn't. Not then.

I waited five minutes.

She didn't seem surprised. "I love your house," she answered, teasing.

"Good." I kissed her with desire for more of her. She was yielding to me again, inviting my hands and mouth to take and enjoy again.

"Natalie," she whispered. "Look at me."

She had her hands in my short, almost curling hair and her thumbs caressed my forehead. Her honey-blond hair was spread out over the pillow. "I'm looking," I said. "I love what I see."

"So do I. I love you, too."

"Sweet," I murmured. "I want you."

"You have me." She laughed with her lips on mine. "I think you had me with the iced tea — do you remember?"

I remembered, though it seemed almost a lifetime ago. "Play your cards right and I'll get you another one just like it on Valentine's Day."

"Tell me exactly what I need to do," she said, teasing again, but the kiss she gave me was serious with desire.

I told her.

I Will Go with You

(2 years)

Don't cry.

Rett had wanted to wait outside until her turn came, but Angel had been holding Rett's hand like a lifeline since the moment they arrived. Even now, when Angel knew that Rett was going to have to stand up, Angel's grip grew tighter.

Their relationship had only two years of history, but two or twenty — time didn't seem to matter. Rett's reluctant return home for her class reunion had brought her and Angel together finally, and in so many ways it seemed as if they had never wasted all those years. They shared a home together near Rochester, Minnesota, where Angel was completing the first of two extensive research studies for the Mayo Clinic. Even though Rett was on the road with the Henry Connors Orchestra three weeks out of five, instant messaging and the Internet kept them in constant contact so that when they were together it was as if no time had elapsed.

Rett gently disentangled her hand because her cue was coming. Angel's lashes were heavy with unshed tears and Rett had to look away or she would cry herself.

The priest paused and nodded in Rett's direction. He had been amenable to interrupting the mass at this point for Rett, even though she was not Catholic and was only there because her lesbian lover was there. The day was not about Rett, but about the family that surrounded her, Angel's family. They were Catholic and had always attended this church here in Woton, been christened here, learned their catechism here, for the most part married here.

They were saying good-bye to their father here, too.

Don't cry.

In the five days since Antonio Martinetta had succumbed to Lou Gehrig's disease Rett had not cried. She had one last gift to offer the man who had changed her life over the past two years, and tears would take it away.

The organist was sufficiently skilled, and the opening strains were lightly presented. The tempo was a little too fast, but Rett had anticipated that. She finished her last deep breath and sent Big Tony, Angel's oldest brother, silent thanks for his help with her pronunciation.

"Quando sono solo," When I am alone . . .

She did not have Andrea Boccelli's lyric phrasing, nor his incredible lung capacity, but she could do the song he had popularized justice. *Yes, I know there is no light.* She sang, averting her eyes from Angel's mother's tear-streaked face. When Rett had suggested the song, knowing how well

238

Antonio had liked it, Angelina had quickly agreed. Antonio had been the light for his family and it was time to say good-bye. She let her gaze move over the assembled mourners. The small church was filled to capacity. Rett knew there were people like her, who had never set foot in a Catholic church before, but they had all come to show respect for the Martinetta clan.

Yes, I know you are with me ... Antonio and Angelina Martinetta had moved to Woton, Minnesota, shortly after they'd married. Even now, surnames ending in vowels were rare in Woton, but everyone knew the Martinettas. In the two short years since Rett had become a part of the family, she'd heard of Angelina's and Antonio's unstinting gift of their time to their neighbors and community. They had also raised an incredible family. Antonio had had a gentle, loving spirit that had infused his children with the same, and his grandchildren, too. They were everything to Rett that her own family had never been.

Even in that bitter comparison, Antonio had made a difference. It wasn't unusual to find him watching an old movie in the middle of the night, and Rett's body clock had often been in a different time zone when she and Angel arrived for visits. She and Antonio had had some interesting late-night chats. The one about family and forgiveness still resonated in her.

The final chorus began with her voice rich and soaring. *Con te partirò, I will go with you*, once in Italian and once in English. The organist repeated the last sweeping theme again and then there was a long silence.

Rett returned to her seat and the mass resumed. Angel laced her fingers through Rett's and gave her a gentle peck on the cheek.

Everyone went back to the house. Angelina Martinetta would not have it any other way, of course. Tia and

Carmella had hired a caterer, ruthlessly overriding their mother's objections. When the struggle had threatened to turn acrimonious, it had been Rett who'd found the right words.

"Mama," she'd said, using the endearment as Angelina had asked her to, "let us be selfish. We need you right now, for ourselves. If you exhaust yourself cooking for a hundred people there won't be any of you left for us."

Even the ensuing tears from all the Martinetta women had not drawn any from Rett. She could not cry then — the damage it did to her voice would have limited her range in the challenging piece she was going to sing to honor Antonio.

Rett felt her throat tightening as she spied the well-loved and worn concertina that Antonio had played so often after family dinners. She could cry now, she thought suddenly. She walked quickly toward the back yard, but there were a lot of people under the trees. The front yard was similarly full.

"Rett."

Cinny Keilor's voice stopped her in her tracks, but not for the same reasons it had during high school. The un- requited longing had finally been vanquished by Angel's love. Cinny had become a better friend these last two years.

She accepted Cinny's comforting embrace and knew she couldn't hold back the tears much longer. Natalie's squeeze of her shoulder was less demonstrative but equally moving. They were a well-balanced couple and Rett had always thought they deserved the happiness they seemed to have found in one another.

She couldn't speak and both seemed to understand. She hurried back into the house — the garage, she thought. It was at least empty. Better still was the backseat of the Oldsmobile.

Tears came. She had held them back for so many days, right from the start at the hospital where Angel had dispassionately checked her father's vital signs and said in a low tone to her mother, "It's any time now, Mama." She couldn't cry, not then. Nor when, a half-hour later, Big Tony had sobbed into his mother's shoulder while T.J. hid his tears in his wife's hair. Angel had remained calm for quite a while, reminding the nurses about Antonio's donor status, but even she had finally gone to pieces when Tia had rushed in only to find she was fifteen minutes too late.

But Rett could cry now. She fumbled in the box of tissues on the floor and mopped her face. She lost track of time for a while and let herself grieve. Family and forgiveness. Gratitude instead of regrets. That was what Antonio would want. The part of her that had found such rapport with him would be forever lonely, but she told herself to be grateful for the time she had had. He'd shone a light into her and it had not gone out.

She was almost composed when she remembered getting the call from Angel to come home now if she wanted to say good-bye. Although she'd been prepared for a month to get that news, it had left her numb. Henry Connors himself had taken charge of her, postponing the morning rehearsal for that night's Seattle performance and then going with her to the hotel so she could pack a bag.

By the time that was done, Jerry Orland, Henry's partner in more than ways than one, called with the flight information and the promise to have the rest of Rett's luggage packed and moved on with the tour. Henry had kissed her like a father and put her in a cab. Rett knew he had to be thinking about the performance that night, and how to cover for the loss of his star vocalist, but it hadn't shown on his face. She had no idea what she'd done to deserve his concern and affection.

She angrily blew her nose. Just when she thought she'd finished with a lifetime's refrain of self-doubt, of wondering why anyone would care for her, of believing she didn't merit love, she would fall back into the trap. *Thanks, Mom.* And kicked herself again. Forty-two was too old to be blaming her mother for her own negative thinking. She was past that — she had to get past that. Family and forgiveness.

She was caught by surprise when the opposite door opened. The dome light made her blink.

T.J. leaned in. "Are you okay?"

"No," Rett said, and she hiccuped.

He sat down and offered his arms. Rett slid across the seat and put her head on his shoulder. "You sang beautifully."

"Thank you." She knew he felt her shoulders shaking.

"I don't know how you kept it together." His voice was unusually gruff. "I couldn't have done it."

"Performer's discipline, maybe. I don't know. I kept thinking how Elton John sang for Princess Diana, without a tear or quaver."

"It's more than that, I think. Papa told me he thought you were one of the strongest women he'd ever met."

Rett gasped. "He didn't know me that well, then." She'd been incredibly weak in her life, accepted bad love and bad advice. She turned her head into T.J.'s chest.

"Or he knew you better than you know yourself. That was certainly true for me. It was never fun as a teenager to realize the Papa had my number, but I'm hoping I develop the knack with my own kids."

Rett knew T.J. was trying to turn her mind away from her grief, and she appreciated it. "How's Angel?"

"She's fine. The second strongest woman in the world." He squeezed her.

"The Martinetta women are all strong," Rett said. "Maybe it's worn off on me."

The door opened again and Angel peered at Rett and T.J. "This looks sort of interesting." Her eyes were puffy and bloodshot, but it didn't look as if she'd been crying for a while.

"We're necking, go away," T.J. said.

Angel shrugged. "Okay." She started to close the door.

"Angel, wait." Honestly, the teasing in this family was nonstop. "Get out, T.J."

He feigned heartbreak. "What am I, a piece of fruit you can cast aside?"

"Yes, now get out. And thanks," Rett added more seriously. She turned toward Angel for a peaceful kiss and cuddle.

"I was catching up on the medical journals this morning. Chromosome twenty-one — they know the defective chain that determines Lou Gehrig's now. They might even know how to fix it."

Too late. "I'm sorry, honey."

She sniffed and Rett proffered the tissue box. "This last week I thought about it so much that CTGA seemed tattooed on the backs of my eyelids."

CTGA were the genetic markers that made up a human being. Rett knew that Angel's mind went far and deep into the vast universe of microscopic biology. It went places she could not follow; few could. Once that had intimidated her, but she was over it, long over it. "It wasn't a waste. You know it's inherited. You could still save a sister or brother's life, a niece or a nephew."

She patted my knee. "Thank you for that. I'd forgotten."

They rested for a few minutes, heads together. Rett realized she was almost asleep — it was warm and cozy and she was exhausted — when Angel suddenly moved.

"I'll be asleep in another minute," she said.

"Me, too. Oh, don't go."

Angel was already getting out of the car. "If I don't start cleaning up, Mama will try to do it."

It was undeniable, and it made Rett clamber out of the car after Angel. They need not have stirred, as it turned out. Tia had organized clean-up crews. Even T.J.'s five-year-old was helping.

Rett washed glasses until her fingers were prunes and kept thinking about Antonio's gift of light. She had chosen

243

the song because he had loved it, but she'd really sung today for Angelina and the rest of the clan. She hadn't yet fully honored his memory. Washing dishes didn't count.

Family and forgiveness.

She knew what she had to do. She'd been avoiding it for two years.

It was early evening when she told Angel she had an errand. She'd never driven directly from the Martinetta place to the house where she grew up, but there was little chance of getting lost. Woton was a very small town.

Left on South Road, right on Road 167. Third house on the right. The last house of the group, separated from the others by a narrow creek.

The scraggly geraniums and unpruned roses should have been in bloom, but they looked almost dead in spite of this year's early spring. The Grand Prix didn't look as if it had been moved in a month. The oil slick underneath it had doubled.

Just looking at it all depressed her. She made herself think about Antonio's light. Family and forgiveness.

Get out of the car, Rett.

In the two years since she'd seen her mother their faces had grown even more alike. That brief sensation of looking in a mirror was unsettling. Knowing she was looking at her own face twenty years down the road was even more so.

"So it's you."

"It's me, Mama." The word had none of the feeling it held when she called Angelina that.

Her mother stood back to let her in, and for once Rett was not immediately overwhelmed by cigarette smoke. The house was heavy with old smoke, of furniture permeated by the smell. The stench of unrinsed beer cans and bottles was as powerful as she remembered, but her stomach wasn't churning like it had two years ago. The pain of that last meeting — their first in over twenty-three years — was still inside her.

"To what do I owe this unexpected pleasure?" Her mother settled into the deeply indented recliner. Rett noticed a collection of cough medicines and used tissues.

"I wanted to see you again. I think I'll always have resentment and problems with our past, but that doesn't have to affect how today and tomorrow work out."

Her mother's fingers twitched as if she wanted to light a cigarette. Rett had rarely seen her without a lit one between her fingers. "Bully for you."

Whatever might happen was all on her, Rett realized. It always had been. She couldn't fix her mother and she had no illusions that her mother would ever change. "You're the only blood family I have. We can go on being strangers, but that doesn't mean I think it's okay."

Her mother seemed to be considering that, but abruptly began to cough. When Rett realized the coughing fit wasn't easing up right away, she went to the kitchen for water. Same glasses, same tap — the memories were harsh and yet they were home, too.

As she left the kitchen a bright red notice caught her eye. During her starving student days at U of M she'd seen one or two final electric notices. Her mother had only two more days to pay or bye-bye lights.

Her mother mumbled a thank-you for the water. "I gave up smokes and have had nothing but colds all winter. Couldn't even work this last month."

"Have you seen a doctor?"

"Yeah. He said my lungs are clearing themselves and I'll probably be susceptible to this kind of thing for the rest of my life."

"You were right to quit. Why did you?"

"Couldn't afford them anymore. It was smoke or eat." Her mother finished the water and nudged the glass into the chaos on the little table next to the recliner. "No matter what you think of me, I don't have that many vices. Men, smoking and beer. Men gave me up. I gave up the smokes. Now all I have is beer."

"As vices go, beer's a virtue."

Her mother laughed and started to cough again, but it didn't last as long as the first attack had. "Don't go making me laugh again. It hurts too much."

"I'll try to avoid it," Rett said drily.

"What are we working at, then?"

"Not hating each other."

"I never hated you."

"I know that now. You just didn't like me much."

Her mother nodded slightly. "I'll admit to that. It was a long time ago and all I remember is being angry most of the time."

"I was angry for a long time. I'm not anymore." Rett could not forget her mother's admission, two years ago, that she'd been too afraid to have an abortion. She'd had her entire life to accept that her mother had no idea who her father was. Bitterness remained, but anger was gone. Family and forgiveness. She gave me life, Rett reminded herself. She might not have loved me, but she fed me and clothed me until I could do it myself.

After a while her mother said, "You've made a success of yourself, then."

Rett nodded. "Maybe I'm not Barbra Streisand, but I'm a long way from nobody." *Nobody* had been her mother's career prediction for Rett's singing aspirations. "The Henry Connors Orchestra is scheduled to perform in Minneapolis this summer. Would you like a ticket?"

Her mother started to shrug that habitual shrug that said she couldn't care less. But she stopped. "I guess I would."

It was enough. It was more than Rett had ever fantasized being possible between them. "I'll make sure you get one. I travel a lot and live up in Rochester now —"

"What the hell is in Rochester?"

"The Mayo Clinic. My partner is a researcher there. Angel Martinetta."

"That mousy Martinetta girl? You're sleeping with her?"

Rett tried not to take umbrage. *Mousy* was hardly the right word to describe Angel's Italian vibrancy. "We're partners, Mama. Two years and counting. She needed to move to Rochester to start a research project and I went with her. My agent still thinks I'm crazy to have left L.A., but I travel so much I wanted to spend all the time I could with her."

Her mother suddenly looked tired and Rett stood up. "I think I'll go now," she said. "I was just trying to say I would try to see you sooner than two years this time. Maybe we don't have anything in common. Maybe I'm only here because I feel like I ought to be. But it's a start."

"At least I raised you to be honest," her mother said. She started to get out of the chair, but Rett waved her down.

"I know the way out, I think." She ducked into the kitchen first. "I'll take care of this, Mama," she said, holding up the electric bill. "It's hard to make ends meet when you can't work."

Her mother didn't say thank you — they had no precedent for gratitude. She didn't say she was looking forward to their next visit, and Rett couldn't bring herself to say it either. She wasn't, and as her mother had said, about such things she was honest. They just looked at each other, two grown women with a bitter history. Rett knew she had changed and did not think her mother ever would. She was only here because Antonio's memory demanded that she get past who her mother had never been and would never be. Family and forgiveness. He had never said it was easy.

* * * * *

247

Cuddled in the impersonal warmth of a motel bed, Rett and Angel shared warm and comforting kisses now that desire had finally been satisfied. "I was afraid to tell you how glad I was to see you."

Rett understood. "Same here. As if I wanted —" Her voice broke abruptly. "As if I wanted there to be a funeral so I could get out of about ten performances and spend an entire night in bed with you for the first time in what, four months?"

"He would understand," Angel said softly. "He loved you, you know."

"I know."

"He'd be proud of what you did today."

"I'd have sung —"

"Not that. I saw the electric bill. It's the right thing to do."

Angel's eyes shone in the dark and their glow warmed Rett in the place where Angel's father had left his presence as well. "She's been sick. Nothing's better. It just . . . is. I can either run or accept it. Running takes too much energy."

Angel yawned with her whole body, then snuggled her head into Rett's armpit. "Will you record it for me? 'Con te partirò'? I want to play it when I miss you. I'll need a CD. A cassette will just wear out in a week."

Rett began to sing it again, softly, until Angel's breathing had steadied. They would both sleep better tonight, finally. Angel murmured in her sleep — she often did — and Rett smiled in the dark. I will go with you, she thought, for this lifetime, for all the rest that follow.

And Now a Word ... or Two

For those of you who have little interest in the blatherings of authors, please feel no obligation to read further. My intent is to answer the Frequently Asked Questions I receive from many readers. I also thought this was the perfect opportunity to extend some deserving thanks and appreciation to some special people who have helped me over the years.

First and foremost in my thanks is of course my partner, Maria. I won't even attempt to describe the quality and depth of her endless support. Never a cheerleader, always a critic, she motivates me to overcome my natural inertia.

I should say right up front that Maria thought the following comments should be with each story as appropriate. I decided to gather them at the end of the book where they would intrude less on the reader's enjoyment. She feels this was the wrong choice. I had the final word. It was a chartreuse Volkswagen, sweetie.

In Every Port

IEP wasn't the first novel I finished, it was just the first decent one, and the first written for myself as a lesbian and for the lesbian reader. I had no expectation that Naiad Press would print it, but one Saturday, just after seven a.m., Barbara Grier herself called to say they wanted to do so. Over the years Barbara and I have had many seven a.m. conversations; I think she realized early on I am generally not alert at that hour. My contribution is usually a half-aware, "That sounds like a good idea." We have, from that earliest conversation, gotten along famously.

After the sheer luck of having *IEP* accepted for publication, I became the most fortunate of first-time novelists: Katherine V. Forrest edited the book. I learned more from a four-page editor's letter and the cogent remarks in the margins of that manuscript than I did in a year of writing classes. Her thoughtful, gentle, supportive approach was everything an inexperienced writer could want. For that, and all the kind words through the years, I thank Katherine from the bottom of my heart.

Even with Katherine's input, there are to this day parts of *IEP* that make the writer in me cringe. But I still love that story. When I wrote "Conversations" for this book, I drew on my own truths as half of an old-married couple. Maria and I are rapidly approaching our 25th year. Our conversations are no longer linear and an outside observer would probably think we're not listening to each other most of the time. They'd be wrong, of course.

Touchwood

Those of you who have read *Touchwood* almost always choose it as your favorite. It's my number one, too, even after all these years. Again, I owe Katherine Forrest thanks for something she did that was, I believe, more painful for her than me: she told me, gently and kindly, that the first draft of the book was unworkable. Barbara Grier flatly used the word *weak*. Many publishers would have at that point abandoned me entirely as a one-hit wonder, but Barbara gave me more time to think about Katherine's comments and what it was I really wanted to do.

Christi Cassidy, who had joined Naiad as an editor, worked on the second draft. Again, I was fortunate. Christi gave me some invaluable insight into what I'd written and suggested several ways I could take figurative doubles and triples to home runs. Every book Christi has edited since includes something she noticed that I had failed to fully flesh out. I am a better writer because of her insights and perspective. Other the years she has tried to teach me the proper use of *lay, lie, laid* and so forth, with absolutely no success.

This will surprise those of you who love *Touchwood* — it is in a close tie for last in sales of all of my books. It was a critical success, however; I keep some of those reviews handy for instant pep talks. I do wonder if the theme, an intergenerational romance, is not really of interest to some women. To each her own, of course. I'll share a wink with those of you who have read it. Not only is *Touchwood* probably your favorite book of mine, but Louisa is most likely your favorite character. Perhaps "Satisfaction" in this book will help those women who didn't read *Touchwood* realize why they just might enjoy it.

"Come Here" was previously published in *The Erotic Naiad*. It has been slightly edited, but for the most part is unchanged since I rather liked it when I was done with it. Judy and Dedric were characters I wished I could get back to over the years. When I began writing *Watermark*, they were right there, ready to be a part of the action. Some characters are like that.

Paperback Romance

I was a serial romance junkie in my teens. I read one a day for at least three years. I still have a collection of my favorites. It was at about this time that I fell in love with Maria (we were juniors in high school; she was reading Faulkner) and began to understand why I gobbled the books up for the heroines, not the heroes. I was intensely interested in the emotional life of nurses on New Zealand sheep stations, ingenues on the London stage, and independent women whose cars broke down in remote places. I wrote *PR* as a gentle satire of the romance genre. It is a lighthearted, far-fetched book to be enjoyed in a bubble bath.

"Key of Sea" picks up on the brief mention of Nick's new lover in the closing pages of *PR*. The closing pages also immortalized a Kentucky Fried Chicken in Sacramento. To those readers who have expressed an interest in finding that KFC, and perhaps participating in a reenactment, there is no KFC on that stretch of Fair Oaks Boulevard. Sorry. Call it artistic license.

Car Pool

I would have to say that *Car Pool* was my first serious romance. (I do not believe that "serious" and "romance" are mutually exclusive.) *Touchwood* had a serious theme, but Rayann and Louisa are mostly concerned with working out the kinks of their own relationship. *Car Pool* features two women with big issues of their own. Anthea's emotional blocks come from alcoholic parents. She wants to quit smoking. She is so closeted she doesn't even see the door — or the closet. Shay's financial straits are extreme and the racist and sexist workplace she endures would crush a less sturdy soul. Before they can hope to solve problems in their relationship they have a lot of work to do themselves.

I am often asked how much of my own life appears in my books. Obviously, I draw on my own experiences for all sorts of inspiration, but *CP* has the one scene that happened to me. For those who have read the book: the chili pepper oil. I was on the receiving end. 'Nuff said.

It has been vastly gratifying over the years to hear from readers that *CP* gave them the push they needed to talk about the frightening, volatile and highly personal topic of *money*. Who says romance novels are just light entertainment? Not me.

"Mechanics" is a story I've been wanting to tell for some time, but not one I wanted to build an entire novel around. It is not how Maria and I became mothers, but is based on the experiences of a number of women and men and my own warped sense of humor.

Painted Moon

I scratch my head and ask myself, "What the heck did I do right?" *PM* was my first "best seller" and that didn't stop it from garnering some nice reviews, too. One thing I do know, Leah Beck's character has more depth because of Christi Cassidy's insights into the mentality of an artist. Some of the elements that work in *PM* I only noticed long after it had been printed. When I reread it in order to write "Smudges" I did at times think, "Hey, I wrote that part pretty darned well." Frankly, it's still a mystery to me.

A frequent question has been in regards to the name. I have one idiosyncrasy (that's right, just one) in that I can't begin a book until I have picked the name. I sometimes have no idea what the book will be about, but the name is chosen. Maria and I were visiting Butchart Gardens outside of Victoria, British Columbia, when I saw this spectacular rose, the only one left on that bush. It was brilliantly white with the faintest hint of silver edging on the petals. In the late afternoon light the silver had a bluish cast to it. The variety was named Painted Moon. For almost a year, I knew nothing more about the novel than that.

Wild Things

Religion can have a powerful effect on people's lives, for good and bad. In *WT* I tried to show the good that Faith desired from her religion — solace, strength, renewal — and the bad — ridicule, abuse, ostracism — that she experienced when she realized she could no longer ignore her feelings for other women. I also wanted to present Faith with a clear choice between a good man who literally offered her the world and a vibrantly alive, notoriously out lesbian. Safety, or the unknown? On a lesser scale we've all stood at that particular crossroad.

In spite of making her choice, and the overwhelming support she receives from Sydney and Sydney's family, Faith's insecurities persist in "Wild Things Are Free."

Embrace in Motion

Just what is romance, anyway? Those who have read all my books will find that the characters often ponder the difference between great sex and a great relationship. *EIM* finds Sarah caught between these two choices and finally realizing the immense underpinnings of affection and respect it takes to make a solid commitment to someone else. I'm certainly not saying that a great relationship can't include great sex. But it is true that great sex can be had without a great relationship. As in "Hot Flash," sometimes life changes can help with both.

"The Singing Heart" was previously published in *The Touch of Your Hand* and has that last moment with Sarah and Leslie that so many readers seemed to need. Okay, I needed it too, but I decided not to append it to *EIM* because I really wanted to underscore how Sarah and Leslie treasured their friendship. Treasured it so much that, at least in the moment of realization that somewhere along the way they had become a couple, it put sex into a distant second place.

I am asked all the time why my own relationship is successful. I usually go on and on about many different reasons, but this is the succinct version.

Guidelines to a Successful Relationship
1) Never begin a sentence with "If you loved me, you would..."
2) Never end a sentence with "... or else I'm leaving you."
3) Romance is not roses and chocolate once a year. Romance is when, at the end of a long, hot day, one person gets up to get the cold drink and gives the *other* person the first sip. Romance is an everyday thing.
4) Share images of the future you dream about. Make sure both of you are in these pictures.
5) (Mixed gender households only) Always put the seat down.

Making Up for Lost Time
Many readers have noticed that I bring food into my books. *Car Pool*, for example, features a dinner party with a chocolate ganache that leaves two grown men almost insensible. My heroines often find comfort of the Ben & Jerry's variety. In *MULT* I wanted to pull out all the stops with one character as a master chef. I've heard from many of you that you were able to duplicate the effect of the chocolate body paint. Congratulations. I don't need more details than that, but thanks for offering.

Though hardly recognizable, the plot of *MULT* was generally inspired by an old Barbara Stanwyck movie, *Christmas in Connecticut.* Barbara of the fabulous shoulders and velvet-iron personality plays a home-and-garden "women's" writer of the 1940s. Her columns are beloved by all, especially the menus and recipes from her gracious and spacious Connecticut estate where she resides with husband, children, a cow and several dogs. She of course can't cook at all, is single and lives in a shoebox apartment. Hilarity ensues when she tries to fake her way through a holiday visit from her publisher, Sidney Greenstreet. Val Valentine's dilemma springs from Barbara Stanwyck's, but the resemblance ends there. I have to admit, however, my mind's eye sometimes saw the lovely Miss Stanwyck in that tool belt.

A little bonus for those of you who have read this far and have a copy of the book. I omitted the temperature setting on the recipe for Simple Cheese Soufflé. Please turn your hymnal to page 106 and write Oven=350°. Thank you.

Watermark

At a bookstore reading I was once asked if I planned to write a sequel to *Touchwood*. At the time the answer was no. A year went by and some ideas I wanted to explore bubbled together and I abruptly saw how *Touchwood* could provide the foundation for another novel. It was not the sequel I think that fans of *Touchwood* were hoping for, but it was definitely the book I wanted to write.

No other book I've written has stirred up so much mail and difference of opinion. Death in a Kallmaker romance? A most beloved character killed off? A kind and caring woman transformed into a heartless bitch? What was I thinking?

My strongest impulse when I sat down to frame the action in *Watermark* was to create a testament to the reality of our love. Too often gay men and lesbians are stereotyped as having relationships based only on the physical. We don't merit "marriage" because when our partners leave us, we hop to the next bed. When our partners die, we don't suffer the same wracking grief because our love is just not as powerful. Those stereotypes are what I wanted to confront with *Watermark*.

I used *Touchwood* as the "back story" that framed the tragedies in *Watermark*, giving me more energy to expend on an increasing list of characters that defined the perilously fragile romance between Teresa and Rayann. One issue raised in *Touchwood* was coping with the shadow of a previous love, of being "second best." I wanted to explore that conflict in greater detail since the shadow cast by the dead lover was immense (one of the reasons I chose her), and perhaps more than a naïve young woman could hope to compete with. "The Tapestry" in this book confronts this theme.

Last, I tried to weave in the reality of random events forever changing lives. Rayann and Teresa are both irrevocably changed by complete chance, which is how life happens. If *Paperback Romance* is the most in line with the so-called romance formula, then *Watermark* is at the other end of the spectrum. Maria, who doesn't like romance novels, and only reads mine because I make her, puts *Watermark* at the top of the Kallmaker heap.

Unforgettable

I can sing and play the piano with great enthusiasm, doing both with only slightly more skill than my three-year-old. The character of Rett Jamison was pure fantasy on my part: a luscious Karen Carpenter voice, perfect pitch, near-perfect recall. Rett ought to be a star, but isn't. It will sound clinical to say that *Unforgettable* is a novel about self-esteem, but there it is. Rett runs from good love to bad, from success to failure because she doesn't believe herself worthy of love or success.

Unforgettable marks the first time since *Touchwood* that I wrote a novel with only one point of view. I think that accounts for the richness of Rett's character. It was a harder job, then, to portray Angel's motivations and explain Cinny's behavior with only Rett's not always accurate perceptions to tell the story. It was well worth the effort. My own pleasure with the finished product has been more than echoed by readers and critics alike.

"Unforgettable, That's What You Are" is a story I really wanted to tell, but couldn't because of the point of view. Natalie started out as a walk-on at a picnic, then she showed up at a slumber party and the next thing I knew she was dancing with Cinny while the whole town looked on. Sometimes characters have their own ideas about what they want to do. She had so much presence that her intentions toward Cinny popped off the page at me, but I just couldn't make it fit with Rett's plot. That was when I conceived the idea for this anthology. I wanted to tell Natalie's story in the worst way.

Never one to mince words, Barbara Grier told me that short stories make many women run screaming in the other direction, but she also urged me to go for it because there's nothing an avid reader wants to know more than what happened after the last page of the book. "I Will Go with You" is a chapter from Rett and Angel's life when the solidity of their relationship supports them during a rough time.

Laura Adams

One Frequently Asked Question remains: Who the heck is Laura Adams? My alter ego, Laura Adams, was actually Barbara Grier's brainchild. Not the name, or the books, but it was her most excellent thought that a second Karin Kallmaker book every year would be nothing but good for both of us and a great many readers and booksellers. I agreed with every word she said, but I think she'll forgive me if I admit what was going through my mind during this conversation. (We were speaking at some time later than seven a.m. for me, which accounted for my lucidity.)

My thought was that with a different persona I could write books Kallmaker fans simply wouldn't expect from me. I already had three such novels in the back of my head and then Barbara so thoughtfully provided me with the opportunity to follow through with them. I know with certainty that she didn't expect first a romantic science-fiction novel followed by a romance-driven supernatural story, then more romance and science fiction. Mea culpa, but oh, it is such fun to write.

My Laura Adams books have all been edited by Lila Empson. Lila has tried very hard to improve my use of commas, but they continue to plague me as I only like to use a comma to indicate a pause for breath if I'm reading aloud which is confusing to everyone but people who talk as fast as I do.

In the years since Laura Adams was born, Barbara and Donna McBride decided to ease back on Naiad's exhausting publishing schedule. For practical yet flattering reasons, they wanted to keep Karin Kallmaker as one of their continuing writers. Laura Adams was free to join many other Naiad writers at a new press, Bella Books. This turn of events seems as wonderful to me as that first seven a.m. phone call when Barbara told me she wanted to publish *In Every Port*. I am a lucky woman. I get to keep writing the romance novels I love with Naiad Press, and I also get to stretch my wings even further as Laura Adams with Bella Books. Pinch me.

Frosting on the Cake

One of the critical complaints about my books I have always found amusing is that I never miss an opportunity to "dally between the reader's legs." Why, yes, thanks for noticing. (How is this a bad thing in a romance novel? Anyone? Anyone?) This anthology is no exception, a fact which I'm sure will delight just about all my readers. For those who are not delighted, I love you just the same.

As I wrote these stories I had different goals unique to each one. But overall, I wrote every single word with all of my readers in mind. Think of this book as a Frequent

Reader Reward, because that's really what it is. I would not write with as much joy if you weren't willing to read, nor would I be as able to take readers in unexpected directions if you weren't willing to go with me. Yes, I write for my own pleasure and to express my own creative impulses, but a large part of my pleasure in my work is knowing that it pleases you, too. As I said above, I am a lucky woman, and I have all of you to thank.

A few of the publications of
THE NAIAD PRESS, INC.
P.O. Box 10543   Tallahassee, Florida 32302
Phone (850) 539-5965
Toll-Free Order Number: 1-800-533-1973
Web Site: WWW.NAIADPRESS.COM
Mail orders welcome. Please include 15% postage.
Write or call for our free catalog which also features an
incredible selection of lesbian videos.

DEATH CLUB by Claire McNab. 240 pp. 13th Detective Inspector
Carol Ashton Mystery.   ISBN 1-56280-267-4 $11.95

FROSTING ON THE CAKE by Karin Kallmaker. 272 pp.The
answer to every romance.   ISBN 1-56280-266-6 $11.95

DEATH UNDERSTOOD by Claire McNab. 240 pp. 2nd Denise
Cleever thriller.   ISBN 1-56280-264-X $11.95

TREASURED PAST by Linda Hill. 208 pp. A shared passion for
antiques leads to love.   ISBN 1-56280-263-1 $11.95

UNDER SUSPICION by Claire McNab. 224 pp. 12th Detective
Inspector Carol Ashton mystery.   ISBN 1-56280-261-5 $11.95

UNFORGETTABLE by Karin Kallmaker. 288 pp. Can each
woman win her true love's heart?   ISBN 1-56280-260-7   11.95

MURDER UNDERCOVER by Claire McNab. 192 pp. 1st Denise
Cleever thriller.   ISBN 1-56280-259-3   11.95

EVERYTIME WE SAY GOODBYE by Jaye Maiman. 272 pp.
7th Robin Miller mystery.   ISBN 1-56280-248-8   11.95

SEVENTH HEAVEN by Kate Calloway. 240 pp. 7th Cassidy
James mystery.   ISBN 1-56280-262-3   11.95

STRANGERS IN THE NIGHT by Barbara Johnson. 208 pp. Her
body and soul react to a stranger's touch.   ISBN 1-56280-256-9   11.95

THE VERY THOUGHT OF YOU edited by Barbara Grier and
Christine Cassidy. 288 pp. Erotic love stories by Naiad Press
authors.   ISBN 1-56280-250-X   14.95

TO HAVE AND TO HOLD by PeGGy J. Herring. 192 pp. Their
friendship grows to intense passion . . .   ISBN 1-56280-251-8   11.95

INTIMATE STRANGER by Laura DeHart Young. 192 pp.
Ignoring Tray's myserious past, could Cole be playing with fire?
                                         ISBN 1-56280-249-6   11.95

SHATTERED ILLUSIONS by Kaye Davis. 256 pp. 4th
Maris Middleton mystery.   ISBN 1-56280-252-6   11.95

SET UP by Claire McNab. 224 pp. 11th Detective Inspector Carol
Ashton mystery.   ISBN 1-56280-255-0   11.95

THE DAWNING by Laura Adams. 224 pp. What if you had the
power to change the past?   ISBN 1-56280-246-1   11.95

NEVER ENDING by Marianne K. Martin. 224 pp. Temptation
appears in the form of an old friend and lover. ISBN 1-56280-247-X   11.95

ONE OF OUR OWN by Diane Salvatore. 240 pp. Carly Matson
has a secret. So does Lela Johns.   ISBN 1-56280-243-7   11.95

DOUBLE TAKEOUT by Tracey Richardson. 176 pp. 3rd Stevie
Houston mystery.   ISBN 1-56280-244-5   11.95

CAPTIVE HEART by Frankie J. Jones. 176 pp. Love in the
fast lane or heartside romance?   ISBN 1-56280-258-5   11.95

WICKED GOOD TIME by Diana Tremain Braund. 224 pp. In
charge at work, out of control in her heart. ISBN 1-56280-241-0   11.95

SNAKE EYES by Pat Welch. 256 pp. 7th Helen Black mystery.
                                             ISBN 1-56280-242-9   11.95

CHANGE OF HEART by Linda Hill. 176 pp. High fashion and
love in a glamorous world.   ISBN 1-56280-238-0   11.95

UNSTRUNG HEART by Robbi Sommers. 176 pp. Putting life
in order again.   ISBN 1-56280-239-9   11.95

BIRDS OF A FEATHER by Jackie Calhoun. 240 pp. Life begins
with love.   ISBN 1-56280-240-2   11.95

THE DRIVE by Trisha Todd. 176 pp. The star of *Claire of the
Moon* tells all!   ISBN 1-56280-237-2   11.95

BOTH SIDES by Saxon Bennett. 240 pp. A community of
women falling in and out of love.   ISBN 1-56280-236-4   11.95

WATERMARK by Karin Kallmaker. 256 pp. One burning
question . . . how to lead her back to love? ISBN 1-56280-235-6   11.95

THE OTHER WOMAN by Ann O'Leary. 240 pp. Her roguish
way draws women like a magnet.   ISBN 1-56280-234-8   11.95

SILVER THREADS by Lyn Denison.208 pp. Finding her way
back to love . . .   ISBN 1-56280-231-3   11.95

These are just a few of the many Naiad Press titles — we are the oldest and
largest lesbian/feminist publishing company in the world. We also offer an
enormous selection of lesbian video products. Please request a complete
catalog. We offer personal service; we encourage and welcome direct mail
orders from individuals who have limited access to bookstores carrying our
publications.